SILVER
IN THE
MIST

**Books by Emily Victoria
available from Inkyard Press**

Silver in the Mist

This Golden Flame

EMILY VICTORIA

SILVER
IN THE
MIST

inkyard
PRESS

ISBN-13: 978-1-335-40670-5

Silver in the Mist

For questions and comments about the quality of this book, please contact us at CustomerService@Harlequin.com.

Inkyard Press
22 Adelaide St. West, 41st Floor
Toronto, Ontario M5H 4E3, Canada
www.InkyardPress.com

Printed in U.S.A.

Recycling programs for this product may not exist in your area.

To my sisters, Sara and Rebecca.
Thank you for being your amazing selves!

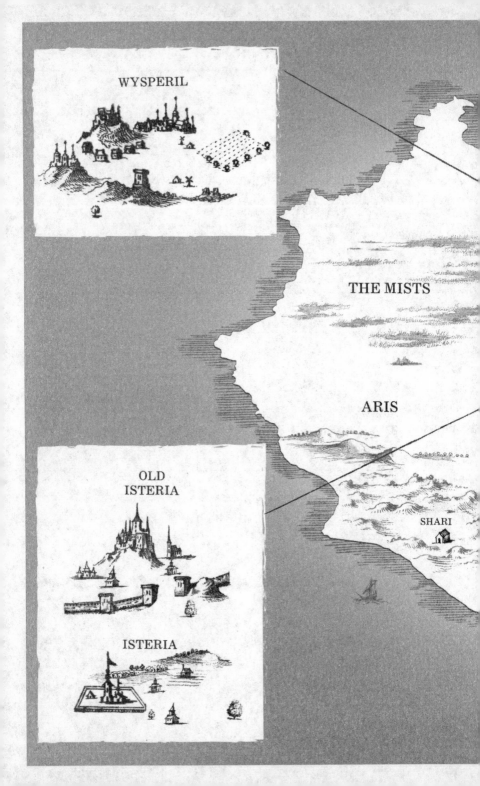

CHAPTER ONE

The camp around me is shadowy and asleep—vulnerable—
just the way I like it. At my back, metal poles hold lanterns
that let out an erratic flicker of a glow. But it doesn't reach
as far in as I am, and even the patrolling soldiers barely stray
from their circles of firelight. It's sloppy, this whole camp.

I feel, rather than see, someone slip into the shadow of the
tent behind me.

"Devlin."

Lochlan's jesting voice is that low tone that barely carries as
far as my ears. I shift closer to the canvas of the tent so they
can crouch beside me. "Fancy seeing you here," they say.

Even though this is serious, my own lips twitch in response.
Like me, Lochlan is dressed in tight-fitting clothes with their
hood up, dark and practical and perfect for getting up to no
good. They tug the strip of cloth covering their face down
as they let out a huff. "This thing gets so itchy."

I raise a brow. "That's not regulation."

They give me a look, but it's edged with that sharp excitement neither of us can hide in the field. It tingles in my own fingertips. I want to get on with it, but as always, the Whisperer's voice echoes in my head, tempering the impulse. *Take the time to observe. Know the lay of the land.*

No matter how many missions I do, how much experience I think I've gained, it's always my mother's voice that sounds in my head out here in the field.

I scan the tents in front of us. There are three of them in the inner circle, five in the outer. If this camp has the usual layout, then the barracks, the mess, and the supplies will be in the outer tents. The scribes and those in command—in other words, everyone important—will be in this inner ring.

The tent on the far left is larger than the two beside it. All are in that deep navy color that is dyed even darker by the night, which only serves to offset the fabric's silver lining. The canvas is thick enough that even if there was light inside the tents, we wouldn't be able to see any silhouettes. It doesn't give us much to go on, but at least it means once we're inside, no one will be able to see us either.

"What did you find out?" I ask.

"Captain's quarters are in the middle. The large one on the left is for the scribes. The last one houses the captain's two pages."

"So are the captain's office and his sleeping quarters the same?"

"Guess."

I stifle my sigh. That will be a pain to deal with, but it's not like we haven't done it before. Multiple times. "The scribes?"

"They sleep with the soldiers as far as I can tell."

That's promising. I scan the area. The captain's tent is the only one with a guard. The man is bored, idly fiddling with his sword's sheath. He wears a tunic of soft blue lined with white, so neat it looks as if it'd get dirty if the guard glanced at the ground wrong.

"We can take him," Lochlan says.

I elbow them. "No evidence outside of the theft, remember?" The scribes' tent isn't guarded, and there's barely a foot of space between it and the captain's tent beside it. That's our best chance. "This way."

We track down the row we're sheltered by, moving from shadow to shadow, aware of the guards and the torchlight hovering just around the corners. At the end of the lane, I wait for the guard's attention to shift and then we're just two shadows slipping over the grassy gap. The canvas of the scribes' tent is secured with thick ties, and I undo the row to let us in.

The space is shadowy in the dark and I take a moment to let my eyes adjust. Rows of portable desks fill the tent so tightly I have to step carefully as I ghost between them, Lochlan behind me.

The desks are littered with papers and worn writing implements, and among them lie pieces of filigree. The delicate swirls of the silvery patterns shine in the darkness, like fallen pieces of moonglow. My fingers hover over them. We aren't supposed to leave any evidence, but I can't resist swiping a couple of the shards into my pocket. This is a Cerenian camp. They won't notice one or two missing pieces of filigree, while we need all the stolen magic we can get.

Behind me, Lochlan pauses as they look at the filigree.

Even though I can't make out the expression on their face from this angle, I know what will be there. Loss.

I nudge them. "Bet you a week's worth of chores I can find what we need first."

Lochlan's eyes glint in the dark as they grin. "You're going to regret that."

"You wish."

A couple more ties get us out the far wall, and I give a quick glance to make sure the guard can't see us before slipping into the captain's tent.

He's a snorer. That much is obvious as we step in and a grinding noise like rocks being smashed together echoes over to us. Lochlan's face contorts in laughter and I grab their face cloth and yank it back over their mouth.

There's not much in here. Besides the bed, the only things are a camp desk and a chest. Well, that and the clothes scattered all over the place. There's even a discarded sword not a foot away from where I stand. He's not a strict captain then. I'm betting he's the type to leave his papers lying out rather than filing them away at the end of the day.

I take the desk and sure enough, it's cluttered with writing instruments and parchment. The Whisperer ordered us to bring back the original orders from the Cerenian monarch that sent these soldiers here. I don't know exactly what they will say, but I can guess. There are a number of patrolling camps that work their way up and down the Cerenian border, making sure it's secure. Normally they follow the exact same route. This camp, though, is well into the neutral territory of the Peaks.

The last true attack from Cerena was decades ago, long before I was born, but that doesn't mean they aren't planning another. I can't see why else they would have strayed so far into the Peaks, when it's such difficult territory to cover. We can't face the Mists and an army.

My fingers shift through the papers, careful to disturb them as little as possible. Then in the dark, I catch the image of a songbird sitting on a branch: Cerena's royal seal. The orders themselves are written in code but that seal means this is what we've come for.

I lift the paper high, so Lochlan can see it.

I win.

The snoring cuts off. I drop to a crouch behind the desk. As I peer around its edge I see the captain blinking sleepy eyes open.

I look at where Lochlan is hiding behind the chest. They're closer to where we entered than I am. They should be able to get out if they move right now, before the captain is fully awake.

I wave my hand at them. They hesitate, but I give them a glare. Moving as silent as a shadow, they're gone.

There's a creak from the bed as the captain gets up, muttering beneath his breath. His footsteps come closer, padding over the canvas floor. My hand finds the knife at my hip. As soon as he's close enough, I'll jab the knife in his leg. Then I'll run.

Fast.

His feet come into view and I'm tensing to move when there's a panicked shout from outside. It's taken up, the sound multiplying.

What did Lochlan do?

The captain grabs his boots and races outside. As soon as he's gone, I slip out the side of the tent. I smell the smoke the moment I'm free, the ring of light at the eastern outskirts of the camp now shining decidedly angrier.

"A lantern has fallen!" someone shouts. "Bring water!"

The camp is a flurry of activity. All of the soldiers, most only half-dressed and with mussed hair, are heading one way. I catch a clear moment and dash in the opposite direction.

I dart between the tents, breaking out of the last line and plunging into the forest at the base of the mountain. It's darker beneath the trees, the branches scratching at my clothes, and even though I'm risking a broken ankle, I don't slow. Better a broken ankle than an arrow in my back.

The ground beneath my feet turns from moss to dirt to stone, and the forest fades as I track up the path.

I turn the corner, and there it is.

A wall of white clings to the mountain like a shroud. It's so thick I can't even make out the rocks in it. All I can see are the flashes of lightning deep in its depths, bright and fierce.

The Mists.

Lochlan sits on a rock just outside the border of white, idly swinging one of their legs. Their hood is already down, showing their auburn hair with the single streak of gray, currently tied back into a ponytail. The filigree lantern we'd hidden on our way down shines at their feet, sparking off their bright green eyes.

I tug the cloth away from my face. "What did you set on fire?"

They grin at me. "You're welcome."

There's a shout behind us from the direction of the camp and we plunge into the Mists.

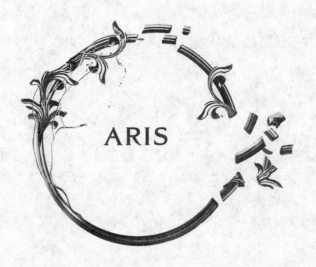

ARIS

CHAPTER TWO

I've always hated the Mists.

Thick and strangling, they smudge out everything: sights and sounds and even feelings. The slight draw of my breath and the fall of my footsteps come out muted and dull. The lantern in my hand reflects dimly on the edges of gray stone swimming in and out of the paleness, each as sharp as the blade of a knife.

Beside me, Lochlan studies the papers we stole, even though they don't know the code any more than I do. They've always viewed things like codes—even secrets, lies, and other people—as puzzles they have this deep urge to crack.

"You know," I say, "you're not going to figure that out by staring at it."

They grin. "Every code can be cracked."

"Not if you don't have the right tools."

Lochlan flips to the next page. "I know you want its secrets as much as I do."

"They aren't for us," I retort. They're for the Whisperer and if she wants us to know them, she'll tell us.

Lochlan quirks their brow at me. I probably could have convinced anyone else of the truth of what I just said. I was most of the way to even convincing myself. But not Lochlan. Never Lochlan.

I just reach out and shove them. They laugh.

Honestly, I don't really begrudge them the distraction. They were once a caster, and even though their connection to the magic is broken, they're still more attuned to it than I am. They told me once that being in the Mists was like slowly suffocating.

Lochlan's low laugh cuts off. I barely have time to pause before they grab my arm and pull us into a cleft in the rocks. A pulse of energy goes through the air, raising goose bumps on my skin.

A phantom.

Every instinct in me tells me to run as the pressure bears down on us, the wisps of white around us turning from eddies into violent gusts. But going out into a Mist storm on a narrow pass like this would kill us.

Just when I think the pressure might split my skull in two, there's a clap, and it appears.

It's hard to look at the thing for any amount of time, its body made of silvered lightning so bright I have to squint against it. This one almost resembles a draft horse, but feral, its mane a wild lash of energy. Sparks dance out from feet that I wouldn't quite call hooves.

I draw out my knife, not the usual one at my hip but the other one from the silver-stitched scabbard tucked into the small of my back. That first blade is plain steel, good for flesh and bones. But my silver filigree knife, born of magic, is the one thing I have that can harm a phantom. It shines in my palm.

The beast steps closer and Lochlan's hand finds my own, still curled around the lantern's handle. I can't fight with their hand covering mine. But I don't pull away.

A charge splits the air, and as quickly as the beast appeared it's gone, taking the storm with it. The swirling Mists are the only indication it ever stood there at all.

Lochlan slumps back against the rock, letting out a shaky laugh. They look even paler than I feel. However horrible the phantom felt for me, it was worse for them.

"Remind me why we do this again," they ask weakly.

I pull in a deep breath, then another, trying to even out my heartbeat. A calm spy is an alive spy. That's what the Whisperer always says.

I clap Lochlan on their shoulder before pushing off the rock behind me. "Because Aris needs us to do this." I slip my dagger back into its sheath. "Now come on. Let's get out of here before that thing comes back."

After close to three days of nothing but white, the Mists finally thin. Every shade of color that seeps back into the world loosens the knot wrapped tight in my chest. Beneath our feet the path winds down and I convince my weary legs to keep going, because we're so close now.

Out of the Mists, the barrier appears.

It's a massive granite wall, crowned with filigree lanterns that each stand taller than I do, their light shredding the last of the white. As we step into their glow, I let out a relieved breath. Lochlan flashes me a smile, bouncing on the balls of their feet. We made it, once again. In the handful of years since we became full spies, Lochlan and I have crossed the Mists half a dozen times already. It seems too many for our sixteen years.

I raise my lantern and flash the pattern of the month up to those hidden by the glaring light above. The ground shudders beneath our feet as the gates pull open.

We step through and as the gates clang to a shut behind us, I stop.

Beside me, Lochlan lets out a long-suffering sigh, but there's a smile tucked behind it, and they pause as well. I don't think they've ever understood why I stop here every single time we come back. I've never told them there's a part of me that is so afraid that one time we'll head back and there will be nothing but a stretch of the Mists obliterating the city I love.

The Peaks give way to gentle hills and then a plain. It holds my home: Isteria, the capital of Aris.

As I see it, that familiar mix of pride and sadness fills me. Isteria's outer wall is capped with battlements crafted from filigree, crowning the city in metal and magic. The light of the lanterns on its towers is reflected among the filigree statues and arches scattered throughout the city, as if they're fallen stars.

To the north, the barrier curves down to the plains a good four miles out from the city's walls. The Mists behind it flash bright with lightning. Somewhere in there is the old castle and the old capital, long destroyed.

Will one day my own city just be crumbling ruins in a mass of white and storm?

Lochlan knocks their shoulder into mine. "Come on. I am starving for some real food."

They head off. I follow, my fingers resting on the satchel at my hip, the papers we stole safely nestled inside.

We head down through the hills. There are still about four miles to go until we reach the city and after the oppressive stillness of the Mists, there's a peacefulness to the darkening landscape, to the hum of the crickets and the soft shush of the wind over the grasses. There isn't much out here, just a few scattered farms. I tilt my head up to take in the sky. I can just see some of the stars coming out. My father used to take me stargazing. I only remember a few of the names of the constellations, though: the Lion, Callian, the Wreath— no, wait, the Bouquet.

Lochlan chats away beside me, as if all their words get bottled up when we're in the Mists. "The full moon festival is coming up. Kai and Janna and I thought we could make a bit of a celebration of it. Janna and Kai said they'd liberate some of the provisions from the kitchen. We're in charge of decorations, but I can handle that, since I know you have a thing against stealing from the palace."

I only half listen, making sure to smile and nod at the right parts. As Lochlan grows brighter the closer we get to Isteria, there's this familiar knot tightening around my chest. As much as I love this city, I know what's waiting for me in it. *Who's* waiting for me in it.

To our left, the sunset is close to blinding as it gives its final burst of light against the hills. I'm starting to turn away as, within the light, there's a flash of silvered lightning.

I whip my head back around.

Lochlan cuts off. "Dev?" Their voice drops low. "What is it?"

I take two rapid steps, squinting to see against the light, but as the sun relinquishes its hold on the horizon, there are only empty hills.

That almost...looked like a phantom.

"Dev?" Lochlan's voice is more hesitant now.

My heart pulses in my throat. A phantom is impossible. We're on the safe side of the barrier. Phantoms can only move and live inside of the Mists—it's what sustains them. Those monsters can't reach us here.

"Sorry." I shake my head. "For a second there, I thought I saw... I thought I saw a phantom."

Lochlan's brows scrunch down. "A phantom?"

I give a laugh. It comes out too nervous. "Just a trick of the light."

Lochlan looks over at the horizon. They turn back, biting their lip. "Are you sure? We can go investigate."

Investigate what? Of everyone, I cannot be jumping at imaginary shadows. Just the thought of the Whisperer hearing what I said makes me feel nauseous.

"It's nothing, and we need to get these papers back."

I hurry off, as if I can outpace my doubts. After a few moments Lochlan's footsteps trot up beside me.

By the time we make the trek to the city's gates it's full-on dark. Up in the pass, the Mists are such a presence. Down here, it's easier to forget that we're a city surrounded by monsters. Isteria is still busy with the evening crowd. There are a couple of market stalls open—not as many as when I was a child but still enough to make a showing of normalcy. The smell of meat pies and spiced cider makes my stomach growl. Lochlan tips a coin into a cup and grabs two steaming pies, sinking their teeth into one before pressing the other into my hand.

I open my mouth because we shouldn't be getting distracted, but they mumble around their mouthful. "Shh... Eat your pie."

I roll my eyes, but take a bite, and after days of dried jerky, it fills my belly with warmth. I should stay alert, but instead I find myself relaxing and taking in the sights. To our left, filigree gear work pulls a load of stones to the top of a wall and nearby a crank-operated hand drill clears space for a new filigree installment.

A caster steps up, and I pause for a moment to watch. The silver light of magic curls around their fingers before they send it into the earth. The magic becomes solid, forming silver curls of filigree, the pattern building its way into the sky.

Even after everything that's happened, there's still something so hopeful about watching filigree grow.

We head on and as we do, the streets widen. The buildings grow larger. Lochlan and I step off into the side alleys, facing foreboding walls instead of welcoming storefronts.

When we reach the palace, we go to an inconspicuous wooden door in the wall surrounded by so much ivy it covers the frame. I used to love this door. It seemed to me a door of stories and secrets, and despite everything, each time I opened it, I wondered if I would find a new world on the other side.

Instead, it opens on a green expanse of lawn. The palace looms over us in the dark. It houses hundreds of people: soldiers and spies, cooks and stable hands, visiting merchants from the smaller cities in southern Aris. But it's still the home I've fought so hard for. Even though I know who is waiting for me in those walls, for one moment I let the triumph of the day be enough. There have been so many defeats lately.

But today we won.

CHAPTER THREE

We're barely through the doors when Reinolds, the Whisperer's assistant, whisks the papers away from me. We're not called in to do a debriefing—the papers are the most important thing—and I'm relieved. I'm a tired I can feel in my bones.

"Want to go out?" Lochlan asks. "We should be able to find some fun in the market district."

As soon as they say it, there's a part of me that wants it. It would be nice to just go out and be free for a few hours. But I can't. "The Whisperer would kill us."

Lochlan clucks their tongue. "You don't always have to do what she says, Dev. You don't have to be her perfect little spyling."

Don't I? I shake my head. "I'm tired, Lochlan. And besides, I think someone else wants to go out with you."

I nod my chin up the hall where Kai leans against the wall. A bottle of deep red liquid hangs from his fingers, catching the moonlight.

Lochlan frowns, tugging at the filigree shard they wear around their neck. They've always claimed they kept that piece because they like the intricate curl of its lines, but I know it's from the attack where they lost their magic. They open their mouth, but I trot away before they can say anything.

As I pass Kai, he reaches out and ruffles my hair. I grin.

"Take good care of them," I say.

"I make no promises."

I laugh, making a mental note to check on Lochlan tomorrow morning so I can drag them out of bed before roll call.

I head off to my room. It's small, tucked into a back corner of a hallway. I step inside, and maybe it's the tiredness or the loneliness, but I'm struck with how bare it looks. Lochlan has their collection of silver filigree shards. Janna has painted bright murals on her walls. Kai has so many plants it's like walking into a garden. But my room... There's my bed, neatly made. My trunk with everything packed inside. My cipher book that sits on my bedside table.

If I hadn't come back from this mission, I'd have left without leaving a mark.

As soon as I have the thought, I wipe it away. I toss my bag onto the bed, hard enough to muss up the sheets. I'm a spy. Not leaving a mark is my job. And even if I didn't really choose it, what does it matter now?

Not even bothering to turn on my lamp, I lie down on my bed and stare up at my dark ceiling. I think of a flash of light, of an impossible phantom where a phantom couldn't be. And despite the fact that I know it was just a trick of the light, I'm still so cold.

★ ★ ★

Lochlan is definitely hungover. They're wearing last night's clothes, sprawled over their bed sideways so that somehow every single one of their long limbs hangs off.

I still remember the first time I saw Lochlan, three years ago. They were a head and a half shorter back then, shorter than even me at that point, and still dressed in their casting robes, as if they couldn't let that part of their life go.

My mother's hand was on their shoulder, even though she hadn't offered me the simplest touch in years at that point. She told me how Lochlan had stopped the phantoms nearly single-handedly when the Mists broke through the barrier. How they'd been forced to pull on too much magic at once to stop the phantoms, and their magic connection was damaged. Lochlan flinched at that, their infuriating smile disappearing for just a moment. Now they were to become a spy, and I was to show them what to do.

I resented them so much, as everyone praised them for what they'd done and they grew skilled so easily.

In that year's trial we were paired together. We were supposed to scale the barrier, sneak past the soldiers, and steal a report that the Whisperer had planted. Only when we got to the top of the barrier, there was a caster there. Lochlan froze, and we were almost caught.

After the trial, I threw months' worth of resentment in their face. I told them this was serious, and if they weren't ready to take it seriously, maybe they should go scuttling back to their distinguished parents. That I didn't see why someone like them would even want to be a spy in the first place.

Anger and pain flashed across their face, when they had

always been so ready with a laugh or a joke. They exploded right back at me.

"Do you think I seriously wanted this? You know that's not why either of us is here."

Their words stole mine away. They had somehow uncovered the truth I'd buried so deeply in my heart that at times even I didn't recognize it anymore.

Neither of us ever apologized for that fight.

But we were pretty inseparable after that.

I yank the blanket Lochlan is lying on, dumping them to the ground. They yelp, spluttering as they haul themself halfway up before they see me.

I smile. "Morning, sunshine."

Lochlan groans, sinking back down. "Why would you do that?"

I throw open the windows, sending light beaming onto their angular face, and they hiss.

"You know," I say, "you really should have noticed when I came into the room. I could have been an assassin."

They sling their arm over their eyes. "I might have had a little too much fun last night."

That's a bit of an understatement. I nudge their side with my foot. "The Whisperer wants to see us for a debriefing."

Lochlan drops their arm. Despite the fact they're in an ungainly heap on the floor, they somehow manage to look serious. They prop themself up onto their elbows and open their mouth but I shake my head. Lochlan knows better than anyone that my relationship with my mother is...complicated.

And they should know that I'll handle it.

SILVER IN THE MIST

I grab a tunic hanging off the bed and throw it at them. They catch it just before it hits them in the face.

"Two minutes," I say. "Do not make me late."

I shut the door, cutting off their sigh.

To Lochlan's credit, they're outside in my time limit, looking astonishingly put together. They fiddle with their filigree pendant as we head down the hall. It's a nervous tic that not even training could knock out of them.

At least I'm not the only one uneasy about meeting my mother.

The Whisperer's office has her own private garden fronting it. As we cross the sun-worn stone path I remember days spent out here, playing among the bushes, or in her office, watching as she decoded ciphers as I did my schoolwork. She'd reach over when she noticed a mistake I made and gently correct me. I don't remember what changed, if it was what happened with my father, but somehow her gentleness and patience died that day too.

I knock on the door.

"Come in."

We step into the office. It's so familiar, and yet the older I get, the more intimidating it grows. Austere bookcases with neatly labeled files loom from the walls. A desk is set near the back of the room, the only ornament on it the small mahogany chest that my father gave her and that I've never seen her without. She even takes it when she goes on missions.

She's never let me see inside. Once—two years ago, on the anniversary of the attack—I sneaked in here and was going to open it before I realized my hands were shaking so hard, I'd never be able to pick the lock. I'd been so scared of what would happen if the Whisperer caught me. Or maybe I'd just been scared of what I'd find.

And then there she is, sitting behind her desk. My mother.

We have the same blue eyes and brown hair, though hers has wisps of gray in it and there are lines at the edges of her eyes. We're both dressed in the same sort of clothes, tunics and pants in dull colors, meant to be practical, not fashionable. Just like me she has her hair back, but only to keep it out of her face, not because she put any effort into the style.

She's a legend in her own right, the Whisperer of Aris. Which, I guess, just makes me one of her whispers.

Her quill doesn't so much as pause as we come in.

"The report?" she finally says.

To my left, Lochlan frowns. The expression is slight, but I catch it. It's always bothered them that my mother never acknowledges me. Luckily Lochlan is smart enough not to say anything.

It saves me from having to do something evil to them later.

I give my report, detailing our uneventful trip east through the Peaks, then scoping out the Cerenian soldiers' camp and liberating their papers. As I tell her about the phantom we encountered on the way back, her quill stills. I think she might ask if I'm all right.

She doesn't. And I know I shouldn't be disappointed, but I am.

The Whisperer finishes her letter. She sprinkles sand on it to dry the ink before slipping it into an envelope and holding it up. Reinolds appears from the hidden doorway in the wall to her left and takes the letter before leaving. Once I thought that might have been me at her side.

"Whisperer?" I ask, because I can't stand the silence any-more. "Are the Cerenians planning to attack Aris again? After all this time?"

Her head tilts as she looks at me, and her face might as well be a mask for how much it shows. "Is that pertinent to your work? It's the soldiers and the casters who defend us from attacks."

I wilt. I don't have an answer, but Lochlan speaks up for me. "You always say, Whisperer, that the more information a spy has, the more useful we can be. I think it's a fair question."

The Whisperer sits back in her chair, glancing between us. "Tell me, why do you think I sent you to that camp?"

I frown. "To collect information on troop movements," I say, "in case of an attack."

She doesn't respond and my stomach gives a horrible swoop. She never actually said that was the reason she sent us on that mission. She hadn't said anything but where to go and who to steal from. I was the one who assumed that was why those Cerenians had been there. I was the one who let my own anxiousness impair my judgment.

"Use your training, Devlin. What did you observe while you were there?"

I want to disappear into the floor. Instead, I force myself to at least attempt to redeem myself in her eyes. The scribes' tent had been strangely large for a patrolling camp, and there were so many sketches and papers in it. Putting that together with my mother's questions…

"They were there to research filigree," I say, wishing my voice didn't sound as unsure as it does.

The Whisperer nods. I can't even feel any triumph because she and I both know I should have noticed earlier. Frustration flickers against my breastbone. Why did I risk my life bringing back some silly papers about Cerenian filigree structures?

The Whisperer gestures to the papers on her desk. "From the information you brought it looks as if the monarch ordered one of her patrolling camps to search for a new site to build a filigree structure. There have been a number of storms along that area of the border and I'm sure they want to anchor more magic there. However, I want to ensure that you didn't miss anything. You saw no indication that they were trying to find an existing structure, did you?"

I don't understand what she's asking. All of the larger filigree installments on the continent are famous. You don't just lose a filigree tower. Plus, there's something different about her voice now: a piercing quality, when I'm so used to hearing perfect smoothness.

"No, Whisperer," I say. "There wasn't anything like that."

"And you sensed nothing strange with either the magic or the camp?"

Strange. I hesitate.

"I won't ask again."

I swallow. "It wasn't near the Cerenian camp, Whisperer. But after I had crossed the barrier back into Aris, I thought for a moment that I saw a phantom."

There's a long, horrible pause.

I shouldn't have said anything.

"A phantom, on this side of the barrier?" My mother's voice is a perfect blank.

"Yes, Whisperer."

She turns to Lochlan. "Did you see or feel it?"

They hesitate. "No, but at the distance Devlin would have seen it there's no guarantee I would have..."

She cuts them off with a swipe of her hand. "I don't have time for this."

"Whisperer," I say, desperate to explain myself. "What if I did see something? Perhaps we should send word to the casters on the barrier or..."

"Devlin."

Nothing changes in my mother's tone, but I go silent as if she had yelled it.

"We will not incite random panic. You of everyone should know better than to follow some fanciful delusion. You are a reflection of me in these halls and will behave accordingly."

Her words are blades and all I can do is stand there as every single one finds its mark.

The Whisperer steeples her fingers. "Now, do you have anything final to add to your report?"

Out of the corner of my eye, I see Lochlan glance at me, urging me to speak up for myself. I want to say something. Anything. Only all my words are gone.

I shake my head.

My mother looks between us and then she says the same words she's always said, so many times they've lost their meaning. "The monarch thanks you for your service."

CHAPTER FOUR

I stride away from the office, cold dripping through my veins. Only Lochlan catches my arm.

Their expression wavers through all the different things I know they want to say. As always, they settle on a bright smile. "Well, she gets more terrifying every visit."

Normally, their jesting tone would be enough to jostle me out of any bad mood. Today, though, I'm sinking into the cold and maybe I don't want to be pulled out.

"Lochlan, I really need to be alone right now."

I turn to go, but they step in front of me. "Don't do that."

"Don't do what?"

"Avoid me. Avoid her." They throw a hand back towards the office. "I know the way she talks to you bothers you, so say that to her."

I bark a laugh. Lochlan's had some ideas that are out there, but this one's all the way off the continent. "Sure, Lochlan, that's what I'll do. I'll just march back in there and say that to her."

I go to step around them, and once again they block me. "Lochlan," I growl, heat now tingling in my fingertips.

"She's your mother, Dev, whether she admits it or not. Whether you admit it or not. So, whatever you think, yes, you can actually talk to her. You have a right to talk to her. In fact, nothing is ever going to get better unless you talk to her."

"That's easy for you to say. Your family loves you. Dotes on you. They even send you care packages every month. Of course, you can talk to them."

Lochlan goes still, and I realize I've hurt them. Guilt wriggles into my chest, and I cross my arms to hide it.

"It's not that easy for me either, Dev," they finally say. "With a family full of casters and me only able to draw on erratic spurts of magic. But the point is I try."

"No, the point is you're the caster who saved everyone, so of course they're proud of you. It's not complicated with you and them like it is with me and her."

"Yes, I saved everyone." I can hear the annoyance creeping into Lochlan's voice. It's good to know we're still the only two people who can get this sort of rise from each other. I've certainly never heard them take that tone with anyone else. "Because they were called away to repair the failing southern barrier, and I was one of the few casters left. I burned out my magic because they weren't here. You think that's not complicated to bring up at family dinners? You think there isn't guilt and regret all over our interactions?"

I should stop. Neither of us wants to remember that day when the massive storm flared up and Lochlan was called out to face it. They did. And they won. But I know the cost they paid. Casters can only pull so much magic through their connection. If they pull too much, that connection can break.

And yet I can't stop. Because I can't say anything to my mother, but I can't contain it either.

"You just don't understand. I made a mistake. Right there in that office. In front of the one person that I just can't—" I cut off, swallowing hard.

We stand there, facing each other. Lochlan sighs. "Dev…" They reach out to me.

I step around them, and this time when they go to block me, I'm ready. I jab them hard in their side where a phantom once wounded them. They stagger back against the wall. It's a low blow, but I am a spy.

Lochlan and I stare at each other. Then they shove off the wall, and walk away.

Just run.

I should be reporting to the yard for drills. After that horrible debriefing, I need to redeem myself. But the hallways are closing in on me, and the only thing I can do is go.

We spies rise early, and even with the meeting, the castle and the yard aren't busy. There's a chill in the air, the soft morning light sparking off the dew. It's a morning I'd perhaps be enjoying in a different life.

I messed up with the Whisperer. I messed up with Lochlan. The failure pounds with every footfall. And here I thought I could impress her.

Around me, Isteria is waking up. Usually, I welcome seeing the busyness of everyone working together. But today I just notice the worn wood on the gates and frames. The cracks in the streets beneath my feet.

Those cracks only grow more distinct the farther I go, as I instinctively stray to the broken-down areas of the city. Until at last I reach the shoddily constructed wall at the city's northern end.

I should turn back but instead I step closer. I need to see the barrier again, despite what my mother said or even what I told myself. I need to make sure it's safe.

There's no door, but the wall isn't monitored since all of the available guards are at the barrier. It's easy enough to scale my way up, and drop down on the other side.

The Broken City spreads out before me, a mess of bricks and beams, long collapsed. I head in between the remains, slower now, even though my run still buzzes in my fingers. Bits of silver filigree stand among the wreckage, old pieces of jagged magic. It makes me think of storms, and screams, and the Mists creeping forward, foot by foot, relentless in their pace.

The memories are faint, scratching at my head. I was young. But I still remember.

The Mists and everything in them, including the phantoms, are a corrupted form of magic. It corrodes our own magic, like water against stone, until our filigree breaks and fails. It had never been as bad as eight years ago, though. There was storm after storm in the Mists that butted against the barrier. One by one the lanterns along the wall began to flicker out.

I remember my mother and father talking, arguing. Letters were sent. I think it was the one time the crown broke and asked Cerena for help. They didn't answer. Then the Mists surged, breaking through a warped hole in the barrier and sweeping over us like a wave.

And my father. He was there, and then after that night he was just gone. He ran straight into that Mist storm. I know he is called a traitor for abandoning his post, by any who dare to speak it when they think the Whisperer can't hear them. And even I can't defend his name against those rumors, when I don't know any more of the truth than they do.

I still remember, though, when Isteria positively shone at night, so bright I didn't see how the monsters could ever come.

We were supposed to work together. Cerena and Aris. In the later years of Moraina, when the continent was still whole and under one monarch, there were problems. The Peaks were never easy to travel, and especially not in the winter. Whichever side of the continent the crown set up their government in, the other suffered. There were coups and attempted revolts. So on her deathbed Monarch Karina decided to divide her country in two. She appointed her elder daughter, Naomi, to rule the newly formed Aris, west of the Peaks, and her younger daughter, Amelia, to rule Cerena, east of the Peaks. There was supposed to be cooperation there, the magic of our two countries bolstering one another.

Wasn't that the whole point?

A charge whips through the air.

I freeze.

Light explodes into existence two streets away and I know what it can only be: a phantom not contained by the Mists.

That's not possible.

I snatch my filigree knife from its sheath and dash forward.

I vault over a half wall and then skirt up to a pile of rubble to look over it.

The thing is like a giant wolf, its back higher than I stand tall, larger than any phantom I've seen before. A shot of energy flies from its feet and hits a nearby building, stones exploding outward.

I adjust my grip on the hilt of the knife, sweat making my palm slippery. I know how little chance there is of beating that thing on my own. But there are no guards on the wall between the Broken City and the rest of Isteria. If I don't stop it now, it's going to breach the city. And I cannot let that happen. I take a deep breath, ready to jump out.

A hand grabs my arm and yanks me back.

Lochlan's face is right up against mine. "What do you think you're doing?" they hiss. "Don't you see the size of that thing?"

My legs nearly buckle with relief. They knew I'd run and they'd followed me. They're now in just as much danger as I am, but maybe, with the two of us, there's a chance.

"The nearest soldiers are on the outer wall," I whisper. "We won't make it to them before that thing breaches the city. That can't happen. I can't…"

The words stick in my throat, images of that night eight years ago flaring in my head: the fear and the screams, and then our too-quiet suite.

I hold out my blade, glowing with power. I look at Lochlan, pleading. "We have to try."

They grind their teeth. "I'll go left, try to distract it. If you miss, I'm coming back as a ghost and haunting you."

Before I can protest that their plan is too dangerous, they're already gone. And the truth is, I don't have a better idea. I creep forward.

The creature is moving in an unsteady path towards the city. No one knows how intelligent the things are—they seem to mostly drive on instinct. It makes them erratic.

I slip over to another half wall and my foot kicks a stone. It clatters away. I freeze as the beast raises its head. Sloppy.

It turns towards me.

"Hey!" Lochlan jumps out from behind a building across the street. They strike the wall next to them with their knife, sending out a spray of sparks. The beast whips its head around and lunges.

I bolt forward, raising my dagger. One chance. It notices me, but it's too late. I plunge the dagger into its side and there's a blinding burst of light. Pain lances through my skull and I fall to my knees, squeezing my eyes shut. A charge of pure energy sizzles over my skin, raising every hair on my body.

Then nothing.

"Dev!" I open my eyes, blinking away the bright spots, to see Lochlan's worried face bending over me. "Are you all right?"

"Yeah." I let the knife fall from my hand, its filigree blade hopelessly ruined from the attack. "You?"

They nod, looking at the patch of scorched earth.

"You were right, about a phantom being inside the barrier." They numbly shake their head. "How is that possible? How was it here, when the Mists weren't?"

I don't know.

And if I don't know how it happened, I won't be able to stop it from happening again.

CHAPTER FIVE

We might technically work for the crown, but it's our job to make sure no one knows that, including the first group of soldiers we run into once we're back over the wall. While most of them head off to report, the remaining two take us into custody for being suspicious.

So now we sit in the barracks at the palace, not two wings over from our rooms, each with an arm cuffed to a chair. Lochlan slouches beside me. They reach for their cuff with their free hand and I knock it away.

"Don't pick the lock," I hiss. I give a warning glance to the two soldiers who are currently hunched in discussion. No doubt about what we saw.

"We could have already been out the window by now," Lochlan mutters. "And they wouldn't have noticed."

"If the Whisperer wants us to break out, she'll indicate so. It's the soldiers and the casters who contain the phantoms.

If we're needed here to report on what we saw, then here's where we'll stay."

Lochlan groans and sinks lower into their seat. "Can't you break just one of her rules?"

That stings. I don't particularly like being cuffed to a chair either, especially when gaining our own freedom would be so mind-bogglingly easy.

But then I see Lochlan's knee bouncing up and down, and how thin their lips are. They're like me. Normally they know how to hide. The fact that their emotions are slipping onto their face means they're really worried. I'm not used to them being the worried one. "It's going to be okay," I say quietly. "We stopped it."

They tug on the shard of filigree at their neck. "It shouldn't have been there, Dev. We both know that. What if something is wrong with the barrier? Really wrong? I'm not a caster anymore. If something happens, I won't be able to—"

They cut off, staring down at their hand so forcefully it's a wonder magic doesn't bloom from their fingers through sheer force of will.

My cuff just lets me reach over and squeeze Lochlan's hand. Looking at them now, thinking of what almost could have happened in the Broken City, I'm so scared of losing them. Lochlan knows me better than anyone. They've seen so many of my sides that I hide from everyone else.

"I'm sorry," I whisper. "About before. I shouldn't have said those things. I shouldn't have gotten angry at you when you were just trying to help."

Lochlan looks at me for a moment. Then they squeeze back.

"It's all right. I know my incredibly wise life advice comes off as intimidating to some."

I choke down my laugh. "You're lucky these cuffs aren't long enough for me to smack you."

The door swings open and I straighten as a captain of the guard steps into the room, with my mother right behind her.

The captain nods at her men. "Unchain the witnesses. We're handing them over to the Whisperer."

The soldiers unlock us, and Lochlan offers them a sickly sweet smile before stretching.

"Come," the Whisperer says.

We follow her as we leave the barracks and go to our own hallways. My bed is a siren's call but it will be hours before I can collapse into it.

Only then the Whisperer stops before the dormitories. "Lochlan, return to your room. I want to speak to my daughter alone."

Both of us freeze. The last time my mother called me her daughter, out loud, before witnesses, was eight years ago.

Lochlan gives me a worried glance, but heads off to their room. The Whisperer keeps going, and I follow her back to her office.

Reinolds is organizing papers in one of the bookshelves. When he sees me, nothing in his face changes, yet I catch the sudden shift in his posture. The tension.

My mother must too.

She walks over to her desk. "If you have something to say, Reinolds, say it."

If it was me, I don't think I'd be brave enough to say anything. But he does, accentuating his words with a respectful nod. "You know my thoughts, Whisperer. I still worry about the risk."

My mother's back is to me. I can't see her expression. But her words are clear in the quiet office. "Sometimes there is no perfect choice, Reinolds. You merely have to go with the best option available to you."

Reinolds pauses, but this time he chooses not to say anything else. "Yes, Whisperer." He leaves.

My mother sits at her desk and I step forward. I want to ask what that was about, but that would be insolent.

She picks up a quill. Puts it back down. "You could have been killed out there," she finally says.

I wasn't expecting those words. A small burn of hope enters into my heart.

"You know we have no people to spare right now," she continues. "You should have been more careful."

The hope snuffs out. I think of the words Lochlan had said to me just this morning. Could I ever be that bold in front of her? "I wasn't killed, Whisperer. I stopped the phantom. I did what I was trained to do."

The Whisperer tilts her head, studying me.

This time, I look back, trying to be the person I'm out there in the field. Because I'm tired of her looking right through me when all I want is for her to truly see me for who I am.

"I have a mission for you."

After what the Whisperer had just said to me, those were absolutely the last words I expected to hear from her. They throw me.

"A mission for me and Lochlan, you mean?" We always run missions in pairs.

"No. They won't be joining you this time. You'll be traveling to Cerena, where you will coordinate with our people who are already there."

I know we have agents in Cerena. The only one I can name, though, is Layde Elirra, a spy who was once close to both of my parents. She's a legend who moved to Cerena decades ago and who's worked her way up to the highest strata of the Cerenian court.

"Devlin, understand that this is not like your previous missions. You will not be merely going somewhere to steal something and then to return. You will be undercover for weeks and if you are discovered, you will most certainly be executed."

Executed.

It's not that I've never faced risk before, even the risk of a painful death. But sneaking into an enemy camp is a far cry from going undercover in the capital, and facing the full wrath of the Cerenian monarch's whims.

As soon as I have the thought, I shove it away. This is what I wanted. A chance to prove myself to my mother. If this is as important as she's making this sound, if she's trusting me with this, then surely...

I straighten, clasping my hands behind my back. "What is it that you want me to do, Whisperer?"

She nods. "I want you to go to Cerena and kidnap the great caster, Layde Alyse."

CHAPTER SIX

Layde Alyse.

I know who she is, of course. Everyone does. She's the strongest caster on either side of the continent. People say she's the reason why Cerena has managed to keep pushing back the Mists all these years while Aris has slowly fallen apart. Even worse, when she's not maintaining Cerena's defenses, she uses her magic to create sculptures and art, wasting it, while we can barely keep the Mists back from our borders. She was the one who taught me it's truly possible to hate someone I've never met.

She also never leaves the capital city.

"You have questions," the Whisperer says.

She's not really asking, and maybe I shouldn't say anything. But I now realize exactly who she and Reinolds had been talking about. I'm the one who isn't the perfect choice.

"Why am I being sent, and not one of your more experienced people?"

"We have been trying to think of a way to get Layde Alyse for years. We don't believe we'll be able to take her by force, not from the heart of Cerena."

I should be following her meaning, but I'm not.

"There is only one way you are getting Layde Alyse out of that city, and that is if you win her trust completely. She will be constantly guarded and watched. We decided that someone close to Layde Alyse's age would have the best chance of befriending her."

Befriend a great Cerenian caster. I don't know how to do that. But I definitely cannot say that to her. "What is the plan?"

"You will play Layde Elirra's niece. As a great noble of the city, she will be able to get you into the highest circles of nobility. In three weeks, the Cerenian crown will host its monarch's twentieth-anniversary gala. While everyone is distracted by the celebrations, you will lure Layde Alyse out of the city and to the Royal Monuments. A force of Arisian soldiers will be waiting just outside of them."

"Wait, the Monuments will react to her magic." Nearby filigree always reacts to casters, and the stronger the caster, the stronger the reaction. Lochlan always says that walking through the city used to herald their presence at every turn. For someone as strong as Layde Alyse, the Monuments will light up like beacons.

The Whisperer nods and I know I've noticed the right thing. "That's why we're sending this with you." She retrieves a wooden box from a drawer and holds it out to me. I open it to reveal a filigree bracelet lying inside.

I don't quite understand. Wearable filigree is too small to offer much protection, although it has saved soldiers and spies in a pinch. But then the Whisperer says, "The casters have created a bracelet with a filigree pattern that can block someone's casting ability. The key is in there as well."

I jerk my hand back. As soon as I snap that bracelet on Layde Alyse's wrist, she isn't going to come willingly. A seed of panic sprouts in my chest.

"Devlin."

I'm still staring down at the bracelet, but the Whisperer's tone pulls my attention back.

"Though you weren't right about your last mission, you are right about the possibility of an attack. We believe Monarch Cora has noticed our filigree thefts. It has made things… complicated. Particularly since there has been unrest in Cerena lately, and Monarch Cora knows that she needs to show herself strong to her people right now." The Whisperer taps the papers. "If Cerena is looking to build a significant new filigree structure, the magic that would give them would be all the advantage they need. The barrier is growing weaker by the day, and the Mists are only getting stronger. We cannot fight a battle both against the Mists and Cerena. Layde Alyse is the one person on the continent strong enough to protect our city. We need her."

Those words sink into me. The Whisperer is right. This isn't about my pride or about winning her approval. This is about our home. "I understand, Whisperer."

"You'll be in a unique position while you're there. None

of our agents will have gotten as close to such a powerful Cerenian caster as you will be. Find out anything you can about Cerenian filigree that we might be able to use against them. And if there is any opportunity for you to sabotage Layde Alyse's attempts to strengthen Cerenian filigree, I expect you to take it."

"I will."

She nods. "I trust you to make our family proud."

There's meaning beneath those words. It calls back a memory, of standing in the main room of our suite, when we still had a suite, when we were still a family. My parents were both spies, and yet they weren't trying to hide their words from my prying ears. Then again, I was supposed to be sleeping. Both of them were exasperated, tipping towards angry.

"Celia," my father said—such a soft-sounding name for a hard woman. "She asked to come. It wasn't dangerous."

My father was gone from the city so often and when I heard he was leaving again, I wanted to go. We went to Shari, the next largest city after Isteria. I rode before my father on his horse. The next morning, we even stopped to get candied apples instead of a sensible breakfast. I didn't realize until that moment, standing in our suite and listening to my parents, that my father had been on duty. To this day, I'm not sure what he'd been doing while I slept.

"You took Devlin on a mission, out of the city…"

"One day you'll have to let her make her own choice, you know."

"My daughter is not going to be a spy!"

I blink the memory away. I know I didn't imagine my

mother saying those words. But a mere two months later there was the attack on the city. And my father...

"I won't let you down, Whisperer," I say.

She slides a packet of papers towards me, bundled together with twine. "This is your mission information: who you'll be coordinating with in Cerena, what we know about Layde Alyse, and your cover story."

I take the papers. For being so light, there's a weight to them in my hands.

She's trusting me with this, and I won't let her down. I'll prove to her that I am the right choice.

"I understand."

I pack light. I don't own much to begin with and everything I need for this new identity will be given to me in Cerena. I certainly don't have anything to wear that would convince a Cerenian high noble to be my friend. However, I will need the tools of my trade: my lockpicks, my steel daggers, a new filigree dagger from the workshops, my cipher book for messages. And I'll need supplies to cross the Peaks. No soldiers can be spared to escort me. Fail or succeed, it will be all on my own.

On my own. This is the first time I'll be gone from Aris for this long. I don't know who I'll be without my mother's watchful presence.

"Was your plan to mysteriously disappear into the air and leave us all wondering?"

I whirl around. Lochlan leans against the doorway, a grin on their face.

My hand has already curled around the hilt of my dagger. I let go. "How do you always manage to sneak up on me like that?"

They laugh as they stroll into the room. "What can I say? I have talent."

I glance at my bag on the bed, half-packed. It already doesn't look like enough to let me do this. I gnaw on my lip. I'm not sure I'm allowed to tell Lochlan about this. But how can I not? "I'm going to Cerena," I say quietly. "To kidnap Layde Alyse and force her to come back here."

That surprises Lochlan. I can tell from the way they pause before they speak. "Wow, I mean... I wasn't expecting that."

I chuckle, but it doesn't come out very light. "I know, right?" I take a seat on the bed, running my fingers idly over the tunic I'd been about to pack. Lochlan sits beside me.

"I was going to find you and tell you," I say. "I was just... nervous. Worried. I don't know."

"We've done missions before."

"Not like this." I toss the tunic into my bag, not caring how messily it's packed. Layde Alyse is our best chance, and I'm the one who's being sent after her. If I fail... If I don't come back with the caster... Aris might not survive that. We're barely hanging on as it is.

I rest my head on Lochlan's shoulder. "I'm not sure I can do this," I whisper.

They wrap their arm around me as they plant a kiss on my forehead. "I know you can. Just promise me to trust yourself over there, and I don't mean the self you think you need to be for the Whisperer. Break the rules. Take the risks." They ruffle my hair. "Go with the strange plans I know are in that brilliant head of yours."

I slap their hand away. "I take plenty of risks, I'll have you know."

A grin quirks up their mouth. "I'm not talking about having a perfectly controlled dive before you jump off the cliff, Dev. I'm talking about flying."

I frown. "What is that supposed to mean?"

"You've always tried to be the perfect spy for your mother. But now, for the first time, you'll be away from her. This might be really good for you. To figure out who you are when she's not watching."

Where is this coming from? I can't change just because I'm leaving. If anything, I need to be more like my mother in Cerena, to ensure I'm making the right choices.

I debate arguing with them, but this is the last time I'll see Lochlan for a while. Depending on how this mission goes, it could be a long while. I don't want to leave with a fight on my mind. I don't want to be worrying the whole time I'm gone about what I said or didn't say.

I don't want any more regrets in this place.

So instead, I sink into their embrace, glad it's just the two of us, without anyone else. I close my eyes, for a moment just enjoying being here. In my room. In this city. Before everything changes and everything is on me.

Because no matter what they think, Lochlan is wrong. I have to be perfect on this mission. There isn't any room for mistakes. So, I will find Layde Alyse. And I will force her back here.

Even if it causes her entire world to shatter at my feet.

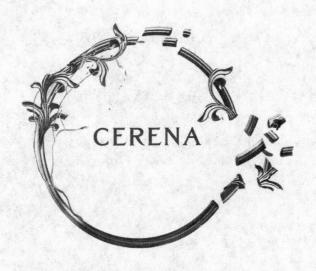

CERENA

CHAPTER SEVEN

Once I'm through the Peaks I slip around the encampment I'd sneaked into only a week ago and join the main road. The hills leading into prairies look much like Aris, only here everything somehow seems a bit brighter.

The road I'm on is loosely populated, but there are still more people here than I've ever seen traveling between the cities in Aris. There are people walking, or riding horses, or sitting in wagons piled high with fruit and vegetables, filling the air with the rich scent of earth. They all chat with one another, relaxed and easygoing.

And why wouldn't they be? In Aris, the Mists have covered the whole northern half of our country, and butt right up against the barrier, four miles out from our capital. Here in Cerena, they've managed to halt the Mists all the way outside their borders, in the neutral territory of the Peaks. That's a good half day's walk from the capital city of Wysperil. They've never had monsters lurking at the edges of their lives. There's no threat strong enough to harm this place, not with their army of soldiers and casters. Not with Layde Alyse.

Won't they be in for a surprise?

The road winds up a small hill and as I top it, I get my first look at the Royal Monuments.

I've always thought of the barrier and the Monuments as the same. Both defenses fully encircle their respective capital cities. Both anchor magic so that the casters within the city walls have a ready supply to draw on.

Only now I actually see the Monuments. Each is a massive tower of pure filigree, stretching so high into the sky, it's as if they want to snare the clouds. Where our barrier is plain, filigree flowers and vines wrap around the sides of the Monuments. There are at least a dozen towers stretching off into both directions, and connecting them are stretches of filigree wall.

It's magnificent.

And I resent myself for thinking that.

It takes me hours to reach the main gate in the wall. Traffic thickens as I go, so that by the time I get there, we've slowed to a crawl. There are three Cerenian soldiers posted at the gate. The Cerenian emblem, a silver bird resting on a thorned branch, decorates their tunics. I feel a spot of pride that where their emblem is a songbird, ours is a large owl, perched on a golden branch.

I reach the front of the line, and school my face into pleasantry as I hand the guard my papers. The woman's gaze flits over the pages lazily before giving them back to me. I nod my thanks and head in, letting out my breath once I'm safely through.

So far so good.

The path I'm on winds between orchards and farmland and everything I see makes me more bitter. The pittance of small farms we have around Isteria is nothing like the sprawling settlements out here. There are even filigree statues standing among the trees: a rearing horse, a bird about to take flight, a fountain.

Then I see Wysperil. The capital city sits on a hill and its walls spiral up towards the center like some enormous pinwheel, filigree silver adorning the towers. The houses are built of sun-warmed bricks. Balconies and courtyards overflow with greenery that I can see even from here. Above it all rises the castle. Spires and towers of silver filigree are set off against the pale stone and the Cerenian flag flaps slightly in the breeze.

A headache throbs into life in my skull.

I hate this place already.

I enter the city on bright cobblestone streets. There are shops selling jewelry and vases and clothing, along with gardens and shale pathways winding among the flowers. Vividly colored murals decorate the buildings. I see one of a forest scene, one of dancers, one of a filigree bridge. The smell of spun sugar wafts through the air, and a beautiful display of pastries makes me remember I've had nothing but jerky for the past three days. There's a shop with beautiful porcelain dishes in its window, and another with a rainbow of dresses. I try to keep my focus light and moving, to be casual, as if

I've seen this all before, but my attention is drawn in every direction at once, to all of the color and shine and people.

Like us, Cerenians wear a mix of tunics and pants, skirts and corsets, except compared to Cerena, our clothes look muted. Here there's a riot of yellows and pinks and blues and greens. Jewelry winks at necks and ears, and there are fine chains woven into elaborate hairstyles. I see capelets made of silk, fastened with beautiful broaches, and finely embroidered vests.

I'd been wondering why my dossier instructed me to wear my most vibrantly colored outfit. I've been uncomfortable walking for hours in an apple red a bit too bright for me, but in these crowds the subtler tone makes me stick out for all the wrong reasons.

This whole city reminds me of a music box, with ornate detailing everywhere.

And as I look at this city, for a moment I glimpse what Isteria could have been. I see beautiful lanterns and machines and all the things we've built, only this time they aren't in a crumbling city, but a whole one. My heart burns with the thought. With Layde Alyse, that could be ours.

I memorized a city street map on my way here, but everything looks different at street level. I'm so disoriented I miss my turn twice.

Slowly I leave the busy, winding streets behind and come out into open avenues, edged on both sides by expansive lawns and stunning mansions.

The house of my contact is a massive building in rich red brick with three stories and six balconies, each one trailing flowers. An iron gate protects it, decorated in a fake filigree style that make me raise an eyebrow. Through it I can see a promenade lined with trees and a water feature the size of a small lake.

I give a man in livery my name—at least the one I'll be using here: Layde Devonia. He bows and opens the gate, motioning me through. I wonder how much he knows. I'm not used to missions with a lot of moving pieces, where I'm not myself. As I head up the walk, I feel off balance and out of place.

Break the rules. Take the risks.

Has Lochlan met me?

I'm halfway up the walk when the door opens and a woman strides out. She's tall and heavyset. Her dress is a shade of autumnal orange that's almost muted for this city, but it brings out her flaming curls perfectly.

Layde Elirra.

She's lived in Cerena for close to two decades and has uncovered more information on the inner mechanisms of the Cerenian court than any other person. Somehow, I have to play her niece. You'd think having my mother as the Whisperer would make this moment less intimidating.

It doesn't.

"Devonia! Darling!" She takes my arm and I get a pleasant whiff of a flower I can't name.

I smile. "Auntie! It has been much too long."

"Come inside, you must be exhausted."

She sweeps me up the front steps and into a hall, which is tastefully decorated with rich mahogany furniture and ornate vases. I've never been inside a Cerenian home before, but as I look around, I see things from home that only someone from Aris would notice: the small statue of a fox that is the Whisperer's personal coat of arms, the tapestry depicting two soldiers who must be the legendary Mara and Kamala, a carved opal, which is the favorite stone of our monarch. It comforts me.

"And this is your only bag!" Elirra tuts. "I must talk to your mother, sending you all this way with so little luggage."

"It's fine, Auntie. It made traveling easier."

We're the only two in the foyer, so perhaps not everyone employed by this house does know. Either that or Elirra is very dedicated to her character.

"Ah, and here's Milla. Come and say hello to your cousin."

A girl my own age steps out from a side door, through which I glimpse a library. Her resemblance to her mother is obvious, with the same build and the same red hair. She's styled it to make her curls intentionally wild, running them through with fine chains of gold. She wears an exquisite green dress with golden embroidery running from hem to collar. A large emerald hangs from her neck, and bracelets drip from her wrists.

For a moment, I wonder if she's turned into just another Cerenian; unlike her mother, Milla was born here. But as she steps towards me, there's a mischievous spark in her eyes.

She clasps my hands. "It will be wonderful having someone closer to my age in this house." She grins. "We'll get up to all sorts of mischief together."

I smile back. "I'm looking forward to it."

I think back to my dossier, about what I know of her. Milla's father, also a spy, died a decade ago, leaving just her and her mother. She is a caster, though her magical connection isn't too powerful.

Elirra leads the way up the grand staircase and Milla loops her arm through mine, drawing me along with her. She chats about the current affairs in Cerena, managing to make a treasure trove of information sound like idle gossip.

I like her.

We stop midway down the upper hall and Elirra opens a door onto a suite. I follow her inside. The space is expansive and rich, with an ornate desk, a canopy bed, and a wide window that looks out over the rear gardens. It's bigger than mine and Lochlan's rooms back home put together. On most of my missions, at the end of the day when I went to sleep, it was either in my own bed or on the hard ground. I feel a little disconnected realizing just how deeply my new life is going to run here and how much Devonia I'm going to have to be.

Because standing in this grand room, as Devlin I feel completely out of place. This glittering world isn't one I've had any experience in. It doesn't fit me. I'm so used to doing my work in the shadows, but here Layde Alyse will be like her own sun. I have to stand in it and not be unmasked.

Behind me Milla closes the door and instantly their personas change.

Milla flops onto the bed. She gives me a wry smile and I'm not sure why until her mother somehow draws herself up even taller and looks over me with a calculating gaze.

"Front and center," she says.

I let my bag slide to the floor and obediently go stand in the middle of the room. Elirra circles me with steady steps.

"The Whisperer's daughter, in my home," she says.

"Yes, my layde."

I stand still, back straight, chin out. Once the Whisperer and Elirra were close, more friends than colleagues. But that was when my father was still alive. They obviously stay in touch even now—their work demands it—but over the past few years I've gotten enough hints to know that something in their relationship soured right around the time my father died. I've always wondered if that was somehow connected to my father's death, but I can't ask. It's not part of the mission.

Elirra stops in front of me and I force myself not to take a step away.

"Welcome to Cerena, Devonia." There is no inflection in her tone. "Everyone employed here is in the Whisperer's service. However, as a great layde of the city I also often entertain many who do not know, so to ensure security and discretion, the only places you may speak candidly are your own rooms, Milla's rooms, the library, and my office should I call you there."

I nod. "Of course, my layde."

"I can't say that I agree with the Whisperer's decision to introduce an unknown element this late in the game, particularly when my own daughter is already here. However, the Whisperer seems to think that you are ready for a mission of such importance. Any failure on your part, though, will compromise both mine and Milla's position and ruin everything we have built. So should I ever feel that your progress is not to my satisfaction, I will ensure that the Whisperer is informed and that Layde Devonia disappears back to her estate in the country. Do you understand?"

Elirra doesn't want me here: she is only consenting to me

being here because she's been ordered to. It's a heavier blow than I thought it could be.

I had wondered what it would be like to be out from under the Whisperer's gaze for the first time in my life. But I'm not. Elirra or the Whisperer: they'll always be watching.

"I understand, my layde."

"We have arranged to introduce you at court tomorrow. Your wardrobe is prepared, and Milla will select your outfit for tomorrow."

Milla, who is currently and unashamedly rifling through my bedside drawer—I haven't even seen what's in there yet— looks up at that, and flashes me a grin that's so wolfish it doesn't exactly settle my nerves. "I can do that."

"Well then, Devonia," Elirra says. "I expect you to prove yourself as your mother's daughter and run this mission flaw-lessly."

Flawlessly. Elirra saying those words only gives them extra weight. She's right. I need to be exactly the spy my mother expects.

I nod. "Of course, my layde."

Without another word, Elirra and Milla sweep out of the room, and I'm left standing all alone.

CHAPTER EIGHT

My trek through the Peaks must have tired me out more than
I thought, because I don't wake up until there's a knock on
the door and a maid delivers breakfast. A spread of dainty pastries and jams and tea so hot it makes my eyes water greets
me, set out on delicate plates. Despite the fact that I know
why I'm here, and I didn't need Layde Elirra to tell me how
serious this is, it's just been so long since I had a morning like
this. With a nice breakfast, and a chair set in the morning
light, and a warm cup of tea in my hands. Without training
or drills, or constantly looking through the window to make
sure the barrier is whole and still protecting us.

As soon as I have that thought I push it down, and pull my
dossier from my pack, studying it as I sip my tea. I don't have
time to sit in the morning sun. I should be preparing for my
meeting with the monarch.

I can't allow this place to make me soft.

There's another knock and before I've had a chance to respond, Milla strides in, followed by a servant loaded down with a bundle of fabric.

The servant carefully deposits the fabric on my bed and Milla ushers her out with a cheerful "I'll help my cousin get ready."

As soon as the door is closed Milla turns on me so quickly I jump, just managing to not scald my fingers with burning tea.

She picks up the fabric from the bed, and as she presents it to me with a flourish, I can see it's in fact a dress. She flashes me an impish smile. "So, what do you think?"

"It's purple." It's the most obvious thing I could have said, but it's really the only way to describe that dress. It's not a peaceful lavender or a deep and subtle violet. No, this dress is a brilliant plum, and the fact that there are at least eight layers of fabric to the skirt only makes the color seem that much more vivid. Even the silver beads that flash in the bodice as Milla gives the dress a dramatic shake just seem too much.

I have the sudden thought of trying to sneak into a military camp in that and being swarmed by soldiers in an instant.

"Yes," Milla says, "and purple is Layde Alyse's favorite color."

"Won't that be a bit obvious?"

"First rule of Cerenian court: always be obvious. Now come on, behind the screen."

I do as she says, since Elirra made it clear Milla was in charge of my wardrobe. I slip from my night shift and somehow manage to stuff myself into the dress. I step back out, incredibly glad Lochlan isn't here to see this. They would never stop laughing. "I feel like a pastry."

"Oh good, then it's working." Milla takes my hand and drags me over to the vanity, making me face my reflection. Somehow the dress looks even brighter on me than it did in Milla's hands.

I bite back my sigh. "I've never understood why Cerena has to be like this."

Milla cocks her eyebrow. "Like what?"

"So—" I gesture vaguely with my hands "—over the top. Garish."

Milla barks out a laugh. "They'd say artistic. In fact, this particular shade of fabric is prized due to the intense dying process and the shade which comes from the shell of a very specific beetle."

"Oh wonderful, so I'm wearing dead beetles. And how do you even know that?"

She tosses her hair over her shoulder. "I'm a Cerenian layde, remember? It's my job here to be interested in fashion and art."

I suppose I should have expected nothing less from Elirra's daughter.

"Now," Milla says, "my mother will give you the full briefing on the way there, but we'll be officially introducing you to the monarch today. Layde Alyse may or may not be there, but we do have to go through the proper channels for this." Milla lifts my hair up, securing it in place with silver pins. They're sharper than usual hairpins, sharp enough to do serious damage if need be. Milla slides bracelets on my arms and clasps a string of pearls around my neck. It makes me feel weighted down, but I try to remind myself that every piece is another layer to who I am now. To survive here—to succeed here—I need to blend in.

"Thank you," I say, a bit awkwardly, "for getting me ready."

"Of course. We all know what's at risk here." Milla looks up and her eyes meet mine in the mirror. She hesitates, her hands stilling over my hair. "Is it as bad as they say? Back in Aris?"

I think of what my mother had said to me in her office.

"It's not good," I say quietly.

Milla silently continues to style my hair.

I glance at her in the mirror. I'm not entirely sure what to think of Milla. She's not as terrifying as her mother, but she is still a spy. I don't know what parts of her are an act, and what is real. I don't even know if the name Milla is an alias or not. Still, I need as much information as quickly as possible so I have to ask. "Milla, why weren't you chosen to do this? You already live here. You already know so much about Layde Alyse."

Milla gives me a rueful smirk. "I'm afraid I ruined any chance of that ages ago."

"What do you mean?"

She sighs. "It was three years ago. The Cerenian court had just heard the news about how the Mists had broken through the barrier."

I wince. That was the attack where Lochlan lost their magic.

Milla shakes her head, her face fierce. "They laughed. The monarch laughed when she heard the news. I was so angry. And there was Layde Alyse, already an accomplished caster with how much magic she had. I didn't even care what she had said in the past. She could have helped us and instead she gave up, just because that was what she had been ordered to do, as if that somehow excused it. So, I cornered her and gave her the tongue-lashing of her life. I probably would have blown my cover if my mother hadn't shown up and pulled me away. Since then, whenever I get near her, Layde Alyse looks as if I'm about to bite her head off. To this day I'm surprised her laydeship has never reported me for it." Milla scoffs. "Really, I should have taken her to Aris right then. I mean, sure the palace was full of guards, and the Monuments were in the way, but I could have done it."

I digest on that before realizing what Milla said. "Wait, what do you mean you didn't care what she had said in the past? What did she say?"

"Layde Alyse has claimed she's wanted to help Aris before," Milla says.

I twist around, so fast my neck cracks. "What?"

Milla shrugs. "When she was younger, she tried to convince Monarch Cora, the court, anyone who would listen that Cerena should send aid to Aris. Not that it mattered. Because everyone refused and Layde Alyse did nothing. She didn't even keep fighting. Words are cheap."

Milla fiddles with some of the makeup pots on the table. I keep staring at her, knowing I'm doing it, but not able to stop. Even with what Milla said about it ultimately being meaningless, I feel a bit off balance. Why would Alyse say that? Was it pride? Was it guilt?

It's not what I expected.

Milla picks up a powder brush and leans past me to fix her makeup. "You should know that Alyse is a bit of an oddball. Even now. It's like she lives in her own world. She spends most of her time chasing fairy tales. She doesn't try to fit in. It's why the monarch hates her so much."

Milla puts down the brush and begins to tidy up. I look at myself in the mirror and see Layde Devonia staring back at me.

I wonder if I'll end up fitting in any better than Layde Alyse herself.

Layde Elirra waits for us in the foyer. She's back to the persona of a caring aunt and even though I should prefer that to the intimidating way she acts in private, at least then I know that the emotions on her face are real.

"Devonia, darling. You look wonderful this morning. And so cosmopolitan."

"It was all me," Milla says, breezing past her mother.

Layde Elirra heaves a long-suffering sigh and even though the joking is an act between the two of them I still get this pang of jealousy in my chest.

A carriage waits for us out front and I try not to gape at the amount of filigree curling over its walls and twining around its wheels. If we could ever convince a horse to go into the Mists, that thing could rumble through the Peaks with no sight of a phantom.

I guess that goes to show animals are smarter than we are.

We settle ourselves on plush seats. The carriage winds up through the streets amid the grand homes, before it breaks out and I get my first real look at the castle.

Filigree curls up the wall like latticework and its towers are topped with delicate glass spheres. Silver balconies curl out from the walls, and walkways made of pale stone and glass bricks connect the various wings.

The carriage follows a wide drive, broken shale crunching beneath the wheels, before stopping to let us disembark. Ornamental soldiers line the walk that stretches before us and courtiers as colorful as flowers dot the lawns. Milla certainly knew what she was doing. I fit in here. Deep down, I'm not sure how I feel about that. I don't even know who Devonia is supposed to be yet. Can I really convince others that she is me?

Inside the palace, Layde Elirra leads the way through the hallways. Each one is adorned with art: a painting of a waterfall that takes up an entire wall; a statue of a young man in a robe crafted entirely from bronze, his hands cupping a small bird; an indoor fountain carved from a single piece of quartz.

We head up a sweeping set of stairs and enter an elevated hallway that connects two wings of the castle. It's lined with windows on both sides, and all of them have been opened, letting in the sweet air from the gardens. Claps and delighted laughter echo up to us through one of them and I drift towards it.

The garden below is crisscrossed with paths that wander among flowering beds and stretches of lawn. A small crowd of courtiers have gathered, lacy parasols held up to block the sun. They form a half circle and in front of them is a girl.

She wears a lavender gown, which is an understatement compared to the intensely brilliant colors around her. She lifts up her arms and silver filigree blooms from the ground.

My feet, which have already begun to turn away, stop.

That pale blond hair twisted into a simple braid over her

shoulder. The blue-green eyes I can just make out. The round face. The age. It fits the description from my dossier perfectly.

Layde Alyse.

Reading that description, I had envisioned those characteristics coming together to make someone bright and brilliant. Someone like Lochlan. Instead, the girl I see looks soft. Weak. She does not look like the single most powerful caster on either side of the continent. And she certainly doesn't look like someone who would speak up for Aris, when everything I know about the Cerenian court tells me they'd only view that as a betrayal.

I lean against the windowsill, trying to portray casual fascination, as if I'd just stopped to take in the show. But then my fascination turns real. I stare as the lacy filigree magic solidifies at her feet. It grows steadily, soon reaching higher than Alyse's head, before bits of it branch off, twining out to kiss the sky. The branches taper off, only for leaves of filigree to curl out from their ends, delicate and shimmering in the sun. Silver apples blossom out between them. And I'm left staring at an honest-to-goodness filigree tree now planted in the garden.

The courtiers all clap as Alyse smiles and curtsies.

She should be the only thing I'm focused on right now. She's my mark. The whole reason I'm here. Instead, I can't stop looking at the tree. I've never seen such fine filigree before. Would Lochlan have been able to make something like that, if we had the magic?

It's beautiful.

"Come along, dear," Elirra calls from farther up the hallway.

I give one last glance at the girl standing before the filigree tree. One of the laydes says something to her and Alyse looks down, her smile feigning shyness, as if she's pretending not to notice the masterpiece she created only a few feet away. As if she is as much an ornament on display as it is.

In that moment, all I want is to wipe that smile off her face and let her see what it's like to be afraid. Because Milla was right. Words without actions are meaningless. She could have saved us and she didn't.

I follow the others through the walkway and down a long hall, only to stop at a grand set of doors carved with the Cerenian coat of arms. The page standing there nods to Elirra and opens the door. Light laughter and the soothing tones of some stringed instrument filter out to us.

Elirra says something to the page from behind her fan before he precedes us into the room. "The Layde Elirra, her daughter, Layde Milla, and her niece, Layde Devonia."

I step through the doorway. Courtiers are spread throughout the room, sitting on low couches. They're all attired in beautiful dresses and expensive suits, or a mixture of both fashions. The musician who plays a delicate lap harp sits on a small raised stage to the right, strumming out light music. Some of the courtiers are playing at a card table, and I make a mental note to ask Milla to teach me the rules later. Servants walk through the room, offering crystal glasses of wine here, or finger sandwiches or strawberries dusted with sugar there.

I'm struck with how strange this tableau seems. That they have time to sit around like this. Not even our monarch has leisure time.

Two of the laydes shift and I see the woman who can only be the Cerenian monarch. The crown she wears is an imperious thing, with twining spires of silver filigree, set all over with sapphire stones.

Her Royal Majesty, Monarch Cora. It's odd, how stately she looks. Our own ruler was six when she took the throne, and she is only fourteen now. Monarch Cora is well into her sixties.

She's dressed in extravagant blue and silver, the embroidery on her dress clearly meant to imitate the curls of filigree patterning. The color complements the silky hazel of her hair and her blue eyes.

This was the monarch who didn't answer our plea eight years ago, when my father left and my mother changed.

She is long overdue for payback.

"Ah, Layde Elirra, it is wonderful to see you and to meet your niece. Come here, child."

I can't think of the last time I was called child. My own mother hasn't called me child in years. I slide into the expression I need, shyly eager, hopefully befitting a Cerenian noble meeting her monarch for the first time. She reaches for my hands and I glide forward, settling my fingers into her palms, which are smooth and lightly scented.

Every eye in the room fixates on me. The courtiers all give me the sweetest smiles, but I see the evaluation and the judgment. A few of them lean in to talk to a companion, hiding their words behind fans.

The monarch smiles as she lets go of my hands. "Tell me, Layde Devonia, did you travel far to join us?"

"Not too far, Your Majesty. I'm from Mirista."

"Mirista!" The woman to the left of the monarch leans

forward. She has a cup of tea and as the smell of nutmeg reaches me, I feel disoriented.

My father always loved the smell of nutmeg. And no matter how many times I've smelled it since his death, it still throws me.

"I've heard that you have to journey near the Central Range to get to here from there," the woman continues. "How terrifying that must have been. Did you glimpse the Hush?"

The Hush. I just don't understand Cerenians. Naming it the Hush rather than the Mists. Wildelights, rather than phantoms. Because obviously calling something by a fancy name will stop it from killing you.

"I was lucky enough to not get that close, my layde," I say.

"You *should* consider yourself lucky, young layde," a man pipes up. "We should all be staying as far away from the Hush, and the country that lies in it, as possible."

The monarch smiles, all graciousness. "I can assure you, Layde Errit, there is no danger to traveling. As always, we advise caution. One never knows what plans Aris might have for the Hush. However, traveling near the Central Range is as safe as ever."

I nearly choke. Our plans. For the Mists. Does she mean other than desperately trying to stop it from killing us?

"Well, I don't believe we have anything to fear from Aris," another layde says. "They are a weak country with a weak monarch. We easily could have blotted them out ages ago if they were worth sending the soldiers."

My hands find each other in my skirts, my fingers clenched so tightly they hurt as my mother's words come back to me: *We cannot fight a battle both against the Mists and Cerena.*

Across the room, I meet Milla's eyes.

The door opens again and the page announces, "The Layde Alyse."

At her entry, every head swivels in her direction, granting me the perfect excuse to do the same. As Alyse steps in, the smile on her face, which looks a bit too carefully put on, slips for a moment. Her pale lavender dress seems even more out of place here. And I resent that I'm in this hideously overstated thing when hers has a simpler cut and no beading to speak of.

"Ah, Layde Alyse, so kind of you to join us."

If there'd been graciousness in the monarch's voice towards me, there's a chill when she says Alyse's name.

They really don't get along.

"My apologies, Your Majesty." Alyse's voice is soft. Far softer than I would have imagined for such a powerful caster. "Some of the courtiers asked for a casting."

"Ah, of course. Layde Devonia, have you had the opportunity to see any of Layde Alyse's casting?"

The perfect opportunity, and the monarch has placed it right in my lap. I let myself think. The monarch must have high standards. Expensive standards. While Alyse was born on a country homestead, nobody special until her talent was discovered. I don't have a lot of time here to get the lay of the land. But a little discord could give me a perfect in. I look at Alyse and force a smile, as kind and cheery as I can make it. It's not exactly a natural expression for me. "I did, Your Majesty, on the way in. Our casters in Mirista could never create such an intricate sculpture as I saw you make. It was an apple tree, correct?"

Alyse glances at the monarch, biting her lip. "Yes, it was."

"An apple tree." Monarch Cora laughs. "How provincial! Could you not have created something more befitting the castle grounds? Apple trees are so very...understated."

The courtiers twitter around the monarch as pain crosses Alyse's expression. It's a look I recognize because it's how I feel whenever my mother stares right through me. I do not like seeing an emotion I've felt so strongly reflected on Alyse's face. At least I know not to let it show.

This caster needs thicker skin.

Alyse gives a small curtsy. "My apologies, Your Majesty. I'll make sure that my next casting meets your approval."

The monarch waves her hand as she turns away. "See that you do."

As the monarch's attention shifts, back to the layde sitting on her other side, everyone else also slips back to what they were doing before Alyse's entry. She is left standing alone in the center of the room and this weariness settles over her face. Then she turns, hiding her expression as she crosses to a chair in the corner and pulls a slim book from her skirts.

In this room of brilliant, vibrant people she looks so...out of place.

Elirra gives me the smallest nod.

It's time.

The monarch has turned back to her companions and I take that as a dismissal. I curtsy and then drift through the room until I stand before Alyse's chair. Looking down at her now, I'm struck again by how small she looks. How unremarkable. This shy, unassuming girl in a corner is truly the most powerful caster on the continent?

Then Alyse looks up at me and for a moment, a bit of defiant shine crosses her expression. It slips away.

I curtsy again, managing to pull off the movement gracefully despite the layers of fabric around my legs.

"My layde," I say softly. "I wanted to come and apologize. I never meant to make you uncomfortable in front of the monarch. I'm afraid I don't understand court sensibilities very well yet."

She shakes her head. "It wasn't your fault."

I fiddle with my fingers, trying to put the perfect bit of longing in my voice as I duck my head. "Actually, I've just arrived here in the capital, and I'm afraid I'm already a bit homesick. We have apple trees in the orchard back home. I love the scent of their blossoms in the spring. It was nice seeing that piece of home here." I look back at her, making sure I hold the eye contact. "I thought your casting was beautiful, and I'm sorry that the monarch didn't agree."

Alyse pauses, a flicker of confusion crossing her expression. She looks down at the book on her lap, her fingers brushing the pages. "Thank you, my layde," she murmurs.

"Layde Devonia," the monarch calls. "Come join us at the card table."

Well, I guess I'm learning the game as I go.

Alyse immediately glances away, biting her lip. I turn, fighting to keep the smirk off my face.

This might be easier than I thought.

CHAPTER NINE

I've been introduced to Alyse, but I only have three weeks to grow a beautiful friendship and steal her away. And I need to do it without the two guards who accompany her about. So, like any respectable layde of the court, I trail her.

This is new to me, spying in plain sight. New and admittedly annoying considering I now have to do everything in an audaciously colored dress. You can only be so subtle in this many gaudy layers of fabric shushing across the floor.

Over the next few days, I track her movements while strolling through the gardens or watching her while idly leaning against a windowsill. I expect her life to be exciting, full of parties and social engagements and events. Instead, she's solitary. She only attends to the monarch once more and only leaves the palace—I'm guessing to maintain the Monuments—once as well.

When she is about, I notice the whispers and looks that follow her from the other courtiers, even occasionally from one of the maids or guards. Milla wasn't exaggerating when she said that Alyse was the odd one out in the palace. I should be able to use that, if I can just find a way to get close enough.

Unfortunately, that is proving difficult as Alyse's days mainly involve going from her rooms to the famed gallery and then returning back to her rooms in the evening.

I sit on a bench in the garden, fanning myself against the late-afternoon heat as I look at the building, knowing by now that she'll be in there for hours. In Aris, aside from the palace, our most important building would be the workshops. That's where our casters make lanterns, and practice their filigree forms, and do the research necessary to protect us from the Mists. The closest Cerenian equivalent is the esteemed Gallery for the Advancement of Filigree Arts. It protects some of the oldest filigree art in Cerena and provides studio space for their casters. It was founded by Monarch Amelia herself, and in her age, it was a public space, open to anyone who wanted to wander its halls.

From the outside, it's an impressive building. Every inch of its walls is decorated with patterns of filigree. Glass spheres top the towers and I catch glimpses of filigree contraptions hanging there.

I want inside. Alyse doesn't take her guards when she goes in—they always wait by the door. It could be the perfect opportunity to get her alone.

Except I'm not a caster and nowadays, only they're allowed in.

I abandon my bench. Normally I'd just sneak inside, but since the whole point is to see Alyse that won't exactly be easy to explain. She needs to invite me. As the country's strongest caster, I'm sure she's allowed to bring whomever she wants.

I wander along the path Alyse usually takes from her rooms to the gallery, winding my way between hedges and beneath a marble arch.

A marble arch. I pause. It's so old I can see the spiderweb of cracks in its sides, some of them quite large. It's still obviously safe unless, say, someone was to change that.

Spies use their environment. That's what the Whisperer always says.

A smile crawls over my lips. There's more than one way to get someone to trust you.

And I'm about to save Alyse's life.

Milla bursts out laughing when I tell her my plan. "You're evil. I like it."

She's lounging on her bed, which has a pale green quilt that looks far more Arisian than Cerenian. She's traded her dress for a loose pair of pants and a tunic but even they're so well tailored she could stroll through the halls of the palace without looking underdressed.

I perch on the edge of Milla's bed, not sure I know her well enough to be sitting here rather than on the vanity chair, but she doesn't shoo me away.

Milla's room is as tastefully decorated as I expected, with exquisite pieces of furniture and an elegant fireplace in the corner made of glittering white stone. The only things that surprise me are the easels in the corner, most displaying finished canvases, though one—of a still life of a vase on the table—is in progress.

Milla might only be studying the arts to fit in, but she's talented. I have no artistic sense to speak of and even I can tell that. No wonder my dossier said that she's also excellent at forgery. I suppose that is one thing that artistic skills might be helpful with.

"I don't have time to waste," I say. "But if I save her, she'll be indebted to me. I just need your help to do it."

"You don't have to explain to me," Milla says. "I think it's brilliant. Now, what's the plan?"

I pull out a rough map I drew of the gardens and spread it over the bed. Milla rolls over to my side.

"Were you being pursued through the castle when you drew this?" she asks.

"Very funny. Just because you've had to fake an art talent your whole life, doesn't mean I did."

Milla looks over at her paintings and a flash of something crosses her face, so small I can't tell what it is. But then she turns back to me and grins. "Well, I've seen children with more talent than you."

I roll my eyes. "Anyways." I trace my finger along the paper. "This is the arch. Tonight, we'll chisel away at the cracks until they make this side unstable. Then tomorrow morning, we wait until Layde Alyse goes to the gallery. She should take this path. You'll be here, hidden by this hedge, and I'll be sitting on this bench right around the corner. As Alyse goes under it, you jam the prybar into the arch and drop it."

"Is it bad that I'm really excited about dropping this arch on her?" Milla asks.

"You don't drop it on her. Just near her." We can't afford to injure Alyse. We need her to fix the barrier.

Milla flaps her hand at me. I suppose that's as good of a promise as I'm going to get. "And then you'll be there to sweep her out of the way," Milla says.

"Her guards will be following her, so we'll have witnesses. They'll see that I've saved the gem of Cerena. I'll gain both the court's favor and Alyse's gratitude in one swoop."

Milla laughs. "I can see why you were chosen for this mission."

A tentative warmth filters into my chest as Milla idly kicks her legs behind her. It actually feels nice to be sitting with her. Even though I know she's her mother's eyes. The truth is, I'm used to being watched. That's just my life. And as spies go, I like Milla. As long as I run a flawless mission, there's no reason for her to ever report anything negative to her mother. Maybe that means we could even be…friends? Undermining the Cerenian crown together. That's something friends do, right?

Lochlan and I had certainly been good at it.

"Was your father like this too?" Milla asks.

The budding warmth in my chest freezes. Was my father like this? Not really. He was a spy, yes, but he had a gentler side to him as well. Not like my mother, who never shied away from doing what had to be done. I've spent so long trying to be the perfect spy for my mother, to be her, that sometimes I forget I had two parents in this line of work.

But then again, my father was the one who abandoned his post.

I shake my head. "Not really. He was a different sort of spy, I guess."

What would he think of this plan? Would he risk hurting Alyse?

I push those thoughts away. It'll be fine. She'll be fine. After all, I'll be there.

This plan is exactly what my mother would do.

So, it's what I'll do too.

I sit on my bench near the archway, the warmth of the morning already prickling sweat out between my shoulder blades. The book I'd grabbed as a prop from Milla's room sits open on my lap, its pages bright in the morning sun. I'm sure it's fascinating—Milla seems like she has excellent taste in every facet of her life—but I'm not paying attention to a word. Despite what I said to Milla, I'm nervous. I can't afford for this to go wrong.

I risk a glance over at the arch. I don't see Milla—she's too good for that—but I can just imagine that grin of hers. We sneaked here last night and chiseled two of the cracks, forming one decidedly large rent. With the proper force, applied at the right angle, it should topple.

Hopefully.

Footsteps sound on the pathway at my back: Alyse, with her guards following a few feet behind. Right on time.

I pretend to studiously focus on the book and catch a history of Cerenian fashion that I didn't expect to be in Milla's collection as, out of my peripherals, I see Alyse step beneath the arch.

There's a crack, more violent than I expected, and the

arch tips. Not in the direction we'd calculated but right towards Alyse.

Not. Good.

I launch myself off the bench at her. I just catch the look on Alyse's face, her eyes wide, before I slam into her. We go down in a tangle of limbs, the crash of stones shuddering the ground beneath us. It's so close I can feel them catch at my skirts.

And then there's silence.

There's this harried buzzing at the base of my skull. I turn to stare at the remains of the arch, a mere finger's width from my feet.

Strange. While I was worrying about crushing Alyse, I never really thought about the possibility of crushing myself.

"Layde Devonia."

Alyse's shaking voice snaps me back to the present. I look at her, still partially pinned to the ground beneath me, the purple and blue shades of our dresses mixing with one another.

"My layde." I scramble back, so that she can sit up. Straggles of hair have escaped her braid, surrounding her pale face. She swallows, glancing at the collapsed arch, and then back at me.

Her eyes stare into me. I've never been this close to her, and I'm struck with the thought that there's more to this caster than I first saw. There is strength in that look.

"You...you saved me," she says.

"My layde!" The guards, separated from their charge by marble remains and dust, are beside us. They help Alyse up and then one of them reaches his hand down to me. I take it, not even needing to fake my wince as he helps me to my feet. I landed harder than I wanted to.

I survey the damage. The arch is down, obviously. And Milla is hopefully long gone. We've already attracted some attention. I see at least five different courtiers gathered farther down the path. Perfect.

Well, perfect besides almost crushing myself.

"Layde Devonia, are you all right?" Alyse asks.

I look back at her. I think she's impressively composed, until I notice the slight way her hands shake. She hides them in her skirts.

"I am, my layde." I glance back at the arch. "I can't believe it fell like that."

"My layde." The soldiers have been conferring, but now one of them steps towards Alyse. "We should get you back to the palace. There may be foul play involved here."

I make sure to widen my eyes appropriately. Foul play. How very concerning for them.

The guards begin to hustle Alyse away. But after a few feet she stops. "Wait, one moment." She turns and looks back at me. "Layde Devonia, will you come to me tomorrow, for tea? I'd like to thank you properly."

I duck down into a curtsy, using the movement to hide my relieved breath. "Of course, my layde. I would be honored."

By the time I'm back up, Alyse's guards are already drawing her away, and she barely has time to raise her hand in farewell before they disappear.

I stand there for a moment, staring at the spot where she left.

Despite the triumph, I feel this pang of unease at how easy

that was to manipulate her. I glance at the broken pieces of the arch, the pieces of rock now sprawled over the path.

At how easily I almost let that all go wrong.

CHAPTER TEN

Elirra gives me the smallest nod of satisfaction when I tell her about my tea date with Alyse. As far as I know, she didn't hear about my nearly crushing the caster, and I'm not sure if Milla was already gone by then or if she chose not to tell her mother about it. I'd like to think it's the latter.

It was just a small mistake. I'll be more careful in the future.

Milla tries to dress me in purple again, but this time I hold my ground. I already have Alyse on the hook. I don't want to act like I'm currying favor.

And by *hold my ground*, I mean I hide behind the changing screen in my room, clutching a dress mannequin to my chest for protection until Milla sighs and relents. She produces a red gown in as pale of a shade as she thinks I can get away with. She doesn't look entirely satisfied with it, but I want to go with my gut.

Besides, if I'm doing this, I'd rather be comfortable.

A page meets me at the carriage drop-off before the palace and I follow her through the halls. As we go, I see courtiers and servants glance at me. I hear the whispers that I've been trained to pick up.

"It's her."

"I hear that she saved Layde Alyse's life."

"Pulled her right out from under the arch."

I try not to preen. Why yes, yes I did. So kind of them to notice.

"Better her than me. Powerful caster or not, I'm not sure I'd want to be alone with someone as odd as Layde Alyse."

I raise my eyebrow, but the layde who spoke is already around the corner.

They're not very subtle, these courtiers.

Alyse's room is in a beautiful hallway overlooking a court-yard with its own waterfall, which has trailing lines of fili-gree running through the water, the droplets of water twining around it.

She meets me at the door. She's dressed simply again—at least more simply than the other nobles I've seen here—in a rose-and-cream gown, with a little porcelain bird on a chain around her neck. Today there are small white flowers braided into her pale yellow hair. I expected the room of Cerena's strongest caster to be dripping with decadence, but instead the space is subtly decorated with couches surrounding a table and a glass cabinet that displays teacups. A small writing desk sits next to a bookcase. The only piece of filigree is something abstract sitting on the desk that has at least a dozen points. I just don't understand art. What is something like that even supposed to mean?

Alyse smiles at me. In court, she seemed as if she might disappear into the floor at any moment. Here, not watched by the monarch, she looks more relaxed. Then again, I suppose I do deserve a smile after saving her life.

I mean, I endangered her life first, but she doesn't have to know that.

She leads me to a table where tea has been laid out on a three-tiered tray. There are cakes with cream rosettes, puddings in delicate cups, and a glass teapot with swirls of silver inside of it. Candied sugar decorations sit scattered about the plates.

Alyse pours the tea with a practiced hand, sending out a waft of lavender and something nutty. I select a cake drizzled in honey, take a bite, and nearly die. The sponge is light and airy, the honey seeped all the way through. I have never tasted anything so delicious in my life. I have meals I love in Aris—piping hot meat pies with Lochlan, fresh porridge on wintry mornings, spiced loaves in the fall—but we don't have anything like this.

Alyse smiles again, no doubt at the expression I hadn't bothered to hide. That cake deserves the truth to be known.

She passes over my teacup. "Thank you again, for saving me. I feel like I didn't get a chance to say that properly yesterday."

"I'm just glad that I was there, my layde," I say. "It must have been a shock."

"Certainly a shock, but I'm safely unflattened thanks to you. My guards and some of the court seem to think foul play might have been involved, but I'm not so sure. It was an old arch." She stirs some sugar into her cup. "Besides, I can't imagine who would want to hurt me like that."

I take a sip of my drink. I don't think those words were an act. Maybe that naive personality of hers is the reason she spoke up for Aris.

"You're here to visit your aunt and cousin, correct?" Alyse asks.

"I am, my layde. My parents have always been eager to see me introduced at court. When my aunt suggested a visit, it seemed the perfect opportunity."

"That must have been exciting." Alyse smiles, but the expression doesn't reach her eyes. It's politeness, nothing more, and that isn't good enough. If I don't leave here forging some sort of connection, there's no telling when she'll ever invite me back.

Alyse is something of an outcast. I'll have to convince her I'm an outcast too.

I allow a grimace to flavor my smile. "*Exciting* is one word for it." I pause, glancing down at the tablecloth. "My layde, if I may, I truly wanted to thank you for inviting me today. I know it's only because I was in the right place at the right time, but the truth is, I've had difficulty these past few days adjusting to court. I worry everyone simply sees me as some country noble." I lift my gaze. "So, thank you. It was nice simply being invited somewhere."

I see it then, on her face: that slip of vulnerability as my words nail the exact spot I wanted to hit.

She runs her finger around the circumference of her cup. "I can certainly understand that," she murmurs. As soon as the words are out, she corrects herself. "I only mean it must be difficult to come here, without your family."

"It has been. You are very lucky, my layde, that your family was able to move to the capital with you."

Her smile falters. She looks down at her plate, hiding it. "Yes," she says, and I can hear the forced cheer in her voice. "It was about a year later, but they joined me here."

That was an interesting reaction. I know she has parents and a brother in the capital. Does she not have a good relationship with any of them?

"They must be proud of what you're working on," I say carefully.

Alyse glances over at the desk on her right, then fixes her gaze back on her plate. She selects an iced cookie and nibbles at its edge. "Yes, they're very proud of me. My mother is a caster too, but she didn't have sufficient powers to even be invited to the gallery to train."

I nod at Alyse sympathetically, but my mind is focused on her reaction. Why would she have looked at her desk in that moment and that context? It's something I want to find out. But I don't know when I'll be invited into her rooms again.

So, I guess I'll just have to figure it out now.

I reach for a cake and in the process I let my hand bump her cup. It teeters and tips, the tea spilling into her lap.

I jump up. "My layde, I'm so sorry." I hurry around the table to dab at her skirt with my napkin. "I can't believe I did that."

But Alyse just waves her hand. "Layde Devonia, don't worry. Please excuse me and I'll ask my maid to clean it out."

She crosses the room and goes through one of the doors at the back. Perfect.

I step lightly over to the desk. The surface is tidy and bare, and when I try the first drawer, it's locked. No matter. I slide my picks out of a secret pocket in my dress and have it unlocked within moments. A quick skim shows nothing in the first drawer. Or the second. A drop of sweat slides down between my shoulder blades. But then, buried at the bottom of the third drawer, I uncover a packet of notes.

The first page has a drawn image of a beautiful filigree tower. I'm guessing from its construction that the real version must be large. Its three feet stand in a triangle formation, but then they twine together until they taper to a point at the top. The filigree pattern that makes it up is extraordinarily intricate.

Beneath the drawing are more papers and notes: ones I don't have time to read. But as I flip through them, the same words flash out at me over and over: *the Silver Spire.*

A book lies at the bottom of the pile. It has a beautifully embellished cover of silver filigree and flowers: *Ancient Tales of Moraina.*

Moraina. It was what the continent was called before it was divided into Cerena and Aris. Looking down at the book, I remember what Milla had said, that Alyse spends her time chasing fairy tales.

Footsteps sound from the other room. I won't make it back to the table, but by the time Alyse steps through the door, I'm admiring the row of teacups in the cabinet, each decorated in a different floral pattern.

"I really am so sorry, my layde, again," I say as we retake our seats.

"Well, you did also save my life. I dare say that excuses a lot."

Yes, and now it's time to see what exactly all my machinations have bought me. What's most important right now is making sure this tea is the start of a beautiful friendship as far as Alyse is concerned. I still think the gallery is the key to spending more time with her, not to mention finding out what she's doing. If I want to be a part of her life, I need to find a way in.

"My layde, I was actually wondering... I heard so much about the gallery back home. I've always dreamed of seeing it. I know it isn't exactly proper for a layde, but is there any chance I might accompany you inside sometime?"

Wariness crosses Alyse's expression. I wonder if others have asked her that, what it is in her past that gives her that expression. I'll need to find out. But for now...

"No, of course not," I say. "It was silly to think that. It's a place for casters, not someone like me."

Alyse blushes. "I didn't mean to suggest..."

"No, my layde, I understand." I flash her a smile, wobbly at the edges, hoping I've correctly grasped her personality. "Of course, I do. This is the Cerenian court. It isn't home. I need to remember that."

Alyse bites her lip, watching me. Then she says, "Well, perhaps a small visit wouldn't hurt."

I flash her a brilliant smile, grinning decidedly wider on the inside. "Thank you, my layde!"

I've secured my invitation to the gallery and I've uncovered one of the caster's secrets.

Not bad for a tea date.

CHAPTER ELEVEN

The library in Elirra's manor is an intimate place. I've just returned from talking to one of Elirra's underlings about my supposed home in Mirista and I've pulled the curtains so no one outside will notice the flickering candlelight and wonder why someone is in Elirra's library this late at night. Rows of shelves and gleaming ladders circle the small room, a collection built up over decades of her working here. I could spend the rest of my time in Cerena just working through these pages.

And yet despite the information at my fingertips, I'm struggling to find any record of the Silver Spire. I look again at the piece of paper in front of me, where I've sketched what I remembered of the structure. I'd been hoping to find some details on it so that I could give Elirra a well-rounded description for my next report, but that's looking increasingly unlikely.

I don't like it. If they have a structure as large as this hidden away, they'd have more than enough magic to get through the Mists and attack us again.

Sitting back in my chair, I look around the room. I know that behind one of these bookcases there's a door that leads to a storeroom with the more confidential papers in this house. Elirra had told me that if I needed access to that particular collection, I could request it through Milla. I assumed that if there was any information on the spire it would be in the Cerenian books, ones that Elirra had no need to hide. But maybe I need to look at the more covert information Elirra has gathered.

I pause, mulling over those words: *covert information*. Once more, I think of my father and how Elirra and my mother fell out right after his death. It could have just been because of the way my mother changed, but as a spy I'm taught to explore all possibilities. I can't shake the feeling that there's a chance it's all related.

Biting my lip, I look at the bookcase where I've already noticed the slight irregularities on the shelves.

Then again, maybe I'm not ready to know.

The door opens, and I nearly start, even though I haven't technically done anything. Milla flounces into the room. She sits down across from me at the table, stretching herself across the mahogany surface and jostling the candelabra. Her usual extravagant outfit has been replaced by drab clothes in gray. She must have been up to no good. I wish I could have joined her.

"Busy night?" I ask.

She grins. "Layde Errit is away visiting his country estate so I took the opportunity to liberate some filigree from his manor. And some secrets. Did you know he's been funneling tax money away from the royal treasury?" She snorts. "He's being sloppy about it too. I can't wait for the monarch to figure it out."

Layde Errit. I remember him from my first meeting with the monarch. I can't say I feel sorry for the man.

"So, how did tea go?" Milla asks.

I push the thoughts of secret doors and my father out of my head. "We have another date tomorrow." I reflect a moment on how late—or really early—it is. "Well, I guess it's today now."

Milla gives me a smile that looks feral in the candlelight. "Look at you. You'll have her wrapped around your finger before you know it."

So far, I haven't found anything in the library, but Milla has lived here her whole life. She might know something.

I slide my drawing across the table so that she can see it. "You don't recognize this, do you? It's supposedly called the Silver Spire."

Milla raises an eyebrow. "I have truly never met anyone with less artistic talent than you." She plucks the picture from my hands. "This is an actual travesty."

I roll my eyes. "Yes. Well, we can't all be the dedicated scam artists that you are."

She sniffs, but there's a grin on her face. "I'll take that as a compliment."

"While I was at tea with Layde Alyse I broke into her desk. There was a book called *Ancient Tales of Moraina*, a drawing of this structure, and notes that talked of the Silver Spire."

Milla's eyes light with interest as she takes a second look at the drawing. "Well, the Silver Spire is a pretty old story." She thinks for a moment. "I know a book that we can find it in."

Milla leaves the room and comes back a few minutes later with an incredibly worn, obviously incredibly loved copy of a children's fairy-tale book. As I open the cover, I see Milla's name written in a childish scrawl. I raise a brow at her and she kicks me under the table.

"My mother wanted me immersed in Cerenian culture when I was young, so I could adapt." Milla flips through the worn pages until she stops at a picture of the spire. "All right. Once upon a time, the magic of Moraina was unbalanced and in chaos. Casters were burning out. Blah blah blah. Death and destruction. Okay, here we go. A powerful caster emerged. She gathered other casters together and they built the Silver Spire, a testament to magic. It was so large that it returned balance to the magic. Only the caster hid the spire so that no one would be able to use it for their own means, and that is where it remains to this day."

I raise a brow. "I might be no good at art, but you're a terrible storyteller."

Milla goes to kick me again, but this time I'm quick enough to jerk my legs out of the way. I take the book and read through the whole story. There are a few more embellishments to the tale, but Milla's version was basically accurate. There aren't many details. The caster isn't even named.

A lot of our tales involve unbalanced magic, of structures or casters. However, if this story is true, as Alyse seems to believe, then I don't remember a period of history where our magic was that chaotic and destructive.

I flip through the book and pause when I reach the back page: *"These tales have been compiled from Monarch Amelia's working notes."*

Working notes. I run my fingers over the ink.

Milla leans over. "Huh, I never noticed that before."

That word, *working*, sticks out to me. I understand having fairy tales in Monarch Amelia's library or even in her personal letters if it was of interest, but not in her working notes. That sounds like she was taking these fairy tales seriously.

That sounds like another caster I know.

"So does this thing actually exist?" I ask.

"If it does, I can't imagine where it would be after all this time," Milla says. "There have been stories of people looking for it: past casters and monarchs. A spire that large would be powerful. But no one has ever found anything. It says it was hidden but where would you even hide something like that?"

"Then why is Layde Alyse wasting her time looking for it?"

Milla shrugs. "Well, that girl has always been a little odd. Temperamental."

"Temperamental. Her?"

Milla grins. "Hard to imagine, I know, but it's true. Layde Alyse was young when she came here. I mean, what's the average age a caster discovers their powers? Ten? Twelve? Layde Alyse is so powerful she got hers when she was six. And when she first got here, she couldn't control it. Any time she got angry, scared, worried: bursts of filigree everywhere. It didn't exactly make her friends. Even once she got control of it, she never tried to rebuild those bridges. She grew quiet and shut herself up in her studies."

That was not the history I was expecting. I think of the caster I know as a child, surrounded by chaotic bursts of filigree. I can't quite reconcile those two sides of her. And now she's chasing a spire that in all likelihood doesn't exist anymore, if it ever did. Why?

I was hoping to find out more about the spire so I could use it. But I guess I'm just going to have to take the risk.

I have this book. I have some sort of connection or at least interest by Monarch Amelia that somewhat resembles Alyse's own interest. That's enough to build a lie off of.

I guess it's time to chase a legend.

The next day Alyse meets me at the door of the gallery. As simple as that I'm inside with her.

The atrium opens up beneath an expanse of glass ceiling that shafts light down into the space, sparking off the creations inside. Filigree statues stand proudly on their pedestals: people, trees, animals, and even a waterfall. Some of it is glowing, but some is just as obviously ancient, with barely a glimmer of light left to its lines. Even the best filigree only lasts so long without upkeep and from the plaques near the structures some of these are centuries old. This hall is absolutely packed with structures: row after row, stretching farther back than I can see.

It makes me think of the workshops back in Aris. I used to go there with my father when he got updates on the work they were doing. I would run my fingers over the filigree, patches of light scattered among the chaotic workbenches. Father would even sometimes slip discarded pieces into his pocket to add to our secret collection. It's one of my favorite places in Aris and yet it is a pittance compared to the filigree around me right now. If the Mists had formed in Cerena instead of Aris, then we could have been the ones with all this.

Alyse takes a few steps before noticing I'm no longer following her. She stops and looks around as if seeing the place
for the first time. Around her the statues glow brighter, re-
acting to her magic. She makes the entire hall go lumines-
cent, and there she stands in the center. For the first time, she
looks as if she owns the world she stands in. "It's beautiful,
isn't it?" she says softly.

Beautiful. A snake slithers into my belly. She thinks I'm
admiring the place. I'm not. There's a thick wad of emotion
stuck in my throat. Cerena has all of this, without even struggling for it. "So much filigree, and none of it used to push
back the Hush."

Dread flushes through my body. I can't believe I just said
that to her.

I scrabble for something to say. "I—I'm sorry, my layde. I
just meant how lucky we are. That we still get to have this
beautiful art, despite everything."

As soon as I say the words, I know they aren't enough.
Only then, Alyse's expression changes. I was sure I had gotten
her personality sorted out: quiet, naive. Easily manipulated,
if I was being honest. But now there's something else in her
eyes. It isn't the confusion or the suspicion that should have
been on her face. Instead, there's this intense focus, so strong
I can feel it rooting me to the spot. As if, for a moment, she's
staring right into me and I have to force myself to remember
that it's Devonia she's seeing, not Devlin.

She turns to the closest statue, a lithe figure with an arm
extended out, as if inviting the caster to dance.

"We really are," she murmurs.

I swallow, my throat dry. That expression on her face wasn't like the Alyse I've gotten to know.

Two casters enter the foyer. They're talking to each other, but as they see Alyse, they stop and bow respectfully.

Alyse inclines her head, and the moment between us breaks.

"This way, Layde Devonia," she says lightly. "I thought you might like to see my workshop."

We take a hallway that branches off the end of the foyer, with rich wooden floors and paneling on the walls. She tells me about the various rooms as we go, her tone casual, as if nothing happened. She points out the rooms for studying the literature on filigree and for practicing casting; the ones for studying the past art forms and the ones for experimentation.

"And this," Alyse says, "is my workshop."

We enter a spacious room in its own tower. There are no windows here, only the glass sphere on the roof, no doubt securing the privacy of their precious caster. The upper floor is a balcony that rings the walls, reachable by an ornate spiral staircase and lined by bookcases. On the ground floor drawings of various Cerenian structures paper the walls: the Starry Arch, the Rose Tower, the Centennial Bridge. Alyse is an accomplished sketcher. The floor is filled with neatly organized tables, which are adorned with filigree pieces. It's peaceful in here, with the silver and the books and the light shafting down through the roof.

I step up to the closest table to examine the menagerie of filigree animals that sit there. There's a peacock, a horse, an elephant, a giraffe. They're all so fine, none more than a few inches tall. But the amount of work that must have gone into these… I pick up a fox. There is such incredible detail in its pointed ears and tail.

It makes me think of home.

Alyse drifts to my side. "There was a fair in the lower city a few weeks ago. I thought I could cast these and send them there. The Hush has been so volatile lately and everyone's been worried. I wanted to make something to liven up their spirits." She shakes her head. "But the monarch said no. She doesn't want me creating in the city. Just in the palace."

"Liven their spirits?" I ask. "But filigree is supposed to be for defense."

Alyse smiles. "It wasn't always. Before Monarch Karina divided her country between her daughters, when the continent was still just Moraina, filigree wasn't used like it is now. Back then, filigree opened new heights. It helped us explore to the edges of the continent and build structures that before we could only have imagined. And everyone was allowed to have that. That beauty and joy and wonder."

I force my frown to stay off my face. Cerena knows more of the continent's history than Aris does, since our original city fell and theirs didn't. I can see the possibility of her words being true. Before Monarch Amelia and Naomi there were no Mists or phantoms or storms. Our magic wouldn't have been needed for protection.

I put the fox back down. But even if filigree was once used for other things, we need it in the fight against the Mists now. That's all it should be used for.

Alyse picks up the fox and holds it out me. "Here, as a thank-you for saving me. If I can't give this to them, at least I can give it to you."

It takes me by surprise, even more so when I realize a part of me wants it. This filigree is intricate like I've never seen before. Even Lochlan, as much as they hate Cerena, would love this. My fingers curl around the warm metal.

I guess it's time to put my plan into action.

"Actually, my layde, there was another reason I wanted to come here today." I put on a bashful look. "Back home, I have a good caster friend who loves rare old books. They recently came across a book on Monarch Amelia. In one of the footnotes, it mentioned how interested she was in the Silver Spire legend. Of course, we had both heard of the Silver Spire before but we never..."

My voice fades away as Alyse's face changes.

I was hoping for a reaction, of course. One of interest perhaps, or eagerness.

I wasn't expecting the sudden desperation that I see there now. And I realize just how truly guarded she's been around me when I finally see an expression that vulnerable on her face.

"My layde?" I ask.

"You found...there's a connection between Monarch Amelia and the spire?" she whispers.

There'd been a part of me that assumed this was just some passing fancy to occupy her idle time, but as soon as I see her expression, I know I was wrong. I'm scrambling to think over my story again, to make sure my lie is as solid as possible before I dig myself in any deeper, when there's a knock on the door.

Alyse glances from me to it, before smoothing her hands over her skirt. "Come in."

A young man enters. He looks a few years older than me, with tousled brown hair and deep green eyes. He wears a richly embroidered waistcoat, beneath which is the tunic of the gallery, only his has three golden stripes. From my dossier I know that gallery casters have one, two, or three silver stripes depending on their magical proficiency. I don't know what gold means.

Out of the corner of my eye, Alyse flashes me a pleading look and gives a small shake of her head.

The man looks between us, and for a moment I see an interest that I don't trust at all before he smiles at me. The expression is far too smooth and easy.

I guess I'm just a real mistrustful person.

"Ah, I don't believe we've met yet..." He pauses, looking expectantly at Alyse. She seems smaller again, her brightness completely dimmed. I resent this man for taking that from her. Alyse is my mark.

I'm the only one who's allowed to make her uncomfortable.

"Layde Kerrin, this is Layde Devonia. She is Layde Elirra's niece."

He comes up to me, close enough that his extra height looms over me. He gives me another smile that I'm sure he thinks is charming and I try not to gag. Even if I was interested in boys, or anybody, I would never want to be with him. "It's a pleasure to meet you, Layde Devonia. I'm the monarch's cousin and the right hand to the head of the gallery."

So he's royalty, or just about. That explains it. I take his offered hand and he bends over to kiss my fingers. As he does, I glance at Alyse and roll my eyes. A hesitant smile flashes over her face.

By the time Kerrin has straightened, I'm back to smiling at him. "Charmed, I'm sure."

"I regret to interrupt your visit, but the monarch has requested a filigree casting for some of her guests," Kerrin says. "She asked me to collect Layde Alyse."

Collect her?

"That's generous of you to come all this way," I say. "As a cousin of the monarch, you must be busy yourself."

"Well." Kerrin looks at Alyse and there is a possession in his face that makes my skin crawl. "I always try to take personal care of my casters, don't I, Layde Alyse?"

Alyse flinches. For a moment I think that whatever I managed to gain here has been lost but then Alyse turns to me. "Layde Devonia. Could you come here tomorrow so we can finish our tour? I'll tell my guards to let you in."

I smile, a real one this time, as I duck into a curtsy. "Of course. I would be honored, my layde."

CHAPTER TWELVE

I follow Milla through the darkened streets, our charcoal clothing blending into the shadows. Milla must have shadows in her blood because she's even better at this than I am. Which injures my pride, but is certainly nice to work with.

She points out different routes I could use to sneak Alyse out of the city: that chain of alleys that reaches between two of the inner walls; that street of shops that will be closed at that hour; in a pinch the side road over there that, while meandering, should be deserted. I inscribe them all into my mental map.

Once we're out of the city walls and heading through the fields and orchards, we both relax a bit. There aren't many guards this far out at this time of night. Just some quiet farms. Out here, I could basically take any path I wanted.

"Thank you for showing me all this," I say, pitching my voice low.

Milla grins, her eyes sparking. She's come even more alive in the night, which is saying something. I wouldn't exactly call her usual self low energy. "Of course. It's my job here to help you. But this—" she runs her fingers over the bracelet the Whisperer gave me "—this bracelet is a marvel. It will really block the caster's magic?"

I feel this twinge of guilt. I think of Lochlan, of the loss behind their expression whenever the subject of magic comes up. I imagine them as a caster and someone putting this bracelet around their wrist, cutting off their connection to the magic.

It's cruel.

Milla nudges me. "Don't worry about it. After all, you just have to lure Layde Alyse away during the party, snap this bracelet on her wrist, and then get her through the Monuments. Easy, right? I mean, that plan really only has three steps."

I give her a dry look, glad she misunderstood the reason for my silence. "Right."

The orchard we're walking through ends before us, leaving a patch of open ground between us and the Monuments. I stop. During the day the towers had been impressive, but at night they're absolutely stunning. Like all filigree work, they let out an ethereal glow, but I have never seen anything built this large. They're towers of pure moonlight, the floral pattern that curls around them shining against the night.

Milla and I shed our dark cloaks, revealing paler clothes. We dash to the base of the wall, where the guards on top won't be able to see us even if they look down.

"All right," Milla says. "So the first thing you'll need to

worry about is timing the guards right. There is one for roughly every mile. This section here is going to be the best place for you to take Layde Alyse through. On the other side, there's a game trail. Follow it to the left into the grove of trees and you'll find the delegation the Whisperer will have sent to meet you."

The Whisperer. My mother. "And how do I actually get through the wall?"

"With this." Milla pulls a slender, pointed filigree tool out of her pocket. It glows bright against her skin.

I recognize it as a tool casters use when doing repairs. They use it to cut off pieces of worn filigree so they can regrow fresh filigree in its place, keeping the all-important pattern as accurate as possible.

Standing here with Milla, knowing I'll need to get through this wall, I realize there's another way it could conceivably be used.

"I'm going to cut my way through the wall," I say.

She grins in the dark. "Brilliant, isn't it?"

I can do that. I'll just have to be quick. And I'll need to find a way to keep Alyse quiet while I'm working. I suppose the threat of daggers should be able to achieve that.

"Have you ever used one of these?" Milla asks.

I shake my head.

"All right, so just jab the pointed end against the filigree you want to cut off. The magic in the tool will react with the magic in the Monument. Then just cut off the piece you want."

She hands the tool over and I slip it into my belt pouch.

"Now," Milla says. "Let me show you a couple of other

places that should be safe for you to cut through, if you aren't able to access this stretch."

We head down the wall, walking in silence before Milla speaks again. "By the way, how did your meeting with Layde Alyse go?"

"Good, until we were interrupted by Layde Kerrin."

Milla glances at me.

"What?" I ask.

"Be careful around him," she says.

"Is he that dangerous?"

"How much do you know about the line of succession here in Cerena?"

"I know it's a bit convoluted," I say, "since the monarch doesn't have any children."

Milla nods. "Right. So it could potentially pass to one of two cousins."

Let me guess. "And Kerrin is one of those cousins."

"Some say he has the weaker claim, except that of the two heirs he is definitely the one with the drive and the smarts to force his way to the crown."

Wonderful. That was not a complication that I needed.

"And what is his relationship with Layde Alyse exactly?" There had been something between the two of them that had made her small, for all of her magic.

"When she first came here, he was set to watch her. Not officially, of course. No one would ever say anything like that out loud. But it was understood that it was his job to keep her in line. It's not the same now that she can control her magic, but I don't think he's ever forgotten." She jabs my shoulder with her finger. "Whatever you do, make sure you don't attract his or the monarch's ire. Because if they turn on you, my mother and I will throw you to the wolves."

"You know, sometimes I can't tell if you're actually on my side."

Milla's teeth flash in her grin. "Good."

A screech splits the night, wrong and strange. Except it's not strange, because I know it. It's a sound I've heard in the Peaks, and inside storms, and during attacks.

Beside me, Milla goes still. And I realize that maybe the sound isn't familiar to her.

Even if I was able to see through the wall, I wouldn't be able to make out the Peaks at this distance in the dark. We're a good half day's walk from the closest Mists here. Before, I would have said that meant the phantoms had to be at least that far away too. Only that's not true anymore.

I look at Milla. "Do you normally hear the phantoms from here?"

She shakes her head. "Cerena thinks it's unbreachable. They think with their Monuments the Mists will never find them. But none of this—" she waves her hand at the closest tower "—is as strong as they think it is."

I'm so used to thinking of Cerena as this untouchable presence. It shifts my world to realize that the problems we're facing in Aris haven't left Cerena untouched either.

Maybe that should make me glad. Instead, I just have this feeling that all of us are running out of time.

The next morning, I head to Alyse's workshop, still not able to shake the uneasiness of last night. I'm reaching up to knock on her door when I hear quiet voices coming from the other side. I glance up the hall, making sure no one can see me, then step closer until I'm right up to the wood.

"I don't think this is a good idea, Alyse." I don't recognize the voice. It's male. On the younger side I'd say. So soft-spoken I can barely catch the words. But the fact that he didn't attach Layde Alyse's title to her name makes him instantly fascinating.

"I know it's a risk, but if Layde Devonia has found another source of information, one that actually links Monarch Amelia to the spire, just like we suspected…" That's Alyse's voice and I'm surprised at how passionate she sounds even from the other side of the door. I've never heard her get close to that tone so far.

"We don't know anything about Layde Devonia. She's barely been in the capital a few days. How do you know we can trust her?"

"She saved my life. Besides, we haven't found a new lead in months. We're running out of time. You need to trust me on this. I think she could really help us."

On the other side of the door, I can practically feel the quiet in the room.

"Alyse." The male voice comes again, hesitant. "I just think that maybe…"

Whoever this is, he obviously doesn't trust me, and I'm not about to let him convince Alyse that I shouldn't be given this chance. I step back from the door and knock.

There's a pause and then Alyse calls out, "Come in!"

I open the door. Alyse is standing with a young man on the far side of her workbench. As soon as I see him, I know he must be her brother. The two of them have the same pale blond hair and blue-green eyes.

He wears a gallery tunic, though his has no silver stripes to speak of. A small topaz dangles from his left ear. He steps protectively up to his sister's shoulder.

Well, at least she has one functioning relationship. I have to admit I'm a little relieved.

I'm not completely heartless.

Alyse smiles at me. There's hesitation in it, but that's all right. Even if she is only letting me into her life because she wants the information she thinks I have, I can work with that. I made up one false clue and I can make up more.

"Layde Devonia, this is my brother, Everett. He's one of the clerks here."

The clerks. They aren't casters but they're still part of the gallery—the lackeys of the gallery truthfully. Actual casters here are too important to monitor the filigree structures and report breaks or worn-away sections, so the clerks do it for them.

Everett bows to me, but as he straightens, there's a too-obvious frown on his face. I'm already regretting feeling relieved. If Alyse's brother doesn't trust me, it could be a problem.

I give him a curtsy, just to be polite, since rank-wise it isn't exactly proper etiquette. It's odd to think she's high nobility while he wouldn't have a title to speak of. In Aris, those crystal-clear distinctions were the first things to go. Phantoms don't care what rank of person they kill. "It's a pleasure to meet you," I say.

Alyse glances at her brother. "Everett and I have also been interested in the Silver Spire, so he wanted to be here for this too."

This is the tricky part. I need to give them enough that they'll want to keep me around, but which won't contradict anything they've already found. Added to which, I don't actually have any idea what I'm talking about.

I can practically hear Lochlan's jesting voice in my head: that this won't be a problem as I never know what I'm talking about.

The Whisperer always says that the way to sell a lie is specifics. She also said one of my jobs here is to sabotage any attempts to strengthen Cerenian magic. I can't give Alyse any clue that might help her investigation—that includes the actual book of fairy tales. However, I do need to give her something that sounds plausible.

"One of my close friends from back home is a caster," I say. "And they love collecting rare books. One of them referenced another volume that spoke of a story of the Silver Spire from Monarch Amelia's time. I should have brought the book or copied what it said. I wasn't thinking. But perhaps we could find the referenced book here?"

Everett folds his arms across his chest. "What was the title of this book?"

I'd be affronted that he so clearly doesn't trust me, if not for how ridiculous that thought sounds even to me. I pretend to think. "It was *Tales of the Time of Monarch Amelia*, written by a Layde Derrington."

Alyse's eyes spark. She turns to her brother. "See, I told you. About Monarch Amelia. That she had to be connected."

She looks so different right now, more excited than I've ever seen her before. Not for the first time I wonder who she really is behind all those courtly manners. She's getting interesting.

Everett taps his chin. "I haven't heard of that book, but it could be in our library."

Not a chance, considering I made it up. But it does offer me the perfect opportunity that I was hoping for. Thank you, Everett. "I'm happy to help look for it. It will go quicker with the three of us."

Alyse glances between me and her brother, looking unsure. I flash her my best smile.

She nods. "All right. Then we'll all go together."

CHAPTER THIRTEEN ·

We spend the next few hours in the library, asking librarians and searching shelves for the book. Not surprisingly, not a single one of them has heard of that book title or Layde Derrington. What a shame.

I make sure to stick as close to Alyse as I can without being too obvious. And I'm both surprised and pleased when, after bringing some books to a table, she's the one who speaks first.

"So, are you interested in filigree too?" she asks. "Like your caster friend?"

I think of Lochlan's laughing eyes and crooked smile, and I can't help but smile too. "My friend has a very…infectious personality. It's easy to get swept up in the things they're interested in."

"Maybe you'll have to invite them here so I can meet them."

I grin. "Don't let me tempt them. They're currently studying for their caster exams. Knowing them, they'd abandon their studies and rush over here, and then their parents would have to chase them down and drag them back."

Alyse laughs. It's soft, but it's real.

Everett pokes his head out of a nearby shelf, his eyes narrowed. I ignore him.

So far this morning I feel like I've been making progress with Alyse. Maybe it's time for some carefully calculated digging.

"My layde," I say softly. "In the few days since I've been here, I've heard rumors. Of you. And of fairy tales."

Alyse, who is looking down at a glossary in a book, freezes.

I wonder how much it would hurt her if I repeated the same harsh words that others must have said to her, over and over. I'm surprised to find that isn't an easy thought to stomach.

So instead, I put hope in my voice. "Do you think the Silver Spire exists? Do you really think we'll be able to find it?"

Alyse looks up, nibbling on her lower lip as she studies me. "I do," she finally says softly.

Maybe I should look down on her for that. But sitting across from her right now and seeing the vulnerability and even the hope in her face, I don't.

"What will happen if we find it?" I ask.

Alyse is quiet for a moment as she runs her fingers over the page. "It would change things. It would change everything." She looks back at me. "You're from Mirista. That's closer to the Central Range than here. Surely you've noticed the way the Hush has grown more volatile."

She has no idea just how aware of that I am. And something must show on my face because Alyse's posture relaxes.

"The spire could fix that. Provide enough magic so that no one would have to fear the Hush."

No one. I know when she says that she means no one in Cerena. And yet, those words dig into this tender part of my heart; the thought of not having to fear the Mists anymore.

I think of the fairy-tale book back at the manor. For a moment, I want to get it and show it to her. In some ways, it would make sense. A solid clue would make her even more indebted to me. And perhaps learning more about something rumored to be so powerful could help Aris too.

Only, there are the Whisperer's orders. She would never approve of that. So I turn back to studying the page in front of me.

Back at the manor, I've barely sat down to dismantle my elaborate hairstyle of the day when Milla pokes her head into the room. "Mother is ready for your report now."

The report. I pulled an all-nighter with Milla studying the Monuments and then I had to be Devonia for the whole day. I completely forgot I'm due to update Elirra on my progress.

Tired or not, I can't afford to slip up like that.

Milla laughs. "My mother isn't that scary."

"Your mother is exactly that scary and you know it." I sigh. My hair is already partly down. I'll just have to finish it. Before I can awkwardly yank out another pin, Milla swats my hand away and does it properly.

"She can't be worse than yours."

True. But at least I know exactly what to expect from the Whisperer. It's usually disappointment, but at least I can see it coming.

Milla rests her chin on the top of my head. "We're quite a pair, aren't we?"

"Did you…?" I hesitate. "Did you want to be a spy?"

In the mirror, Milla pauses. It's actually reassuring that she doesn't have a ready answer.

"I don't know," she finally says. "It was expected, so I did it."

I look at the two of us who are so similar and yet so different. The truth is, when I was young, I wanted to be a spy. Even if my mother wasn't open to the idea, my father was. I remember sitting with him on a rock out by the castle lake in the evening, when there was a castle lake. Where the sound of the water and the evening crickets would hush our words. His hands turned over the picks, showing me how to tease the lock open.

Back then, I wanted so badly to join my parents in their work. Until it happened. My father left, in all likelihood he died, and I became a spy and somewhere along the line it became a cage.

The thought surprises me. The truth of it.

My gaze finds the painting hanging on the back wall of my room, a beautiful one of a forest glade in the morning. I know from what I saw of the easels in Milla's room that she painted it. "What has it been like living in Cerena all of these years?" Just being Layde Devonia for a day was exhausting. Milla's had to play pretend her whole life.

She shrugs. "It's the only place I've known. But it's not my home. Not for me, and certainly not for my mother."

It's the answer I expected. And yet, as I look at Milla in

the mirror, a flash of something crosses her face. A longing, maybe? A regret?

It throws me.

Milla pulls me up and spins me towards the door. "Now, go on." She grins at me, all sharp teeth. "My scary mother is waiting."

I make my way to Elirra's office. A richly embroidered rug is spread out on the floor. Bookcases full of leather-bound volumes line the walls. A large mahogany desk sits in one corner, and there's a table with low couches in the center of the room. I wonder how many hidden compartments are in this room alone.

Elirra sits at the table, but as I come in, she looks up at me and smiles. "Devonia, darling. It's so nice to see you this evening. Come, shut the door after you so we can talk."

I do as I'm told, and at least now I'm expecting Elirra's sudden shift from welcoming aunt to cool general. She gestures to the couch across the table from her and I perch on its edge. As she looks me over, I wonder if I'm Devonia enough for her. Her gaze catches on an ink splatter on my inner arm and she frowns. I tuck it into my skirts.

"My eyes in the city tell me that you've struck up quite a friendship with Layde Alyse," she says.

I expected Elirra to keep tabs on me, but it bothers me that I haven't noticed who exactly has been watching me. "Yes, my layde."

"What other progress have you made?"

I update Elirra on what has happened the past few days, detailing my meetings with Alyse, as well as all I know about the Silver Spire.

When I'm done, I can't read Elirra's expression at all. "Yes, Milla has told me about Layde Alyse's current preoccupation with that particular legend. Have you discovered exactly why she is so interested?"

"She thinks it exists and that it can change things. According to the legend it did save the waning magic of Moraina. A spire such as that could give Cerena even more of an edge against the Mists and against us, should they find it. I think it may be in our best interest to keep a close eye on this investigation."

Elirra tilts her head, studying me. That look bores into me and I fight the urge to either shrink or straighten against it.

"Assuming that the investigation in no way threatens your main mission here," Elirra finally says, "I would agree. So far, the crown hasn't yet recognized the ways that even their magic is growing weaker, at least not officially. However, perhaps they have noticed and this is an attempt to shore up their power. The monarch herself might have assigned this task to Layde Alyse."

That would be the most logical explanation for all the secrecy. Alyse doesn't want others to know about this because the monarch ordered her not to tell anyone. Yet I have a hard time believing that, particularly after seeing how strained things were between Alyse and the monarch. And why was Alyse so desperate to grasp at information offered by a complete stranger, despite her brother's and even her own misgivings, if she does have all the resources of the monarch and the palace at her disposal?

I'm missing something.

"By the way," Elirra says. "I've just received word that a

messenger will be coming from Aris in a few days, to carry your progress back to the Whisperer. You'll make sure, of course, that I have a good report to send. We both want to avoid any more embarrassment for your mother."

I go stiff. More embarrassment. There's only one thing—one person—Elirra could be referring to.

My father.

There's a sharp edge in Elirra's eyes. Is he the reason she doesn't trust I can do this? The thought is cutting.

Elirra doesn't say anything more and I stand, assuming the conversation is over, but then she speaks again. "Devonia."

I stop.

"Obviously, it won't be in Aris's benefit for Cerena to find a spire of that size, should it exist. You know how heightened the tension has been between Aris and Cerena. I think you should continue to watch Layde Alyse as she searches for information. But should there be an opportunity to ensure that her project remains fruitless, I want you to take it."

I think of what Alyse said in that library and of that phantom's scream that I heard with Milla. The magic is growing weaker here too, whether Cerena openly admits it or not.

And I wonder if they might actually need this spire.

CHAPTER FOURTEEN

The monarch had arranged a garden viewing for the next afternoon. It's on the western lawn where every flower possible seems to be in full bloom: carnations and lilies, crocuses and azaleas. It's a rainbow of brilliance settled against a bright wash of green.

Seemingly a full half of the court has turned up and Milla and I wander among them, taking turns carrying the conversation while the other person listens in to the gossip.

"…a wildelight."

My ears perk up as I glance at the trio of laydes beside us, hiding their words and faces behind their fans.

"My cousin was staying in an inn at the edge of the city. She heard their cries again last night."

"Shh," another scolds. "The monarch has it in hand, I'm sure." But as the woman looks towards her monarch, I see the nervousness in her eyes.

Milla leans in to me. "You'll never get them to admit that anything is wrong." There's a bitterness in her voice, so surprising that I glance at her. "They won't fight for this. Any of this."

"Milla—" I begin.

She straightens. "Layde Alyse."

I look over and sure enough, there's Alyse on the far side of the group. She hangs back by herself, and those nearby skirt around her, leaving a space between her and them.

"You're up." Milla slips her arm out of mine and strolls away.

I put on my best smile as I head over. "My layde." I duck into a curtsy.

Alyse nods back. "My layde."

"I was wondering if you would like to walk the procession together," I say.

Alyse hesitates. "Wouldn't you prefer to be with your cousin?"

I look over my shoulder, relieved to see that Milla has already joined up with a few other laydes. She says something and her companions laugh. They're real laughs, not simply polite ones. Milla looks like she fits here among these beautiful people in this beautiful garden. I don't.

I turn back to Alyse and smile sheepishly. "My cousin has her own friends. She doesn't want her sad little country relation tagging along."

"Layde Devonia," Alyse says quietly. "You were kind enough to speak your mind at tea, so perhaps I should too. You said that you were struggling at court and that you were feeling alone. But if you've heard the rumors, you know there are those here who don't view me kindly. Being seen with me will only increase your isolation. It's one thing in the gallery but out here…you might not want to stand so close to me."

Her words dig into me, that she's warning me about this for my own good, considering what I'm here to do to her. She recognizes the way others treat her, and she doesn't want someone else to go through that, even if it means she stays alone.

"Maybe I'd rather be here with you," I finally say. "If that's the way they treat others who they don't feel belong."

Alyse looks surprised. She ducks her head but I catch a tentative smile on her face, before the expression is hidden away.

"All right," she says shyly. "Then let's go together."

The monarch begins the procession, leading us all deeper into the garden. Kerrin is by her side, of course, engaging her at every opportunity.

Then I see Elirra, who, for all intents and purposes, looks like she's holding her own court. There's a pack of a good dozen courtiers hanging off her every word. She catches my eye from across the path, and there is evaluation there.

I take a deep breath. I can do this.

Slowly the groups and trios of courtiers distance themselves from one another: close enough to still roughly be a single crowd, far enough for some privacy. Alyse tells me about the plants as we walk, and I'm impressed with how much she knows. There truly is a country girl still in there somewhere.

Our garden path ends at a glass pavilion. It's obviously a new installation from the scuffed grass around it, and its walls send out brilliant prisms in the sunlight.

"It's my turn now," Alyse says with a sigh.

"Your turn?"

Alyse shakes her head and when she speaks, I'm surprised at the exhaustion in her tone. "To exhibit, for the courtiers."

Before I can say anything, the monarch sweeps around to face the milling crowd.

"And now for the centerpiece of the viewing! Layde Alyse." She even manages to keep the distaste from her tone as she calls for her caster.

Beside me, Alyse looks a little sick.

"Just be yourself, Alyse. You're the strongest caster in Cerena. You deserve to be seen for who you are."

Alyse glances at me in surprise, and only then do I realize that I said those words. A smile slips onto her face before she heads off.

Good job, me.

Alyse steps up to the pavilion, her hands dancing through the air. Filigree sprouts from the ground, curling up the glass supports before crowning the roof in beautiful waves.

I should hate this: filigree used just for beauty. Instead, I feel a stab of pride. Let these posh snobs disrespect Alyse after that.

Around me the courtiers clap. Alyse bows, and I frown as I notice the beads of sweat at her hairline.

She steps back to join me. "Good job," I murmur.

She gives me a relieved smile. "Thank you." She glances at the monarch, who is regaling us all with tales of the work she put in commissioning others to make the pavilion. "At least she's happy today."

The monarch does seem happy. And she is certainly droning on. It's hot beneath the afternoon sun and I regret not bringing one of the parasols that so many of the others have.

Sweat prickles beneath the material of my dress. I shift, pluck-
ing the fabric away from an indiscreet area of my body.

There's a gasp from a nearby layde, who stares at me. She
waves her fan furiously in front of her face while whispering
to her companions. As soon as her back is turned, I stick out
my tongue at her.

There's a snort beside me.

I glance at Alyse as she claps her hand to her mouth in embarrassment.

It's strange. Devonia still doesn't seem to quite fit me, certainly not here in this place. So why do I feel so at ease around
Alyse, even now?

It gives me an idea. "Want to go?"

"What?"

The monarch is still talking, the courtiers closest to her
pretending to be enraptured. "Come on." I grab her hand.

I steal away, pulling Alyse off across the lawn and through
the bushes, branches tapping at our shoulders. I glance back
at her, and to my surprise, she actually looks a bit excited.

We go through the closest door of the palace, leaving behind
the echoes of the monarch's words. A carpet runner parades
down the hall's center, light beaming onto it from the tall windows set in the walls. In between those windows are nooks, and
in the nooks are statues of those who can only be the past royalty of Cerena.

"What is this place?" I ask.

Alyse looks around and despite the fact that she doesn't have
a good relation with the current monarch, when she speaks,
her voice is hushed. "The Hall of Royals."

We walk slowly down the aisle. The first statue is of Monarch Levi, the current monarch's late father. I know the names of the next two royals, but not many after that. Some of the faces are old. Others young. One just has a pedestal bearing a vase of fresh flowers. The mysterious Monarch Rina, who was crowned young and never once left her rooms until the day she vanished, or so the stories go. Each statue is built from marble, the only point of color the silver pendant on their chests, imprinted with the Cerenian crest.

This place reminds me of the portrait hall in Aris. Sometimes while my parents were busy discussing official business, I'd wander through the hall, imagining the lives behind the portraits. Even if we lost a lot when the Mists formed, we still had stories—parts of history that only belonged to us.

The hall ends at a sunny alcove of curved windows and stone benches. We stop at a statue of what can only be the first monarch of Cerena: Amelia.

I've seen many depictions of our own first monarch, Naomi, in cloth and canvas and stone, and looking at this statue now, the sisterly resemblance is obvious. Monarch Amelia looks younger and softer, but they have the same eyes and the same shape to their faces.

Her statue is carved so her fingers reach up, cupping the royal crest at her heart. Her crest is different from the others. Two curved lines around the border meet at the top and bottom, curling around each other in a pattern reminiscent of filigree. It signifies Cerena and Aris, separate but together. Monarch Naomi's pendant had that exact same symbol. It was dropped from future royal crests after the Mists formed...for obvious reasons.

"Do you know the story of the sister monarchs?" Alyse speaks softly, but in the silent hall it still seems loud.

I adjust my skirts, using the movement to buy myself some time. I know the story as much as anyone does. But Layde Devonia would only know the side I don't want to tell.

"When Monarch Karina divided her country, between Amelia and Naomi, it was meant for the monarchs to rule independently of one another but to still work together. At first all seemed well." The next words stick in my throat, but I force them out. "However, Naomi was jealous of her younger sister, who had taken half her birthright. Naomi had always been interested in filigree, and she tried to grab too much of the magic. There was a magical explosion. On this side, it took out a wing of the castle, where Monarch Amelia sadly was. On the Aris side, though, something formed. The Hush. It eventually obliterated the entire palace and city."

The words taste sour in my mouth. I refuse to believe that a monarch who was such an inventor, and who gave us the foundation that Aris stands on to this day, would have done something that could cause such harm. But any opportunity at studying their legacy was erased in those early days of primal panic when the Mists first appeared, bringing with them storms and phantoms.

Those secrets died with the sisters who made them.

Alyse watches me, her head cocked to the side. I see it there in her eyes again, that evaluation. That intensity. And then, to my surprise, she smiles.

She turns back to the statue. "You know, that story has always seemed so strange to me. Monarch Karina was a wise monarch: she obviously trusted her children to rule well together or she would never have divided her country. Somehow I've always felt there had to be more to that history than what we know."

That isn't what I expected from a Cerenian, and certainly not from the strongest Cerenian caster there is. Something kindles deep in my chest.

"What more could there be?" I ask.

She shakes her head. "The truth of what exactly went wrong all those centuries ago."

The truth.

Whatever truth there is, no one cares about it anymore. Whatever happened, its scars have dug too deeply to be healed. Neither side wants to go back now.

Neither side. As soon as I have the thought, I hate myself for it. Aris isn't like Cerena.

"You know," Alyse says. "I like to come here, when I need to think." Her gaze drifts back to the statue, a regretful look on her face. "I always think about how Monarch Amelia never had a choice. Neither of them did. They were monarchs because that was what they were born to be. Some people even thought that Amelia wasn't fit to lead them. There were some who just wanted to use her."

I frown. Every version of Cerenian history that I've heard has made Monarch Amelia seem so beloved. Then again, all those accounts came after her death. The poor young monarch murdered by her sister's spite is much easier to mourn and to love than a living monarch. Besides, I get the feeling that Alyse isn't just talking about the sister monarchs anymore.

It was just last evening when Milla and I were talking about why we chose to be spies, if there was even a choice for us. It's odd to think that might be something we share in common with the caster standing beside me. She had to come to the capital at six years old, and she said her family couldn't follow her for a year—not even Everett.

"Well, anyone who thought that about Monarch Amelia would have been wrong," I finally say.

Alyse smiles. She closes her eyes, lifting her face towards the light coming in through the windows. "I've always felt close to Monarch Amelia when I stand here. She feels like magic to me." Alyse shakes her head. "Which is silly, of course. Monarch Amelia wasn't a caster. But still. It helps, being here."

"Helps?" I ask.

She shrugs. "It helps to know that maybe she was a little bit like me." She twists a thin ring on her finger. "Sometimes I feel that everyone at court just wants to use me too."

Use her. It gives me a pang of guilt.

"I'm sorry." Alyse glances away. "I shouldn't have said that."

Maybe she shouldn't have said that, but I shouldn't have felt that. I'm a spy. Guilt shouldn't be in my vocabulary. She trusted me with something personal and I should use it. "Honestly, my layde, sometimes I feel the same. I was happy at home. I didn't necessarily want to come to court. However, it was so important to my parents that I was presented and that I make a good impression. Sometimes I feel like who I am as a potential layde is more important to them than who I am as their daughter." I let myself pause as I shake my head. "I know it's not the same…"

"It is the same…" Alyse murmurs. There's something so kind in her face, and it hits me hard. Because Alyse wasn't just talking about the sister monarchs, and maybe I'm not just talking about Devonia either.

My fingers find the book of fairy tales in my hidden pocket. I have Elirra's orders. But for the first time, I let myself think of what I want to do. If I want Alyse to keep working with me, I'll need some real proof soon. This could be it. It could help me learn more about Cerenian filigree too. The risks are worth it; I'm sure of it. I can still contain the investigation. I'll make sure to contain it.

Maybe it's time to start trusting myself more.

I pull out the book.

"My layde. I wanted to show you this. It belongs to my cousin, and I found an inscription inside."

I open it to the back page. As soon as Alyse sees the words, she notices the same thing I had. "Her working notes," Alyse murmurs. "Monarch Amelia is connected."

"I know it's not the original book I was talking about," I say, "but at least it's something. Honestly, I've felt bad these past few days. As if I've just been wasting our time on some fruitless search."

Alyse shakes her head. "That isn't your fault. The palace library is large, but that doesn't mean we have every book. And even if the library does have it, I wouldn't be surprised if it was sitting in Layde Kerrin's room right now."

"Layde Kerrin?"

Alyse runs her fingers over the inscription. "Layde Kerrin… He's always been possessive about everything that I do. Everett and I were able to hide that we were specifically searching for the Silver Spire from him for a long time but I think… I'm pretty sure he knows now. Because one day we went looking for resources in the library and they had all disappeared. We think he has them in his rooms."

That was not a complication that I needed. Kerrin already has a good deal of power at court. I cannot afford for him to get any closer to Alyse. No matter what, we have to stay ahead of him in this investigation.

Which means I have to find out exactly what he has.

CHAPTER FIFTEEN

I slip up through the city, feeling so much more at home in my close-fitting outfit than in any dress. Normally getting past the palace wall would be the hard part, but when Milla gave me our clandestine city tour earlier, she had shown me a way in. I go until I reach a chink in the wall hidden by the manor sitting in front of it.

I pull off my gloves. I should keep them on, but I've always felt steadier climbing when I can feel the imprint of the stone beneath me. Besides, the Whisperer isn't here to see.

I start up, reaching for a bit of exposed brick above my head. The wall doesn't have much to grab—what I'd give for a helpful piece of ivy—but I grit my teeth and continue on. By the time I reach the top, my muscles are shaking, but on the other side, right where Milla said it would be, is the roof of the stables. It cuts the amount I need to climb down by half, and soon enough my feet are on the solid roof below.

In front of me the castle is quiet and still, but my blood is pumping, and I can't help but smile. Maybe I don't enjoy everything about being a spy anymore, but this...this I still love. These wild midnight hours of secrets and stealth.

It makes me remember the night my father took me to a garden wall, teaching me to climb. I can still feel the rough stone beneath my clumsy fingers. It wasn't a high wall, but at the top I'd slipped. Even though my father was right there, his hands cupped to catch me, I'd been so determined to complete the climb that through sheer force of will I'd managed to stay on. My father had laughed, tossing me into the air once he helped me back down. His little silvershade, that's what he'd called me—the delicate flower able to grow in the harshest conditions and that famously glows at night. The flower that is also extremely poisonous.

My mother would always shoot him a look when he called me that, but he never stopped.

I blink, and the memory of that night dissolves, back into the Cerenian palace.

Slipping my gloves over my now-chilled fingers, I flex them as I slink along the stable's roof, making the short drop to the ground when I'm as close to the castle as possible. There's still a good stretch between me and a side door, but it's late and there's no one about. I dash to the door. I slip out my picks and relax at the familiar weight of them in my gloved hand. The lock only takes me a few seconds, and I grin as I slip through.

During the day the castle bustles with life, but in the dark it's ghostly still. It turns out that even this place, filled with glass and silver and beauty, can turn eerie at night. The slivers of moonlight coming in through the windows tease shadows at every turn.

There's a patrol outside the courtier's wing and I wait for the glow of their lantern to disappear before I slip inside.

I count the halls and the doors until I reach the one that, according to the map I commissioned from Milla, is Kerrin's. I press my ear against it. There's no noise, and not a hint of light beneath the door.

I pick the lock and slip inside, making sure to flip the bolt on the other side. Then I pause to scan the room. I'm in a richly decorated sitting area. There are three doors, but only two are closed—a bedroom and bathroom probably. The other is open to a darkened office.

Perfect.

I step inside. A desk is off to my left, bookcases and a side table to the right. As soon as I see the table, I know it's what I want. The fairy-tale titles on the pile of books gleam out at me from the bit of moonlight coming in through the window.

I pull out my notebook and get to work, making an inventory of the titles, authors, and any clues I can find as I do a quick scan of the pages. Most are classical tales of the spire legend. Some of the wording is slightly different, but the core story remains the same. Next to the books, though, is a pile of reports.

I go through them and immediately see what captured Kerrin's interest. The reports, which cover centuries of Cerenian history, all talk about a mysterious filigree structure. Yet, by the end of each report, every one is a false lead, either referring to a structure that definitely isn't the spire or leading to a dead end. Kerrin has helpfully written the conclusion to each branch of his investigation at the end of the various reports. Until the last one in the pile.

There, Kerrin has just scribbled a question mark. I catch a glimpse of the text: *"They would need the power of the spire beneath the roses."*

The door to the outside room opens.

I snatch the page as I scan the room. There. I slip to the nearby shelves, where there's a wedge of hidden space by a bookcase corner. I crouch down.

Footsteps cross the main room, more than one pair, and then candlelight comes into the office.

"Put them there." Kerrin. I'd recognize his grating tone anywhere.

Footsteps, lighter than his, cross to the table and there's the soft sound of a pile of books being settled. I carefully shift down farther, even though it makes my legs burn.

"These are all the books she has been looking at lately?" Kerrin asks.

"Yes, my layde." The new voice sounds like a woman's, and it's clipped and professional.

There's the rustle of pages flipping and then a cover slamming. "Nothing. No new hint of the spire."

There's a pause. "The spire doesn't exist, my layde."

"Then why is she looking for it?" Kerrin snaps.

The woman doesn't respond.

"What have you found about that country girl she's been hanging about with?" Kerrin asks.

That country girl. Me. I grimace. As much as I don't want Kerrin's attention focused on Alyse, I can't afford for it to be focused on me either.

"Not much. She's never been to the capital before. She's from Mirista. So far, my investigation has been solely confined to the capital. I could go there to find out more, if you wished."

Silence stretches out. As far as I know, there are no clues to my existence planted in Mirista. I wasn't supposed to allow anyone to ever question my story.

Who is this woman?

"No. For now, watch her here. Layde Alyse too."

I slowly let out the breath I've been holding.

"Yes, my layde."

"Depending on how things go, we might need to change our tactic. Now I need to get ready."

Kerrin's footsteps retreat.

The woman stays at the table and there's the shush of pages being flipped.

I lean out, just enough to catch a glimpse. As soon as I see her, I can tell she's a spy. It's the way she stands poised, ready for anything.

It's not just Kerrin who's after me and Alyse. It's a spy like me who is trained to pay attention to things that don't quite fit. Someone who is trained to catch mistakes.

My legs cramp and my knee taps the bookshelf as I try to balance myself.

There's dead silence.

My heartbeat thuds in my ears as I don't even dare to breathe. Sloppy. Unbearably sloppy. I shift so that I can grab the hilt of the knife tucked into my waistband.

Then footsteps cross the room and there's the click of a closing door.

I shift down, leaning back against the wall and closing my eyes.

What am I supposed to do now?

Milla is waiting for me in my room. Well, *waiting* might not be the most accurate word. She's flung herself over my bed, in a set of dark clothes, perfect for sneaking, her flaming curls spread out over the bed coverlet now that they're released from her hood. I'm sure she's asleep until she cracks open an eye.

"You're back. I was just thinking I'd have to run a daring rescue mission for you."

I press a hand to my chest. "Aww, you'd come and rescue me?"

She snorts. "Well, no, but it's the thought that counts, right?"

"Thanks." I pull my curtains closed, not wanting the reminder of the morning sun and how close I cut it. The earliest servants were starting to clean by the time I was out of the palace. I wish I could sleep until I meet Alyse and Everett in the library, but energy buzzes beneath my skin. It'll take me that long just to calm down enough to so much as sit still.

Milla lazily drags herself up to a sitting position. "So, did you find anything good?"

I bring out the paper with a flourish. "I found something." I smooth it out, already concocting the best, least suspicious way to plant it so we can "find" it this morning, when I actually read the whole paragraph. My breath swoops out of me.

Milla rocks off the bed. "What is it?"

I stare at the page:

Monarch Eliron knew their country was under threat. A group of rogue casters from the forests of eastern Moraina had been gathering support for years and were ready to attack the capital. Eliron decided they would need the power of the spire beneath the roses to defeat the threat to their crown. So they called on their casters and created staves of filigree. They went to the silver tower, twin to the one across the stony ridge, and they reached deep into the magic, imbuing the filigree weapons with even more magic.

"Devlin," Milla snaps, "what is it?"

"There are two spires," I whisper.

Milla's brow furrows.

"There are two spires… And I think the second one is in Aris."

In a moment, Milla is at my side, snatching the paper and hungrily scanning it.

I stand there, stunned. I can't be sure. But what else could the stony ridge be referring to except the Peaks? Which means there's one of these on both sides of the continent. Which means there's one on our side.

Milla looks up at me, and in the gleam in her eyes, I see she thinks the same.

"This could change everything." My heart thuds. "A filigree structure of that size. It could push back the Mists."

"It could keep Aris safe."

I'm already yanking off my shirt as I step behind the screen, for once eager to make the switch from Devlin to Layde Devonia. This sharp hope grows in my chest. I want this to be true, so badly I can taste it.

And I would have never discovered this if not for Layde Alyse.

"What are you going to do?" Milla asks.

"I'm going to tell your mother." I poke my head out from behind the screen. "And then I'm going to help Layde Alyse find as much as she can about these spires before that messenger arrives."

CHAPTER SIXTEEN

Elirra looks over the report I stole from Kerrin, as I force my-self to appear calm in front of her.

In that moment, I don't even care that this clue comes from Kerrin and that he obviously knows about it. I don't even care who he might have told. Alyse and I can beat whoever else is looking for the spire. I will make sure of it. With this clue, Elirra cannot argue with my working with Alyse.

"You wish to tell Layde Alyse about what this report contains?" Elirra finally asks. "You do not believe that is a risk?"

"It is a risk, but a manageable one. Layde Alyse knows more about the Cerenian spire than anyone. In less than two weeks, I'll be stealing her away. After that, she will no longer be able to tell others of what she has found. Her brother, Everett, is powerless at court. And even if he discloses every-thing the moment we disappear, this very report came from Kerrin. He could also tell Monarch Cora at any time, if he hasn't already done so. I do not think the monarch believes in the spire's existence, but our strongest chance of controlling this situation is to make sure that our investigation stays ahead of any others."

Elirra's look bores into me, but I don't quake beneath her gaze. I'm right, I know I am. This is a chance for Aris and I will not let that go.

"What happens if Layde Alyse gets too close to the Cerenian spire?" Elirra asks.

I know what I have to say. "Then I will make sure she doesn't find it."

The silence stretches out as Elirra looks at me. I wonder who she sees in me: my mother or my father. The commander or the traitor. I straighten.

"Very well, then," Elirra says. "Proceed."

I can barely keep my steps measured as I head to the library to meet Alyse and Everett. They're already in the library, poring over books at their usual table. I smile as I come up, barely able to keep the expression from widening unnaturally.

Because they wouldn't find that suspicious at all.

"I have some good news," I say. "I've been trying to think if there was anything else about what my caster friend found, and I just remembered there was. The book referenced was written during the reign of Monarch Demetria. I know it's not a lot to go on, but it narrows it down."

"Monarch Demetria," Everett says. He leaves, returning with an armful of books, including the one where I planted the sheet of paper I found a few hours earlier.

We work at the stack of books for a good half hour, and

even in that time I'm debating taking the book and accidentally discovering the clue myself, when Alyse opens it and the paper falls perfectly out into her lap.

She picks it up and as she reads it, her eyes go wide. She gives a furtive glance around the library then spreads it out on the table. "Look at this."

I lean over the paper, not even having to fake my eagerness.

"Two spires?" Everett says.

"Didn't I say?" Alyse's excited whisper is on the loud side of quiet. I wince. "If Monarch Amelia had a spire, then Monarch Naomi must have had one too. The Silver Spire must have had a partner because that's the only way it—"

Everett reaches out and touches her hand. Alyse cuts off. "Well, it makes a lot of sense."

I want to know what she isn't telling me. But asking right after she cut herself off is clearly not the way to go about it.

"Look at this part," Everett says. He points to the line: "...*beneath the roses.*" "Perhaps that refers to the Rose Garden."

"The Rose Garden?" I ask.

"Roses were Monarch Alexander's favorites," Alyse says. "The Rose Garden, out by the East Wing, has stood there for centuries."

It seems a bit of a stretch, but this is why I wanted to work with them. I wouldn't have made that connection. "Well, why don't we start there?"

I had imagined the Rose Garden as some small corner of the main grounds. Instead, we step through an intricate golden gate adorned with rubies carved into roses. Inside, low brick walls barely contain the explosion of flowers inside of them. There are bushes of roses, and beds of roses, and roses trailing up walls and arches. In reds and whites, in yellows and purples and blacks. Their scent flavors the air, as thick as honey. In between the flowers are beautiful statues, large marble vases, even filigree sculptures.

I can actually feel my mouth drop open.

Is there no corner of Cerena that isn't completely gorgeous?

Alyse smiles at the look on my face. "This garden actually has a long history. Monarch Alexander loved roses, so his brothers came together and built this place. But when the explosion happened, it took out the closest wing of the castle. The gardens fell into disarray. Then two hundred and fifteen years ago when Monarch Myra took the throne and began to restructure Cerena, she resuscitated the garden and brought it back to its former glory."

But when the explosion happened. I knew this part of the grounds was once connected to the old wing. I didn't realize we were that close to that particular piece of history, though. Monarch Amelia would have died very near here, and it changed everything.

I smile back at Alyse. "I'm impressed that you knew that off the top of your head."

"Gardens remind me of home."

Ah, of course.

Then I see Everett. At Alyse's words his face goes tight.

Interesting that he obviously doesn't want the same reminders of home that she does.

Alyse drifts over to a space between two bushes, and I follow her. As we kneel down, I see a small filigree flower nearly overrun by the bushes beside it. At least I think it's supposed to be a flower. It's a bit…abstract.

But the way that Alyse is looking at it, with familiarity…

"Is it one of yours?" I ask.

Alyse props her chin in her hands. "Yes. When I was just learning. This was one of the first pieces they let me do."

"They let you do?"

She reaches out, brushing one of the petals. The little flower responds by glowing brighter. "When I was young, every bit of my power had to go into the Royal Monuments and the filigree structures at the border. I'm not sure if the monarch let anyone from the other cities hear about it, or even if you would remember from that long ago, but the magic of Cerena was weaker then. The Hush was wearing down our border and the monarch needed all of her casters, including me, to strengthen the filigree.

"I wanted to make something different, though. Not something that loomed over us, but something that was beautiful." She laughs. "Of course, I was used to making these bulky things, and it was hard to craft something so small and fine."

The flower is indeed fine. There's even something beautiful about its flaws. Yet, if I were to compare it with the Monuments, there would be no comparison.

A smile quirks up the sides of Alyse's mouth. "You don't like it much, do you?"

Heat spreads across my cheeks. "Well, it's just…using filigree to make a flower, something so small with so little magic in it…" I struggle to find what I'm trying to say. "It's not very practical, is it?"

"Practical?" There's a playful spark in Alyse's eyes.

To my surprise, I feel an answering smile play around my own mouth. "Being practical is useful."

"Boring you mean."

"Reasonable."

She grins. "Uninspired."

It's the first time I've seen that expression on her face and I'm a little proud that I was able to bring it out. I don't have an answer, so instead I scoop up a handful of dirt and sprinkle it in her hair.

For a moment I freeze, and so does she. My own surprise is reflected on her face. I'm opening my mouth to apologize when she laughs. She brushes the dirt out of her hair, only for it to fall onto her shoulders.

I can practically feel Everett's dagger eyes boring into my back. I pretend not to notice. This is actually nice being here with Alyse. I'm not having to watch my every word because perhaps right now Devonia wouldn't be watching her words. There are no eyes more dangerous than Everett's judging me.

"That's right," she says. "Avoid my obviously superior argument."

"Obviously superior?"

"Art is important too, Layde Devonia, just as important as defense. It makes us strong in different ways. Once magic was everywhere, for everyone. It wasn't just to push back the Hush or the wildelights. It wasn't used for defense or war. It was just there, to build and explore and inspire. Everyone deserves to have that magic in their life."

Her words draw me in, tantalizingly sweet. Only I don't have room for any of that. Inspiration. Exploration. With the Mists pushing so close to Aris, those things don't have a place in my life.

Do they?

Alyse looks down at the flower and it pulses with a new power. I think she's correcting the wayward art, but instead she's adding a leaf. Its delicate body glows with light, only for darkness to shoot through it.

Alyse jerks back, gasping.

"Alyse?" Everett drops to his knees beside her. "What is it? What happened?"

She stares down at her hand and in her eyes there's a cold, bright fear. "I just…for a moment…" She flexes her fingers. The leaf glows again and continues to grow until it tapers off at the end. "Sorry." She shakes her head. "I must be more tired than I thought."

Everett nods worriedly. I stay silent. I've seen those fluctuations of casting magic before. It happens when the magic starts dying. When a caster reaches for magic through their connection and that magic isn't there. It started happening in Aris years ago.

Alyse can't save my home if her magic disappears.

"Has that ever happened before?" I ask quietly.

Alyse shakes her head. "No," she whispers.

I scan the garden, which seems darker than it did before, because then at least I feel like I'm doing something useful. My gaze catches on something. "Wait, look over here."

I step over to a wall covered by climbing roses. Being mindful of the thorns, I brush them aside. It reveals an imprint of the royal pendant, stamped into the stone. Only this one has the two intertwined lines. Faint flecks of silver decorate the stone. "This is Monarch Amelia's pendant."

Alyse steps up beside me. "It looks like there are words beneath there."

Together we brush the dirt out of the grooves.

"A gift of a bouquet of stars points the way to the spire of silver."

I frown. "A bouquet of stars?"

Alyse's face lights up. She turns to her brother, taking his arm. "The gift, from the Rose Suitors story."

Everett smiles at her, and it makes him look so much less judgmental. But then he turns to me, and sees my still-confused look. His brow furrows. "You've never heard it?"

I wonder if I've made a fatal mistake, if this is some common Cerenian tale, but Alyse shakes her head. "I don't think that many people know the story. You always just told it to me because I loved it so much. Tell it again?"

I don't particularly like Everett, but as he starts speaking, I have to give it to him: he has a voice that was made for stories. It's low and steady and melodic.

"Once, long ago, there was a monarch who was of age to be married. One by one suitors came to her, and one by one she sent them away. Eventually, feeling pressured to take a partner, she decided to set a challenge. She invited anyone in her country who wished to bring her a rose of their choice and she would wed whichever suitor brought her the most beautiful flower.

"Some of the suitors brought red roses or white or black or blue. Some brought roses made of ice, of wood, of sugar. Some brought intricate roses of gold or of gems. But one wasn't a rose at all. It was a delicate necklace of filigree lines with a note asking the monarch to go out to her garden that night and hold it up in the light of the spring moon. The monarch did, and the outline of the silver traced the shape of flowers in the stars. When she lowered the pendant, she saw a beautiful woman there in the garden. So the monarch married her, the suitor who had gifted her a bouquet of stars."

Alyse sighs happily and Everett reaches out to muss her hair, making her laugh. I have to admit: it's a nice story.

"All right," I say. "So, we somehow find or make this necklace. Then what?"

Alyse bends down to look at the imprint of the crest in the brick. "We put it here." She splays her fingers over the stone and a flash of silver shudders through it. "I can feel silver filigree in the brick."

"Can you wake it up?" I ask.

Silver light blooms around Alyse's fingers but then she shakes her head. "I can feel it, but not its shape. Not accurately enough."

So, we just somehow find a centuries-old pendant that traces this obscure bouquet pattern in the stars.

I pause. Stars. A bouquet. Why does that sound familiar?

The tread of footsteps comes towards us, muffled by the grass but still there.

"Someone's coming," I say.

Alyse steps from the wall, the flowers falling over what we found, right as Kerrin comes into our section of the garden.

As soon as Alyse sees him, she fixes her stare to the ground, her shoulders hunched. And I hate Kerrin, for making her look like that. I hate him for the influence he still obviously has over her.

Kerrin smiles, that smile that is so pleasant and sure of itself because he knows exactly where the power in this garden lies. "Layde Alyse," he says. "It's interesting to find you so far from your usual pathways out here in the Rose Garden."

Alyse fiddles with the hem of her sleeves. "We thought we would go for a walk and enjoy the weather."

She doesn't know that the clue we're chasing right now came from Kerrin's room. I'm so aware of the words hidden by the thorns just beside me.

Kerrin reaches over to a bush and plucks a flower. Alyse flinches at the sound of the stem snapping. "Surely you have better things to do than exploring the gardens. Unless, of course, that's not actually why you're here."

Alyse shakes her head. "Why else would I be here?"

He twirls the flower, the thorns flashing past his fingers. "Some say you're back to chasing fairy tales again. That isn't exactly the best use of your time, now is it?"

She swallows, the movement too vulnerable. Doesn't she see that he relishes knowing how much his words are getting to her?

"I'm not under your charge, Layde Kerrin, not anymore."

He steps closer, leaning in towards her as he says in a soft voice, "Will you answer to the monarch then? We could get her involved."

Alyse's hands clench at her sides, but she doesn't say anything. The person she is around Everett, or even me, is so different from who she is around others. I want to see her stand up to those who so obviously scorn her, like the monarch and Layde Kerrin. But she's too scared. She hesitates when she needs to act. The Whisperer would call that a weakness.

Luckily, it's not a weakness I possess.

I clear my throat.

Everyone's attention turns to me. Kerrin smooths down the front of his embroidered vest as he smiles. "My apologies, Layde Devonia. I didn't see you there."

I give him my most brilliant smile. "I can see that. Would you rather I leave so that you could bully Layde Alyse in private?"

Alyse's mouth drops open. Everett's eyes grow wide. Kerrin, though, stills. I had just been in his library and I'd heard what he said. I know he's already watching me. And yet, I couldn't just stand there and say nothing. Not with Alyse looking like that.

The thought surprises me. There's a part of me that's ashamed for taking that risk. But there's another part that, for the first time, feels like myself.

Layde Kerrin looks back to Layde Alyse. Then he smiles again, as if I didn't speak. "The monarch wants you to exhibit a casting. I'll tell her you'll be along shortly."

He gives a bow to Alyse, not an inch too deep, and then goes to leave, only to stop in front of me. He offers me an easy smile. "I can only imagine how difficult it must be to understand Wysperilian customs when you've been living in the country for so long. I'm sure Layde Elirra will soon be able to instruct you in them. It's important to choose your allies wisely in this city." He leaves the garden.

I glare after him, surprised at the intensity of the heat throbbing in my head. I can't believe he just called me some country bumpkin.

I am going to relish pulling that man's world down around his head. And I really hope he realizes it was me who did it.

CHAPTER SEVENTEEN

The Bouquet.

I don't have much interest in astronomy, but I'm sure I've heard of a constellation called the Bouquet before. I look at a star chart in Elirra's library but as I scan the sky, I can't find it.

The Rose Suitors story could be old enough to have happened when Moraina was one country and the two cities of Isteria and Wysperil took turns being the capital. Maybe only Aris remembers the constellation?

I head upstairs and poke my head into Milla's room, only to pause when I see that she's painting. I watch her for a moment, her brush dancing over the page, spilling out color and light. She's painting the glass-and-filigree pavilion, and somehow Milla makes it just as beautiful on canvas as it was in that garden.

"I know you're there," Milla says without turning.

My neck goes hot and I step into the room.

Milla washes off her brush in a cup on the easel before turning to me. "Do you need something?"

"Have you heard of a constellation from back in Aris," I ask, "called the Bouquet?"

Milla frowns and I realize my mistake. She wouldn't know that constellation because she's never lived in Aris.

"I mean," I say, "would your mother have any star charts from Aris here?"

Milla stands and brushes past me. "This way."

We go back to the library, only this time, Milla pulls forward the bookcase I noticed before. She unlocks the door hidden behind it and leads the way in.

It's a small room, and even when Milla lights the candle sitting on a shelf, the space is still dim. Bookcases and cabinets with cubbyholes line the walls. They're filled with papers tied with twine and thick volumes of books. A worn table with two chairs sits in the middle of the room.

"These are the records we've collected during our time here in Cerena as well as the information from Aris we need to keep hidden." Milla points to a cabinet in the corner, the only one with doors on it. I can see the lock on it from across the room. "That belongs to my mother. If you value your life, don't touch it."

"Understood."

"Now, star charts." Milla shuffles through some rolls of paper, the parchment crinkling beneath her fingers. She pulls one out and spreads it over the table. The deep navy of the background ink is offset by the golden leaf used to denote the stars.

"When and where would this constellation appear?" she asks.

"Spring, and right over Wysperil."

Her fingers skip over the stars. "Well, here it is."

Sure enough, there's a constellation of flowers painted out in golden lines among the stars on the paper. It's labeled *The Bouquet* in a neat script.

"So, Aris does know of it," I murmur.

"And why is that important?"

I tell Milla about what Alyse, Everett, and I had discovered in the Rose Suitors story.

Milla looks back at the paper. "Huh. To think we knew all this time, while they didn't."

Her words match my feelings exactly. We remembered, while they forgot. That makes me feel a little vindicated, when we're usually the ones who weren't able to keep any of our history.

I lay the Cerenian chart on the table as well. "It looks like what we call the Bouquet, they call the Crown." The two constellations occupy the same spot in the sky, though who-ever decided on them connected the star patterns in very different ways. Hopefully this will be enough to let Alyse make the pendant. But first, I need to hide where it comes from.

"Milla, you're good at forgeries, right? Could you draw up something that connects the Crown constellation to the Bouquet, without implicating Aris in it?"

Milla grins. "Gladly."

The next day, all the courtiers have been invited to the opening of a new art gallery. Windows placed between each painting and sculpture beam natural light into the room. The courtiers, most as colorful as the paintings themselves, wander about admiring the art, some even looking through tiny golden binoculars. And yet in the room I sense an undercurrent of tension.

Of fear.

"I hear that the Hush broke through the border."

I pause to admire a stone bust as I intentionally don't look at the pair of courtiers at my back.

The voice speaks again, so low that even though the crowd is fairly quiet as they murmur compliments about the art, I can still barely make out the next words. "It nearly reached one of the cities on the border before the monarch's casters arrived to push it back."

"What is Layde Alyse doing?" a second voice says. "It's her job to stop this from happening and instead I hear she's back to chasing fairy tales."

My hackles rise at those words. I can't believe they expect Alyse to solve this problem all by herself, when the monarch refuses to even recognize it.

The courtiers move off and I take a breath to calm myself. I go to find Alyse.

She stands near the far end of the gallery, looking at a painting of an ocean shore. I know now that she does notice when others say things about her and I don't want her to have to face that. So, as I step up beside her, I smile and go for a distraction. "See, this is art I can appreciate. I can tell exactly what this is."

Alyse laughs. "Maybe we'll make an art lover of you yet."

The flowing lines of the painting remind me somewhat of Milla's work. Perhaps hers is less polished, but there's still something about the art styles that are reminiscent of one another. "I wonder if Milla might one day have a painting here."

Alyse looks at me in surprise. "Your cousin paints?"

My stomach drops. Was I not supposed to mention that? No, neither Elirra or Milla had said to hide it. Yet, it isn't common knowledge. Why? I assumed the only reason Milla would paint would be to fit in better with high Cerenian society. "Sorry, I'd assumed she'd told everyone. Please don't say anything."

"Of course, I won't. For some people, art is a very intimate thing. A private thing."

That I can understand. I wouldn't want my horrible drawings to see the light of day. But Milla is a good painter.

A trio of courtiers pass us and I can feel their eyes bore into our backs. Beside me, Alyse plays with one of her rings. "They're all talking about me, aren't they?"

I struggle to find the right words to say to her. "Has the monarch ordered you to go there? To where the Hush broke through?"

"No. She wants me here in the capital, just in case."

Just in case. It's the closest indication I've ever heard of Cora admitting that all is not right in her country.

Alyse shakes her head. "You know ten years ago, this exact same thing happened. The Hush was beginning to break through. And then the monarch found me and I was able to push it back. Monarch Cora could have spent the past decade looking for other ways to fix this problem, but she didn't. And now it's becoming too much for even me, and nothing has happened or changed and I just—" She cuts off. "We need to find this spire. It's the only way."

The only way.

I glance at the crowd around us, all of them pretending to live in this beautiful world that hides every problem they don't want to deal with. There is nothing real in this place.

And I'm struck very intensely that I might be the least real person here.

Another pair of courtiers goes to pass, not even bothering to hide their whispers. I whirl on them. "You know, a fan in front of your mouth doesn't actually hide your words. And if you weren't such cowards, you wouldn't bother with the fans at all."

The laydes gape at me before giving me furious looks and scuttling off.

I turn back to Alyse only to see that she's gaping at me too. "Layde Devonia, you can't just say that."

"Why, because we're at court? Don't you think this place would benefit from a little more honesty?"

I don't get the chance to hear whatever Alyse might have said, because at that moment, the monarch's voice floats towards us.

"Layde Alyse!" The crowd parts to show Monarch Cora, surrounded by her usual entourage. I can make out Her Majesty's too-tight smile even from where I stand.

"Come here, my dear."

Alyse gives me an apologetic grimace before heading off. The crowd swallows her in a moment.

I stifle my sigh. Now what do I do? Look at art?

"That is quite the sour look on your face, Layde Devonia."

Layde Kerrin. Of course.

I turn to the side, and then I have to force myself not to

stiffen. Kerrin is indeed standing there. And beside him, in the dress of a court layde, is the spy.

He gestures to his companion. "Layde Devonia, may I introduce Layde Gianna. She has recently come up from the country and I've been escorting her around."

Gianna—if that is anywhere close to her actual name—is perhaps only a few years older than me, just like Kerrin. She has light brown hair, beautifully styled with golden ornaments, and deep green eyes. A splatter of freckles crosses her cheeks and the bridge of her nose, making her look deceptively innocent.

This is not good.

"It's a pleasure meeting you, Layde Devonia," she says, ducking into a curtsy. "Layde Kerrin has told me much about you."

I'll bet he has. I return the curtsy she gives me. "It is a pleasure to meet you as well, my layde."

Gianna loops her arm through mine. "Will you take a turn about the gallery with me? We are both new here in court, after all."

She pulls me forward and I have no choice but to walk beside her, Kerrin trailing smugly a few feet behind.

"Layde Kerrin tells me you are from Mirista," Gianna says after we've walked a few paces. "I hear it is beautiful country out there."

It's a good thing I had prepared for this. I prattle on, telling Gianna how much I love the old bridge, and the annual fall celebration in the town square, and taking picnics by the forest's edge. Before she can ask another question, I give her a bright smile and say, "And you, my layde? Did you travel far?"

"Quite far. My family's estate is on the eastern coast. I've only been here a few days and already I miss seeing the ocean in the morning."

We stop at a painting of a glittering crowd all facing the crowned monarch in the center. I would guess from the outfits that the painting is well over three centuries old. The crowd looks happy, enjoying a summer's morning in a garden, except for the figure standing at the edge of the gathering. That man stands in the shadows and silver light gathers around his fingers.

I look at the plaque beneath the painting: *The Rogue Caster.*

"Do you know the story?" Gianna asks.

"I do not, my layde."

"It was during Monarch Curren's reign. The capital had been placed in Wysperil for the summer, and there was a party to dedicate the building of a new filigree structure. The monarch's head caster, Cina, was power hungry. When he stepped forward, supposedly for the casting, he instead sent a spear of filigree straight towards the monarch."

Gianna gives me a smile. "Well, luckily he was a caster, not a soldier, and his aim was off. Monarch Curren was merely injured, not killed. Still, it does illustrate the power a caster can have."

Heat flares against my breastbone. "Are you implying something, my layde?"

"You are good friends with Layde Alyse," Gianna says. "Anyone can see it. However, Layde Devonia, I hope that you and I can also be good friends. Layde Kerrin tells me you have had a somewhat tumultuous relationship with one another, but I would hope you wouldn't allow that to become a barrier."

Gianna squeezes my hand and her rings dig into my fingers. "Cerena must ensure that all of our casters are focused on loyalty to the crown. I'm sure you would agree with that."

Loyalty. I smile. "Of course, my layde."

"That is all Layde Kerrin wants too. Simply to ensure that the gallery and all of its casters are working together. I'm sure I speak for both of us when I say that we would always be happy to listen to you and to hear anything you have to say. You'd find us very grateful recipients."

"I'll keep that in mind."

Gianna finally lets go of my hand. "We'll be off then."

She takes Kerrin's arm and the two of them head off.

I watch them go, before looking down at my fingers where there are still the crescents of her rings imprinted in my skin.

This could be trouble.

CHAPTER EIGHTEEN

The next morning, Alyse is called off to attend to official caster duties. It's not surprising, considering the news of the Hush breaking through the Cerenian border yesterday. So, I take to the city. I tell myself it's because I want to review the best paths to escort Alyse to the Monuments the night of the gala, but maybe there's also a part of me that wants to see Wysperil now that I'm here.

I decide not to go as Devonia, but as close to Devlin as I can, foregoing a dress and instead wearing some of the more casual clothes Elirra provided me. A laced tunic in turquoise. Soft pants with an orange scarf as a belt. It feels strange to be wearing clothes like this. Strange but nice.

It's a warm morning, and the city is already alive. I pass a group of children wearing school tunics and a couple of women with shopping baskets. Before I know it, I'm following them.

The road opens up into a central square with a filigree fountain as its centerpiece. The morning market stalls are all brightly decorated with bows in every color. There's fresh fruit and loaves of bread hot from the oven. A troupe of street musicians are tuning up their brass horns. One stall has beautiful porcelain figurines, though none are as fine as the silver fox sitting in my pocket now. I rub its head, not entirely sure why I brought it with me, except that it's become a habit while in Wysperil. It's a reminder of what I'm here for and of who I need to be. It's a reminder that I've seemed to be losing sight of lately somehow. For some reason, I don't seem to mind that much.

Because right now, I just want to take this all in. The colors. The music. The smells. This is all so different from Aris. There's none of the scurry or the desperation. We didn't get to have this back home. But I do, for this one moment.

I purchase a fried treat, crunchy and dusted with sugar on the outside, gooey and hot on the inside. As I gingerly eat it to avoid burning my tongue, I stop in a corner of the market to watch a puppet show that's waylaid a group of schoolchildren.

Three of the puppets wear colorful armor: one in red, one in yellow, one in blue. I recognize them, the jewel knights, because this is a story that predates the separation of the continent, back before Monarch Karina. The three knights had been tasked with recovering the crown jewels after they'd been stolen by a powerful caster.

It throws me back. A festival had set up its tents in the field outside of Isteria. I'd been so young the memories are blurry around their edges. I was walking there with my parents, all of our fingers sticky from eating caramel apples. We went to the carnival games and my parents won every one: they were spies after all. We stopped at a stage where this very play was being performed. I watched, my heart pounding in my throat as the knights had to navigate the deathly caverns, a stretch of underground catacombs in what is now northern Aris, and outsmart the caster they found at its end. The same story plays out in front of me now, even if it isn't exactly the same and some of the details have been changed.

At the end of the play, the crowd had jumped to their feet, cheering as the caster revealed herself as the monarch, and that the trial had been to pick her very own knights.

And my parents, they had cheered too.

They had, even my mother.

I remember.

The sugary treat turns my stomach. I step away. This is what I get for giving myself over to a nice day at the market.

An angry shout rips through the air.

I tense, my hand subtly moving to press over the hilt of my knife that lies beneath the scarf at my waist. The band's music cuts out and the show comes to an abrupt stop as a stir of unease goes through the market. Parents hustle their children away while others press towards the security of the wooden stands.

I slip closer.

Two people who look to be shop owners, judging from their aprons, are shouting and gesturing to the side of a building. They've cornered a group of young folks, students probably, only a few years older than I am. There's a drop cloth at their feet, which I'm guessing they just pulled from the wall beside them for their big reveal. A demonstration then.

Painted on the wall behind them is a terrifyingly depicted

picture of a silvered phantom. It looks like a massive bear with spiky fur of pure light. It's painted blazingly white with jagged, erratic edges, and it's devouring the crest of the Cerenian crown.

It's art. But it's subversive. Powerful.

And it sends goose bumps all over my skin.

"The monarch is hiding something!" one of the students shouts. He's at the back, his companions blocking the shopkeepers who are attempting to shove their way through to him. "We've all heard the cries of the wildelights at night. We need the truth!"

One of the shopkeepers swings his fist at a student.

The square explodes. People scream, some running from the fight, others dashing towards it.

I see one child, frozen at the edge of the brawl, and snatch her out of the way before she's trampled.

Another shout sounds across the square, and hoofbeats too, a moment before a squad of mounted soldiers bursts out of a side street. It only takes them a few moments to restore order, forcing the students and shopkeepers apart.

The captain swings their horse in front of the painting. "Who did this?" they ask the suddenly silent crowd.

Everyone looks at the small but still defiant group of students.

The boy who'd been shouting—their leader, I assume— throws his shoulders back, obviously preparing for a fight, but the captain just smiles. They raise their voice, so it projects over the crowd. "We understand that there have been rumors about the Hush. However, these are all natural fluctuations.

The monarch, as always, is watching over the situation and there is no need to worry."

No need to worry? As I look around, I see the worry everywhere, in the creased brows and the clenched fists and the fact that no one is quite meeting the captain's eye or standing still.

"Please." They gesture to the band. "Continue. It would be a waste to ruin this morning."

Slowly the band starts up. The students, under threat of the guards, slink off. Around me the market resumes again, but there's a different flavor to the air so unlike the earlier merriment. Everyone heard what those students said, and the captain's words have done nothing to change that.

And I realize, in a society like Cerena, if the Monuments fall, it will be the people here who'll face the phantoms first, while the courtiers hide in their glittering, filigree castle.

It's wrong.

There's a sniffle and I look down to see that the girl is still standing there.

She stares at the image on the wall, which even now the soldiers are covering up with the cloth. I see myself in the fear in her eyes. The child I was. When I couldn't have known how bad it would get, but I was still so scared. I didn't expect to see that here. To see that maybe Cerena is broken just like Aris.

I pull the little fox from my pocket and hold it out to her.

She gasps in delight and tentatively takes it. Her eyes light up as she gently turns the little figure in her hands, all thoughts of the painted image and the brawl forgotten. I think of Alyse, that I actually did what she wanted.

Then I slip away before the girl has a chance to raise her head again.

CHAPTER NINETEEN

Alyse is beyond excited when I show her the forgery of the report, linking the Crown constellation to the Bouquet. She immediately begins to cast based on the lines of the constellation while Everett, knowing what he does of filigree patterning, also draws up some options.

I quickly realize this is going to be more complicated than I thought. It's not enough to simply cast filigree over the lines of the constellations. The pattern within the filigree, the size of the swirls and curves, is also important.

I don't like just sitting there, so after a few moments, I tentatively draw a sheet of paper towards me. I might not be the best at art, but surely I can do something helpful. I start my own drawing, trying to remember what I've picked up about how filigree patterns work over the years. When I'm done, I sit back, only to see a page of lopsided scribbles.

Suddenly I understand the appeal of abstract art.

Alyse lets out a burst of laughter. "What is that?" she gasps when she can talk again.

"It looks like flowers," I protest. "If viewed at the right angle."

"And in the dark," Alyse says.

Really, she's sassing me now? I wad up the piece of paper and lob it at her head. It bounces off with minimal damage but it does elicit a satisfyingly startled yelp from her.

"All right, so I might be a little bad at art."

"I didn't think anyone could be that bad," Alyse laughs. She pauses. "That didn't come out right."

"Why don't you tell me how you really feel?"

Alyse grins at me. And I grin back. This actually feels nice. Being bad at something. And having that not really matter, when usually it matters so much. Alyse doesn't care that I'm so obviously failing at this.

Failing. My hands still.

I think of my mother, sitting across from me at her desk. Her expression giving away nothing, and yet somehow still not being able to hide her displeasure.

My throat closes up.

"Layde Devonia?" Alyse asks. "Is everything all right?"

I have no idea what is on my face, or even what's supposed to be on my face. So, I say the first thing that comes to me. "Sorry, I was just thinking how bothersome Layde Kerrin has been lately."

The temperature in the room plummets. Maybe I feel a little guilty about that. But I also feel relieved because I can control coolness.

Everett's jaw twitches, and suddenly he's very focused on his drawing, which is a perfect image of a bouquet of flowers.

"I hate him," Alyse says, and then immediately blushes.

I'm actually impressed. I didn't think she had that much fire in her.

She fiddles with the piece of filigree in her hands. "He thinks I'm out to steal his position from him. As if I would ever want to be the head of the gallery. As if I ever asked for any of—" She cuts off.

There's a heavy silence. She looks at her brother, her expression tired and small. "I didn't mean that."

Everett glances at me before looking away. "I know," he says quietly.

As if I ever asked for any of this. Is that what she was going to say? Just like what she said in the Hall of Royals.

Even though I'd want casting powers like hers more than anything, because that would mean I could save Aris, I understand being given a life you didn't choose. A life dictated more by the circumstances around you than what you might have wanted.

I didn't expect her to look at her brother as she said that, though.

Everett shakes his head. "In any case, I think we're going about this the wrong way. Even with the constellation, there are just too many ways filigree can be patterned. And that's even assuming that the pendant followed the exact lines as this image."

Alyse taps her fingers on the forgery of the report. "Well, this constellation's name was changed at some point, and there must have been a reason why. What if we looked up more about the Crown?"

"I can check to see what we have in the gallery library," Everett says. "If this does have something to do with filigree, maybe it's in there."

"I'll look in the main library then," Alyse says. "Layde Devonia, do you want to come with me?"

I feel a flush, that she invited me. She's starting to value my company for its own sake. And I manage to ignore the fact that I'm beginning to feel the same.

Alyse and I grab any book that looks useful to send back to her workshop. Neither of us want to risk Kerrin getting any more of our research.

It's late by the time we've commissioned two poor librarians to carry our books to her workshop, the candles lit long ago in their sconces. Not for the first time, I wonder if Cerena wouldn't benefit from, at the very least, the knowledge of how to make filigree lanterns. Surely that's safer than putting fire together with books.

Alyse stretches, wincing as she lifts her arms above her head. "I've kept you too late, Layde Devonia."

"It's fine, my aunt knows where I am." That statement is far truer than Alyse suspects. It's probably far truer than I suspect. "Besides, I enjoy libraries."

She smiles. "Well, I have quite the personal collection, if you'd ever like to look at it."

"Truly, my layde?"

"I'll bring you some tomorrow."

Alyse pushes back her chair and together we head out.

We've almost reached the main doors when I hear a distinctive voice: Layde Kerrin. Beside me, Alyse stills.

And then he says her name.

Alyse and I glance at each other. I should leave it. But Kerrin is a problem, and the more I know, the better equipped I'll be to handle it.

"Wait here," I murmur. "I'll see what he's talking about."

I step lightly forward until I can peer around the end of the bookcase. Kerrin stands next to a table piled high with tomes and Gianna is next to him.

Kerrin flips through a volume and I realize it's the one Alyse had been looking at the last time we were in the library. Clearly, we should have taken those as well.

"These are all the new works she was reading?" Kerrin asks.

"Yes, my layde, at least the ones I could find. Everything since she's struck up a friendship with Layde Devonia."

They're talking about me. Again.

There's a shadow at my back and I give a startled glance over my shoulder. Alyse did not stay when I told her to, and there's an edge of determination in her eyes.

"The ones you could find?" Kerrin repeats, turning to glare at the spy. "That isn't good enough. You're here to find everything. That's your job, isn't it?"

Gianna's expression doesn't even flicker. "Yes, my layde."

"Then find answers for me."

"Yes, my layde."

"Take these books back to my room."

Gianna picks up a pile and slips away as if she'd never been there. Kerrin looks through one of the remaining books, the flipped pages showing all our past research. Just how close is he? I hate not knowing. Nothing I'm doing here will mean anything if Kerrin finds the spire first.

Kerrin shuts the book and heads back into the library stacks again.

The light of his lantern disappears and then, to my surprise, it's Alyse who steps over to the table. I follow, looking down at the books we browsed through the last time we were here.

"I thought the fact that so many people view the spire as just a legend would keep others away," Alyse murmurs. "But he's getting closer."

The candlelight on the table flickers over her face. It catches her expression, drawn and tired. I haven't asked what it was like to be forced to do what Kerrin wanted, to be who he wanted her to be.

"Well," I say. "We'll just have to find this spire first then."

Alyse smiles. It's a whisper of its usual brightness, but it's there and I'm glad. "We should go."

I nod and turn, but then I notice the pot of ink settled on top of a pile of books.

I nudge it closer to the edge of the pile, just enough that if anything on the table is jostled, it'll come down.

Alyse's eyes go wide. "What are you—" she begins, right as we hear footsteps.

"Shh." I grab her hand and pull her away, ducking behind a bookcase where we can still see.

Kerrin comes back. He thunks the books down on the table and the pot tips beautifully. It smashes into the table, ink flying over his hands. He lets out a yelp, jumping back so fast he trips and falls.

Beside me, Alyse lets out a very loud snort of laughter.

Oops.

Kerrin's head whips around. I take Alyse's hand again and we run.

"Who's there?" he shouts.

I pull Alyse behind me, out the doors and down the hall, bursting into a garden. We duck behind a grove of trees. Huffing, I glance over at Alyse, and only catch a glimpse of incredibly bright eyes and a wide smile before she's bent over in half, practically shaking from how hard she's laughing.

And then, before I know it, I'm laughing too.

Why not? We both needed a win.

"I can't believe we did that," Alyse says when she can finally straighten, brushing the tears from her eyes. I wonder if this is closer to who she might have been, if she hadn't been forced to come here and was ostracized. I wonder if there is a bit of strength in her.

"Did you see his face when he fell?" I snort.

Which just sets us off again.

"Ah…" Alyse slides down until she's on the ground, her back against a tree, looking more relaxed than I've seen her yet. I sit down beside her. "I never do things like that."

I grin. "Things like what?"

"You know." She waves her hand. "Rebellious things."

Rebellious things. I wonder how many of those I have truly done. It seems odd to think, considering how much I'm undermining the Cerenian crown on a daily basis. But it's true. Normally I'm so busy weighing risks, making sure I decide on what my mother would approve of. But I know that wasn't the reason I had nudged that inkpot. I'd done it simply because I knew it would annoy Kerrin.

What would my mother think of that?

What would my father?

I tip my head back against the tree, looking at the stars that are peeking out between the branches. Despite what I just learned, about Kerrin and even a Cerenian spy watching me, there's this loosening in my chest. What did Lochlan say: Trust myself?

Maybe I want this: the chance to be out of my mother's shadow for the first time in my life.

So I say probably the most honest thing I've said to Alyse yet. "Well, maybe we can learn to break the rules together."

She looks at me, and for a moment, sitting there, we're just two girls, out in a garden.

She grins. "I'm not sure, you seem pretty well versed in rebellion already."

"You're right. I'm an awful influence."

Then Kerrin goes stomping past the doorway we just left and we both duck down farther, dissolving into laughter.

CHAPTER TWENTY

"Devonia, darling. Come into my office."

Elirra's voice halts me halfway to the stairs. I smooth my hands over my skirt and head in. Elirra sits at her desk, and her expression shifts to coolness as I close the door behind me.

"Come closer."

I step up to the desk and halt, only realizing after I finish the movement that this isn't my mother's office. There's a chair here for me to sit in and the woman behind the desk isn't the Whisperer, as much as she reminds me of her.

I perch on the chair's edge.

"My spies tell me your friendship with Layde Alyse is advancing rapidly."

That could be a compliment if not for Elirra's clipped tone. "In fact, your friendship with her seems to have grown so strong that you've begun to break cover to defend her."

"My layde?"

"Speaking up for her at the art gallery viewing, rather rudely. Interfering with Layde Kerrin, who, I might remind you, is one of the potential heirs to the Cerenian throne."

She was watching me. One of her eyes was watching me even then, in that dark, quiet library.

Just last night, I was thinking of how nice it was to feel a little bit free around Alyse. Only I wasn't free.

"You need to get a hold of yourself, Devonia. You are becoming too erratic. Yes, getting close to Layde Alyse is of the utmost importance, but right now you are walking a very thin line. You will get nowhere with Layde Alyse if Layde Kerrin or the monarch truly turns against you, and all of your actions reflect on Milla and myself, potentially damaging the work we've done here." She looks me over. "Perhaps you're just not suited to this undercover work."

Every word she says makes me sit more rigidly in my chair. I can feel it all creeping back in: Elirra's words; my mother's words.

I wet my throat. "I'll improve my performance, my layde. I promise."

"You had better. The messenger from Aris is arriving tomorrow. They will be here for a few days before returning. Currently, I am unsure about what report I will send back. You have three days to help me decide."

"I understand," I whisper.

She waves a hand. "Then you are dismissed."

If it were Lochlan here, they'd stand up for themself. But instead, it's just me, burning with shame. And as cowardly as it is, all I can do is use the opportunity to flee.

★ ★ ★

"I don't care if you don't like bright colors," Milla says. "There's a certain dress code to functions like this and you are going to properly represent the great house of Layde Elirra."

She holds an audaciously orange thing up to me and I give her such a pleading look that she huffs and turns back to the selection of dresses on the bed.

It's the garden party today, one of the high points of the court's summer season evidently. I haven't even changed yet and I'm already dreading it.

"You know," I say, "you could come with me." Maybe I want her to come. After my talk with Elirra I need Milla to remind me what I'm doing here, because too often Alyse makes me forget. I'm supposed to focus on the mission and the mission only. It shouldn't matter what anyone else at court thinks of Alyse. It shouldn't matter what I feel about Kerrin's butting in. Elirra was right. That stunt with the inkpot was immature.

"And while away hours in small talk? No, thank you. Besides." Milla picks up a turquoise dress that's so much better than any other option she's shown me, I snatch it out of her hands before she has a chance to change her mind. She rolls her eyes. "And besides," she repeats, "we both know I have more important things to do."

Like research. We're both going to need our reports ready for the messenger, and the more information about the second spire that we can send back with them, the better.

Milla does my hair and decks me out in fine jewelry and

though I feel ridiculous, she declares I look the image of Cerenian nobility.

Huzzah.

The garden party is being held on the North Lawn. Overhead, blown-glass balls dangle from tree branches, in between blossoms of pinks and whites. Filigree poles line the walkways, wrapped around with brightly colored streamers. On the main lawn, tables are set up with lacy cloths, holding frosted punch drinks and spun-sugar decorations among plates of mouthwatering treats.

This party is full of brilliance, as if they really are trying to make so much light they can't see the shadows biting at the edges of their world.

And yet… I think of Aris. A year ago, the monarch had decided to hold a party, to raise people's spirits. My mother even gave us spies the evening off to go. It wasn't fine like this. The tents were from the army. The food was street food: meat pies and spiced cider and roasted nuts in greasy bags.

I wasn't going to go, but Lochlan dragged me along. And everyone at the festival was so happy. Listening to the rowdy bands, playing tug-of-war, throwing balls at the dunk tank. Eating food until our stomachs hurt. The party brought the city back to life. And I never forgot it.

Couldn't this high Cerenian event be that too, if it was shared with everyone?

The memory dissolves, back to delicate laughter and distinguished guests. I wander among the milling crowd, dressed in their best finery and bedecked with jewelry. I listen in to conversations as I pause to enjoy some flowers, or take a sip of my drink, or rest for a moment on a bench. I overhear information on how Layde Veranna's daughter gambled away her favorite coach, how many exquisite ruffles are required for the latest fashion, how the plans for the gala celebration are coming along. The party is set around the edges of a lake and a small stage on its shoreline holds a string quartet, their music twinkling out over the water. It gives me an idea.

Afterward, I'm searching the edges of the party, with still no sign of Alyse, when I spy someone familiar, fiddling with one of the poles.

Everett.

I'm debating slinking away but by some unlucky chance he looks up and our eyes meet. I hide my grimace as I walk over. In all fairness to him he smiles courteously enough back, giving me a bow. "Layde Devonia."

"Everett, I didn't realize you'd be here today."

He brushes his fingers over the pole. "Layde Kerrin wanted someone to watch the poles."

Of course. That's just like Layde Kerrin, to force Everett to come here to this world that he doesn't belong to but his sister does.

"I'm sorry," I say. "I shouldn't have brought it up."

"It's fine, Layde Devonia." But his voice has that tightness it always holds around me.

I've made good progress with Alyse, but I haven't gotten anywhere with Everett. I want to know why.

"You don't like me very much, do you?" I ask.

Everett stares down at the pole he's fiddling with, even though he isn't doing much more than wiggling it in its hole. I guess Alyse isn't the only sibling who avoids confrontation. "No," he finally says. "I suppose I don't."

I wait a moment before prodding, "May I ask why?"

He straightens, and truly looks at me. His expression, rather than being disdainful, is serious. Searching. "Layde Devonia. There have been many who have tried to befriend my sister here, particularly when she was younger and first came to the capital, even with her magic being the way it was. It didn't take her long to realize they only wanted to be her friend because of her position and the prestige that she could give them. And as bad as that was, what was even worse was the way that they all, every one of them, eventually turned their backs on her. So, I'm sorry, Layde Devonia. I thought my sister had decided not to let people in so easily anymore, but for some reason she has decided to trust you. But I don't. Not yet."

I know I should lie to Everett. Tell him that of course I would never turn on Alyse and that they can trust me. Yet the words curdle, and I can't get them out.

Because they can't trust me.

"I'm sorry," I say, "that she had to go through that. But I wouldn't tell the monarch about this. Or anyone at court. I don't know why you're hiding this but... I trust you both to have a reason."

He studies me, and his expression seems softer now. Then he turns back to the pole. "If you're looking for Alyse, our parents caught her at the Willow Gazebo. It's in that grove of trees over there."

It's something of a peace offering that he's willingly telling me how to find his sister. Then I realize what he said. "Wait, your parents are allowed at this party and you're not?"

He rolls his eyes. "Our parents are excellent at forcing their presence into places they aren't necessarily welcome. They've always wished to be great laydes. But when I got here… I wanted to be allowed in the gallery, since that was where Alyse worked. Since I'm not a caster, my only chance was to become a clerk. And the courtiers who grace this place aren't interested in having lowly clerks mingling with them."

"What snobs," I say. Clerks are an important part of the network that keeps Cerena safe.

Surprise and then an actual pleased smile crosses Everett's face.

Another clerk calls Everett from farther down the path, and with a nod, he heads off.

I go in the direction Everett indicated. It doesn't take me long to find the gazebo, hidden away from the party. Considering the rest of the palace, I was expecting some grand structure. Instead, the gazebo is made of plain white wood with a massive willow standing over it.

Alyse stands inside with two people who can only be her parents. Despite what Everett said, I was still expecting some family resemblance. They all came from the same provincial background, a mix now of two worlds. Instead, these two are so obviously court. Her mother is in a vibrant green dress, with three different ribbons trailing down the back, and a capelet with beaded gems woven into it. Her father's waistcoat is embroidered with golden flowers and he has five massive rings on his fingers. Alyse, in her pale yellow dress with a single drop necklace, looks so subtle compared to them.

"Darling," her mother says, lifting Alyse's chin. "All we're saying is that we're worried about you."

"Now you choose to be worried?" Alyse sounds surprisingly forceful. "You didn't seem concerned when you first came here."

Her mother's fan snaps shut and Alyse flinches. "This is what I'm talking about, Alyse. Since when have you spoken to your parents like this? And the rumors that have been going around? That you've gone back to chasing silly stories, shirking your casting duties. Have you not heard the whispers about you? The way people are talking again?"

"We simply want to avoid a repeat of when you first came here, button," her father puts in. "You remember how that felt. How that reflected on us. You can control your magic now. You could be an upstanding member of court if you let yourself."

I see each of those words hit their mark. I thought Alyse had been making progress and maybe growing a bit bolder. But all that has been stripped away.

"Now," her mother says, "if you'll excuse us, we have to go and mingle."

Her mother sweeps past her, and her father tips his hat to her of all things.

I watch them go before turning towards Alyse again. She stands with her back to me, staring at the garden wall I can just make out through the trees, as if she wants nothing more than to be far past it.

This is what I should want. If she's vulnerable, it will be that much easier for me to gain her trust. Instead, I feel as if I'm intruding on something painful, that perhaps I should just go. And feeling just as strongly that I can't leave her like this. With everything I'm going to do to her, maybe I owe her something in this moment.

"Layde Alyse?" She doesn't answer. I step up into the pavilion and place my hand on her shoulder.

She jumps, spinning around. "Layde Devonia." Her eyes are red and she glances away to hide them.

"My layde," I ask, feeling very awkward. "Are you all right?"

She nods, but doesn't look at me. "Of course."

I hesitate then reach out, taking her hand and drawing her down onto the bench. "Did something happen with your parents?"

She plays with the single ribbon on her dress, and I don't think she's going to answer. "I disappointed them." Alyse takes a breath then lets it out. "I... They're my parents. I want them to be proud of me, I do. But at the same time, I don't know, I just..." She trails off.

"You just want them to really see you."

I hadn't meant to say that. But Alyse is suddenly looking at me so kindly and openly. I'm not used to that. The world of spies isn't gentle, and it certainly isn't open. Before I know it, I keep talking, skirting as close to the truth as I dare. "My father died a few years ago. Things were different when he was alive." I remember the warmth. From him, yes, but also from my mother. As we walked through the palace gardens, or they surprised me with a horseback ride that ended in a picnic, or even as we just sat in our suite, reading stories. She was a different person when he was alive. Before he took her heart and didn't come back with it.

"Ever since then I've had a...complicated relationship with my mother," I say. "And sometimes I feel like she expects so much of me, and who I really am gets buried beneath all that. Sometimes I feel like she looks right through me without seeing me at all."

Alyse gives my hand a squeeze. "I'm sorry," she says. And I'm surprised when, more on instinct than anything, I squeeze back.

I've never had someone like Alyse. Lochlan has my whole heart, but they're too much like me. We don't let ourselves be gentle with each other because gentleness doesn't belong in our world. Our ribbing, sarcastic sort of friendship is the strength that keeps us going.

"You know," I say, "you shouldn't always give in to everyone. People will take advantage of that. People like your parents and the courtiers." People like me. "You should stand up for yourself."

"Is that what you do with your mother?" Alyse asks.

Her words throw me, because it's not. All this time, part of me has been blaming Alyse for not being stronger or fighting harder, when I've done exactly the same thing. I've always followed orders, no matter what they were or what they asked of me. I was never strong enough to break out of the rules that others put in place for me.

Am I the one who needs to be braver?

"No, I guess I haven't."

"It's hard, isn't it?"

And I say something I've never admitted out loud to anyone, not even Lochlan. "I'm so scared of making mistakes around her. I always feel like I have to be perfect. They bother me, mistakes."

Alyse twirls her fingers. "You know, that's one thing I love about art." A silver flower grows in the ground at the edge of the pavilion, its petals and leaves twining up. "Art doesn't have to be perfect. It just has to be there, to make people smile. To bring them joy. When it comes to art, mistakes can open up possibilities. They can lead you to something new."

I look at the little flower. The truth is, I can see beauty and strength in it. In her. I always thought she was weak and naive. But maybe I wasn't seeing all of her.

"Can I just call you Devonia?" she asks. "You could call me Alyse, if you wanted. Not around the other courtiers—that would make the monarch angry. But when it's just the two of us."

Alyse looks at me with such hope. And I know what I have to say, because Layde Devonia would only say one thing. No matter how guilty Devlin feels. So, I smile. It's easy, because it's what I trained for and yet it's so painfully hard when my body is an ice block and I feel in over my head. "I'd like that."

Alyse smiles as well, and the brightness of it makes the guilt that much worse.

From far off, I hear the band change songs, and as soon as Alyse's eyes light up with recognition I know they're playing the song I requested.

"I read a bit about your home village," I say, "in the books you lent me. This is a popular song there, right?"

Alyse laughs. Then she grabs my hand and we're spinning in this garden, with the trees and the bushes whirling around us. I'm happy, even though I shouldn't be because of this friend who isn't my friend at all and this relationship that is built on lies and yet is feeling more and more real. Alyse gives me the space to voice the thoughts that I've never allowed myself to say before.

I don't know when that started happening.

It's hours later, when I'm heading away from the party towards the line of carriages, that I realize what I've done. It's a shot of panic into my brain, so intense I have to stop, bracing my hand against a tree trunk.

I told Alyse that my father was dead.

But both of Layde Devonia's parents are supposed to be alive.

CHAPTER TWENTY-ONE

The carriage comes to a stop. I rush into the house, hoping I'll be able to slip upstairs unnoticed only to find Milla waiting for me in the foyer.

She's going to ask about the garden party. I'm scrambling for a lie when she says, "Our visitor has finally arrived. They're waiting for you in Mama's office."

I'm so rattled it takes me a moment to remember what visitor Milla is talking about: the messenger from Aris. They were set to arrive today to report back my progress to my mother and tell us what's happening in Aris. I don't want to see them. I can't take any more bad news, and I don't know how I'm supposed to give a levelheaded report after what I just did. At the very least I want out of this dress. But the messenger is waiting and I can't say something unprofessional like I need time, not even to Milla. We're both here to do a job.

So, I cross the foyer and step into Layde Elirra's office. The messenger is standing with their back to me by the desk, idly flipping through the papers there. Layde Elirra's papers.

But that's not what causes me to freeze. Because even from the back, I know them. That auburn hair with the gray streak. That confident posture.

They turn, and a smile curls onto their lips. "Now who might this fine layde be?"

At that look on Lochlan's face, so familiar, something inside of me crumbles.

"Lochlan!"

I run at them and they lift me off my feet with a laugh. "Did you miss me that much?"

For a moment I just let myself cling to them, because I'm off balance and I just made a huge mistake. But they're safe and they're home.

Finally, I let go. I slap them on the arm. "You're the messenger?"

"I mean, clearly I was the best choice." They settle back onto the edge of the desk.

It's only then that I get my first good look at them. Their clothing is still dusty from the long journey. There's a fresh bandage on their arm. And their eyes...there's a heaviness to them that they're trying to mask, but they just can't.

Something's wrong.

"Lochlan, what is it? What's happened?"

They glance away, even though they usually never hide anything from me. It isn't like them.

"Lochlan?" I take a seat beside them on the desk, folding my fingers around their own. This time when they look back, they let me see the sheer exhaustion and grief on their face.

"Kai is dead."

Dead. Around me, the world goes hazy. I stare at Lochlan, the feel of their hand in mine gone distant. "What?"

"He's gone, Dev." Lochlan's throat works for a moment. "Another phantom broke through the barrier. A large one. The casters…they think that's it, that once those things grow that large and powerful, they no longer need the Mists to sustain them. The phantom made it into the city and Kai went out with the casters to stop it." Their voice catches. "And he was killed."

Kai. I think of how he was always ready for some fun and yet never made me feel badly when I said I couldn't go. We trained together since we were both twelve. And now he's gone, because of this job that pulls us in so young only to snuff us out like candles.

I wrap my arm around Lochlan's shoulder and pull them close. "I'm so sorry, Lochlan."

They grip the filigree shard around their neck, white-knuckled. "It's all because of the barrier. It's failing. There are gaps in the magic, and the casters are being pushed to their maximum trying to fill them. Two had already burned out by the time I left."

"How long do we have?"

"If you don't get Layde Alyse through the Monuments at the gala…" They shake their head, and I see the fear in their eyes that normally we both try so hard to mask. "It's not going to be good."

Just a few hours ago, I was in that pavilion with Alyse. I was laughing and dancing. Now, I've been yanked right back into desperation. How could I forget, for even a moment, the stakes that Aris is facing?

"You shouldn't…" I stop, try again, to speak around the grief weighing down my body. "You should have stayed in Aris. With the others. Given yourself time to rest."

"I couldn't let you hear about this from someone else. That's why I asked the Whisperer to let me go. That's why she consented, I think."

I'd been wondering why Lochlan was the one who came. They're a burned-out caster. While their connection is damaged, it's still possible for them to get erratic spurts of magic. Which means it's possible for filigree, like the Monuments, to react to them. But my mother wouldn't care about something like that.

I squeeze Lochlan tighter, as if by doing that I can block out everything around us. "I'm going to fix this, Lochlan. I promise. And when I do, we won't have to lose anyone else."

I take those words deep into my heart. One way or another, I will find a way to keep that promise.

For both of us.

I want to spend time with Lochlan while they're here, because we only have a few days. They need enough time to report back to Aris before the soldiers leave to reach the Monuments by the gala. However, I need to also keep things as routine as possible with Alyse.

I head to her workshop filled with renewed determination. Elirra is right. I need to be perfectly Devonia: no breaking cover and no letting personal feelings get involved. If I can just do that, then maybe this heaviness that's weighed down my heart since I heard the news about Kai will ease.

Everett, Alyse, and I sit around a pile of books in the workshop. Everett successfully discovered that the Crown constellation was named by none other than the mysterious Monarch Rina I had glimpsed in the Hall of Royals. She only ruled for a decade, and in that time, she never left her private rooms. We search through every book on the royal line we can, but the most she ever has is a paragraph or two. There is nothing to indicate why she would change the name from the Bouquet to the Crown.

Everett finally pushes his book away. "Nothing."

Every minute that's ticked by has made the frustration in my chest grow. I'd just promised Lochlan to fix things. Now here we are at a dead end. There has to be something. "This is the palace. How can there be no information on one of the monarchs?"

Alyse taps her fingers on the workbench. "There might be something in the Royal Library. I could petition the monarch to go inside."

She hasn't even finished speaking before Everett shakes his head. "Alyse, no."

I glance between the two of them. "What's the Royal Library?"

"It's a special collection of books and knowledge, all about past monarchs," Alyse says. "It includes diaries, personal papers, letters. Usually, only members of the royal family are allowed inside but exceptions are occasionally made. I've actually been in once, a long time ago. If there's anything on a lost monarch, it would probably be there."

"That's not a good idea," Everett says. "You aren't exactly in the monarch's good graces right now."

Alyse stares down at one of the rings on her fingers. "I suppose that's true enough."

Just a few days ago we'd been at the art gallery when Alyse had said how much Cerena needed their spire. That doesn't even come close to how much Aris needs ours. Alyse can't just give up at the first sign of trouble right now.

"I think we should try it," I say. "This might be our best chance."

Everett glares at me. "It isn't our best chance. If Alyse asks for permission to go in there, she's going to have to tell the monarch why. That didn't go so well the last time."

"She doesn't have to tell the monarch the truth. Alyse is her strongest caster. The Hush is volatile. Alyse doesn't need any more reason than that to go in."

"And if something happens? The two of us aren't going to be with her."

"What could happen?" An edge creeps into my voice. I try to smooth it out. "It's a secure library in the middle of the safest place in Cerena."

Everett shakes his head. "Just because there are guards and filigree, it does not make this palace safe. And you haven't seen what Alyse has been through here." He looks at his sister. "It's too risky."

Alyse looks between us and for one single moment, I think she might disagree with her brother and side with me. But then she sinks back into her chair.

"Everett is right. The monarch will probably just say no. Maybe we should try something else."

"Or maybe we shouldn't give up at the first sign of trouble."
As soon as the words are out, I can hear they're harsher than I
meant them to be. Alyse startles. I need to stop this right now.
I can't afford to alienate them or make them distrust me in
any way. But Aris is dying. The spire could save it. And Alyse
is giving up, without even a fight.

Like she always has.

I shove my chair away from the table and stand up. "I'm
sorry," I mutter. "I have a headache."

I leave the room, knowing I'm running away, and not even
managing to care.

"Devonia."

Alyse's voice sounds behind me, because of course, she followed me. I debate ignoring her, but something in her voice
makes me turn.

She stands there, her expression just so concerned. Behind
her, Everett steps into the hallway too, placing his hand protectively on her shoulder.

Well, he's never letting me near her again.

"Are you all right?" Alyse asks.

Am I all right? I nearly laugh. No, I am not all right. Aris
is falling. Kai is dead. And we need help. We need *her* help.

"You need to do unpleasant things sometimes, Alyse. You
can't just go around covering everything messy up with art.
That's not how the world works."

Everett's face goes stormy. He steps up to stand in front of
his sister, but she reaches out to stop him.

"And what about you, Devonia?" I thought Alyse would
be hurt because of what I said. Instead, she looks straight at
me. "You do the exact same thing, burying everything com-

plicated in this world beneath the lies you choose to believe. You won't even tell the truth to your own mother. You are just as scared as I am."

Those words strike me, breaking apart something deep in my chest. And I don't have an answer for them.

So I leave, and this time no one calls me back.

CHAPTER TWENTY-TWO

Lochlan is working in a spare room Elirra granted them, studying Cerenian filigree forms when I get back. They open their mouth to say something, but I beat them to it. "Will you help me break into the Royal Library tonight?"

Lochlan pauses. "Dev...?"

They know something is wrong. But I can't tell them this. Because how am I supposed to say that I trusted Alyse when I was supposed to be making her trust me? That I might have just ruined my progress when the only chance of saving Aris lies in my ability to steal her away.

I squeeze my eyes shut. "Lochlan. Please." I don't want it there, but even I can hear the desperation that creeps into my tone.

There's a pause, and then, "Of course."

We leave in that still part of the night when the rest of the world is asleep. I wrap the dark around me, ignoring the way my heart still pounds and Alyse's expressions play out in my head. I guess I'd just been wrong about her.

Lochlan and I crouch by the outer wall as we look over at the tower the Royal Library is housed in. It's taller than I thought it'd be.

Lochlan cranes their neck to look up at it. "Well, this is a terrible idea." There's a smile tucked into their words and I know they're ignoring how something is obviously wrong. I'm grateful for it.

I point. "There. That spot is just at the right angle that we shouldn't be seen by the guards on the wall."

"*Shouldn't* be seen?"

"Stop whining. You know I'll go up first."

I steal off across the lawn. Behind me Lochlan grumbles. "This would be so much easier if I had my casting. I could just make handholds. Nice and easy."

If only.

At the base of the wall, I look up. It's four floors. Lochlan is right: this won't be easy. Then again, we've never gotten used to easy.

I reach for a hold above my head and pull myself up. I keep going and after a few feet hear Lochlan begin their ascent below me, still muttering beneath their breath. Nice to have some consistency.

It's hard work, and every foot of the way I expect there to be a shout from a patrol I didn't notice that's spotted us. This high, the only way for them to get us off this wall would be to shoot us off with their crossbows.

I should not have thought that.

My muscles are screaming as I reach the window for the

library. Even though the sill is narrow, it's so much larger than the purchases I've been finding that I'm grateful once my fingers curl around it.

The window is locked, but I can see the catch on the inside. It's precarious reaching down and grabbing my knife, but I get it and slide it between the window and the sill.

"Take your time," Lochlan says from beneath me, their voice strained. "It's not like we're defying death here or anything."

"I will kick you," I mutter back. My knife tip hooks onto the catch and it releases. I give a perfunctory scan of the dark room beyond the glass before sliding open the window and slithering in. Lochlan is right behind me.

They collapse onto the ground, leaning against the wall. "Why can't we ever just use the door like regular people?"

I'm shaky too, but on the other side of that shakiness is a thrill. This is my element—both our elements. And after misunderstanding Alyse so completely, I desperately need to be in my element.

I reach my hand down to them. "They'd be expecting that."

Lochlan heaves a dramatic sigh but clasps my hand and lets me pull them to their feet.

Together we range between the bookshelves, painted pale by the moonlight coming in through the windows. Beautiful hardwood shelves are slanted so that each book or packet can be displayed face-out. Others lie on tables or pedestals. There's a tantalizingly archaic smell to this place. Among the shelves are busts of monarchs. They all gaze imperiously at us.

It doesn't take us long to work out the system. The shelves

are organized by rulers with the most recent ones near the door to our right and the older ones farther back in the room. We follow the years until the decade-long span of Rina's rule.

There isn't much. Where other monarchs fill shelves, Rina has a single sheaf of paper wrapped in a leather folio.

I unwrap the cord and open it on a shelf so that Lochlan and I both can see it.

There are official reports tucked inside, as well as one or two decrees that evidently Monarch Rina did sign. I suppose she was still a monarch even if she never left her room. Then I see a letter to one of her advisers.

I understand your concerns. However, after uncovering the report that I did, I must protect our spire from ever being discovered. It is the two-hundredth anniversary of Cerena, which will provide the perfect opportunity to rename the Bouquet to the Crown.

All I can say is that if I am rewriting history, at least I will prevent it from repeating itself. If the spires can truly be used in such a way, then it is good that they remain hidden. Our own people debated taking Arisian magic once. We cannot allow that to ever happen again.

My insides go cold.

Debated taking Arisian magic.

What is this?

Lochlan takes the page. There's something dangerous in their eyes that I haven't seen in a long time. "The spires…" Their voice trails off.

"They can steal magic," I finish.

There's this throbbing in my head. Does Alyse know? No, I'll give her enough credit to assume that she doesn't know this. But some Cerenians knew in the past. And if Monarch Cora ever finds this out and gets her hands on this spire, she will use it that way too. She would doom Aris.

And everything would fall.

"Dev, look at this."

Lochlan has flipped to the next page. This one isn't in Monarch Rina's writing and it looks much older than the other papers in the sheaf.

I am interested in seeing if the spire still stands after everything that happened. There was so much turmoil when Monarch Amelia took the throne as a second child, and she chose to hide the entrance to the spire. I know that her blasted rose necklace is the key, but I do not know where it ended up. Not all of Monarch Amelia's staff is cooperating with the transition of power and if any of them know where it is, they won't say. There were supposedly drawings in her letters with Monarch Naomi. I shall have to search for them.

"The necklace," I say. "It really did exist. And there are drawings of it." Drawings in Monarch Naomi's letters, which I have no idea where to find.

Alyse would probably know, if I could convince her to tell me. Only, I'd have to get that information without tipping her off.

Outside, the next watch is called. The shout echoes through the quiet room.

Lochlan slips the page into their pocket. "We should go."

I nod, and then we're just shadows, heading back out the window.

CHAPTER TWENTY-THREE

Two days aren't long enough to see Lochlan, but they have to head back. I told them everything Alyse and I learned and now if they can just find the spire, this won't all be on me. Even if I fail here, which frankly is looking increasingly likely at this point, Aris can still be saved.

I wrap Lochlan in a hug in the foyer, knowing Elirra wouldn't approve. Glad she isn't here to comment. Lochlan squeezes me back.

"You'll be safe, right?" I ask, pulling away to look at them.

They just smile that ever-confident smile. "Of course. You too?"

They don't say all the words they could have said. As a spy in Cerena, I'm playing a dangerous game. We both know what might wait for me at the end of it.

Only I smile back. "Always."

Lochlan gives my hands one last squeeze, and then they

step out of the house and they're gone. They take a piece of me away with them.

I head off to report to Elirra. I'm dreading telling her that I've been helping Alyse get closer to a weapon, but she needs to know of the threat. However, I'm intercepted with a letter from the house messenger. It's from Alyse.

This could be it, Alyse unceremoniously booting me out of her life, without giving me a chance to trick her into taking me back. But when I open it, I see a single line.

"Devonia, I need to talk to you in my workshop."

I don't know if the note is promising or not, but after just saying goodbye to Lochlan, distracting myself by facing Alyse seems preferable to hanging around here. Besides, if I meet with Alyse before my report, I'll be able to tell Elirra I successfully misled the caster away from the spire. Which will be much easier than admitting I was helping her get closer.

I go over my plan as I head to the gallery. First, I need to apologize. I hate the thought, when I know I was in the right, but it's important for Alyse to see that I'm sorry. Then I'll tell her that I found something that says the information we need is hidden in the gallery's library. I'll help them scour that place to their heart's content and they'll stay distracted until the gala. Lochlan will find our spire and I will not allow anyone in Cerena to get close to theirs.

When I reach the workshop, I arrange my face to make it clear how afraid I am of the mistakes I've made. Alyse already knows how much those scare me. It should be a good-enough opener. I take a deep breath and step inside.

Alyse is alone today, and I'm glad Everett isn't here. His obvious disapproval is an obstacle I just don't have the energy to deal with right now. Alyse is bent over the star chart, still working on that piece of filigree, but as I come in, she looks up.

Time for my act.

I step forward, dipping down into a perfect curtsy. "My layde, I wanted to apologize for yesterday." The words stick in my throat, but I force them out. "It was wrong of me to simply leave like that and…"

"Devonia." Alyse's voice is soft, but there's something so serious about her tone that it makes me pause. She gets up and gestures to the window bench. "Will you sit with me? I need to tell you something."

I do as she asks, but as I take my seat, there's something off about Alyse. She's nervous. I can see it in the tense set of her shoulders, the way she's playing with her fingers while not quite meeting my gaze.

I'm not that scary.

Then she looks at me. That intense focus is back in her eyes, and once more it pins me. In some moments, she seems so weak, but this gaze is steady and strong. It's like she's looking right into me and even though she can't possibly know who I am, she still seems to see me.

"Devonia, I need to tell you something about the spires, and I hope I'm not wrong about you. I don't think I'm wrong about you. Because ever since you came here, even as long ago as when we first went to the gallery, it seems like you haven't agreed with wasting filigree, with cloistering it away where no one can use it. That you've always wanted more from magic."

I wish I could go back and slap myself. How could I have

been that careless, to say that to her? "My layde, I can assure you..."

"The spires can steal magic from one another."

The words I'd been about to say dissolve in my mouth. Alyse knew. She knew and she didn't tell me. Which means that Cerena's strongest caster knows the spires can steal magic.

I need to control this situation right now, convince her that what she knows isn't true. "My layde, I'm not sure what you've discovered but I think..."

"I would never allow that to happen." Alyse studies me for a moment. "And I think that you feel the same."

This is a trick. It must be. She's Cerena's head caster and one who feels trapped by her position. If she could find a way to grant Cerena such a supply of magic, she'd embrace it. And I know that if these spires can truly steal magic, then it's either going to be Cerena or Aris. Just like it's always been Cerena or Aris. I am not letting my country be the one that falls.

So maybe that's why I say what I say next. Because Everett isn't here, and I'll be stealing Alyse away, so what does it matter if I skirt a bit too close to the truth? If I can make Alyse hesitate, it will buy Aris time. "If you really meant that, you would stop looking for the spire right now. Because you know there are others here who wouldn't hesitate to use it."

"Why do you think I haven't told the monarch about this? Why I haven't told anybody about this outside of you, me, and Everett? Devonia, the spires aren't just filigree towers. They aren't just samples of powerful casting. They are two of the most ancient sculptures on the continent, perhaps *the* most ancient. And the magic in the two of them was always meant to be connected. They were built to balance the magic, to hold this all together."

Alyse draws herself up straighter. "And if we can connect them again, it will destroy the Hush."

CHAPTER TWENTY-FOUR

It will destroy the Hush.

I stare at her, not able to form a single coherent thought. What?

At the expression on my face, Alyse relaxes slightly. She goes on, her voice softer now. "Everett and I have been re-searching casting for years together. We searched through books of fairy tales, through decrees and reports and history to try to find a way to push the Hush back. As we did, we began to see these hints that talked of a set of spires. That their magic was different and that they were connected with each other. What we found in these past few days has all but confirmed that. If I'm right, these spires were disconnected when the Hush formed. But from what I know of filigree, if we manage to light both spires, we could send a magic charge between them. It would reawaken the connection they once had. And if that happens, it would be powerful enough to destroy the corrupted magic. The Hush would be gone from Cerena, from Aris. If we did this, we could save everyone."

Save everyone.

Alyse is trying to save Aris?

That can't be the secret she's been hiding from me all this time, that she's been hiding from everyone.

She's trying to save Aris.

I think of the Mists, which have been such a heavy presence my whole life. I think of my father, stolen away because of them. Could it actually exist, a future where the Mists and the phantoms were gone for good?

My fingers brush my pocket, where I've hidden the page Lochlan and I stole. I wasn't going to show it to her, but I still brought it along in case I needed the leverage. Alyse notices.

"Devonia?"

I need to think. As much as I want to believe that Alyse means what she says, I don't know if she's strong enough to defy crown and country. I've learned enough of her history here to realize she's failed at doing that before.

The Mists gone for good.

I pull the paper from my pocket and hold it out to her. "I found this. It was in a misfiled book in the library."

Alyse unfolds the paper. She reads the letter before she looks up at me.

"How exactly do these spires steal magic?" I ask.

"The connection between the spires should mimic the connection a caster has with the magic of this continent. Just like we can pull magic from all around us into our casting, it should theoretically be possible to pull magic between two connected structures." Alyse shakes her head. "But we could also stop that from happening. We could reactivate the connection and share the magic instead."

"So, do you know where we can find Monarch Amelia's letters?"

She bites her lip. "All of Monarch Amelia's personal effects were stored in the Royal Vault."

Alyse seems to realize what she said and her face falls. The Royal Vault is the most secure place in this entire castle.

Would I be able to break in? As soon as I have the thought, I know it's impossible. The Royal Vault is in its own tower and it has no windows, just one thick door. The only access to the vault is the raised walkway that is always guarded at both ends. We'd have to get through both doors and the two sets of guards that are stationed at them.

But then something Lochlan said comes back to me. *This would be so much easier if I had my casting.*

There's no way I'm getting into that place alone. But what about if I had the help of a powerful caster with powerful magic?

"We could break in," I say.

Alyse stares at me. Breaking into the most secure vault in the country probably isn't something that Devonia should have suggested. It's a far cry from tipping over inkpots or petitioning the monarch to go into her library. But the words are already out, and this could work. The vault might not have windows, but the walkway does. With casting we could get high enough to bypass the first set of doors entirely. There would only be one set of guards to deal with. It would take the impossible and make it merely incredibly difficult.

"We could break in," I repeat. "Using your casting."

Alyse's mouth drops open and now I'm the one who's surprised her. My heart pounds in my chest, because what am I even asking of her? But I don't have time for her to hesitate right now.

The door bangs open. My hand slides to my knife's hilt, but it's Everett, his face pale.

"Alyse. You need to get to the throne room. Something's happening."

Alyse jumps to her feet and runs out the door. I'm right behind her, but clearly I'm not as used to running in this many layers of skirts that trip at my feet, because I lose her. By the time I get to court I worry I won't be able to get in, but the doors are open. The guards don't even blink as I calm my racing heart to appear somewhat dignified, and I walk inside.

The throne room is a vaulted hall, with long windows set high up in the walls that fill the space with light. Banners attached to the sconces hang in pale Cerenian blue. The space is filled with courtiers, all facing the front of the room, where I'm sure the dais and the throne are obscured by the crowd. There are whispers hidden behind fans and a restless shifting all through the hall.

It's a risk moving to the front of the crowd, but I have to see. I shift between the courtiers, slowly making my way to the front of the room.

As I get closer, I can make out Layde Kerrin's voice. Of course, he'd be the one bringing up trouble. "Your Majesty, we caught this rat trying to sneak out of the city."

"I wasn't sneaking anywhere. I was simply leaving the city to see my family."

At that voice, my stomach plummets down to the floor.

No.

I don't care about being subtle or quiet anymore. My heart pounds behind my eyes and I can't think. I can't breathe.

I slide through the last line of the crowd and see them.

Lochlan.

CHAPTER TWENTY-FIVE

Lochlan is on their knees, their wrists shackled together. Their jaw, from the angle I can see, is puffed and swollen. A guard stands on each side of them.

"Going to see your family?" Kerrin steps closer to the dais and at the look of his smug face it takes everything in me not to fly at him. Alyse stands off to the side, worrying the hem of her sleeve. "Your Majesty, the Royal Monuments pulsed with brightness when this rat passed. It's clear they're a burned-out caster." Kerrin looks down his nose at Lochlan. "And we don't have those here in Cerena, do we?"

Lochlan needs to say something, right now, to get out of this, but pain splits their face and they falter. At the worst possible moment, they falter.

"See!" Kerrin says. "They aren't denying it. Your Majesty, what would a burned-out caster be doing here if not to spy on us?"

The monarch stares imperiously at Lochlan. In that moment I truly despise her. "Of course, your monarch would attempt such a misguided affront on Cerena. She's young and weak and desperate to prove herself strong. Just like your whole country. Tell me, Arisian, did the Whisperer send you?"

The Whisperer. A shot of panic goes through me at the sound of my mother's alias, with Lochlan chained and on their knees. I wish they would look at me, so they'd know I'm here, but they stare down at the floor, their face painted in a stubbornness I know far too well.

"Do you need some convincing, rat?" Kerrin asks.

He nods at the soldier on Lochlan's left. The man steps forward, raising the butt of the spear he holds.

I know it will be a death sentence for both of us. I know I'm supposed to be like stone, hard and unyielding, but I don't care. I can't let this happen. I'm about to lunge forward when filigree blooms from the ground next to Lochlan, knocking the soldier off his feet.

For a heart-stopping moment, I think somehow Lochlan got a burst of magic right when they needed it, but then Alyse places herself between Lochlan and the dais. "Your Majesty," she begs, "please, don't do this."

My heart burns at the sight of her standing up for my best friend. At the sight of both of them suddenly in danger.

"Layde Alyse," the monarch's voice whips out. "Are you suggesting we let spies run freely around our country?"

"Your Majesty, Aris is in crisis. They need help. Help we could give."

The monarch's eyes burn with rage, but the rest of her face

is so unnervingly still. "Draining our own resources, and dragging us down with them."

"What do you think will happen when Aris falls?" Alyse cries. "Their magic helps to weaken the Hush, just like ours does. When Aris falls, when we lose all of the protection and magic that they give, do you think that won't affect us here? When we are carrying the weight of defending against the Hush all on our own? You know what's happening with the magic even here. You know and you're not—"

"Layde Alyse!" The monarch pushes herself to her feet, her voice cracking across the hall. "Desist. I have put up with your peculiar ideas long enough and if you weren't—"

The monarch cuts off. I expect Alyse to be cowed. But her eyes meet mine. She squares her shoulders as she stands up straighter. "If I wasn't what? Cerena's greatest defense against the Hush? The only person who makes us different from Aris, which you seem so ready to let crumble?"

A nervous whisper goes through the courtiers.

But I am so proud.

The monarch stretches up to her full height, and for the first time I see a woman who's ruled this country for twenty years. From the dais, she glares down at Alyse.

"Guards," she says smoothly. "I'm afraid the capture of this prisoner has upset Layde Alyse's delicate sensibilities. Take the spy down to a cell. Layde Alyse, I suggest you return to your rooms."

The soldiers grab Lochlan and haul them to their feet. As they're hustled off, our eyes catch for the smallest moment before Lochlan looks away, even now protecting me. But I see the fear in their face.

We both know what happens to captured spies. The normal rules of war do not apply to people like us. We work in the shadows and, if caught, we suffer in the shadows too.

I am not letting that happen to Lochlan.

The moment the monarch releases the courtiers I rush back to the manor. Somehow, they already know. I can tell when I burst through the front doors and see Milla talking with one of the servants. She waves him away, and the man disappears down a side hallway.

"Milla," I say, crossing to her.

Her face is grim. "I know." She looks soft for a moment. "I'm sorry. I know you two were friends..."

"*Are* friends. We have to get them out. The dungeons will be tricky but..."

"Devonia."

Elirra stands in the doorway to her office, and she doesn't look rattled at all.

She smiles at me. "Come into my office, dear."

I don't want her to give me the order that I know is coming, but I have no choice, so I obey. Before she even has a chance to speak, I say, "We can't leave them there."

Elirra raises one eyebrow. "Tell me, will Lochlan divulge Aris's secrets?"

"Of course not."

"Then this isn't a problem, is it? It's unfortunate to lose an agent as skilled as them, but it seems that is what has happened."

I knew this was coming, and yet it hits me with a physical blow. Is that all we are to her? Expendable agents to be used and then thrown away?

If it was me in that position, would the answer be the same? Is that what my mother told Elirra when she sent me here?

"You aren't going to help save them," I say, flatly.

"*We* aren't going to save them," Elirra says. "I'm sure Lochlan relayed to you the news they carried. The barrier is failing. Pulling off a rescue mission would risk everything we are doing here. You know better than any that our loyalty to Aris must be paramount."

I grit my teeth. "I know, but…"

"Devonia." Elirra's voice is as sharp as a knife. "You are forbidden from trying to rescue your friend. You need to remember what you were trained for and sent here to do. And that is not to risk everything on a doomed rescue mission. Do you understand?"

Of course, I understand. My whole world is back in Aris, and it's about to fall.

Break the rules. Take the risks.

I've tried to follow the rules all my life: the rules my mother set for me, that her spies set for me.

But now, I won't. This is Lochlan, who was always by my side when we were running missions, ready with a laugh or a joke whenever I felt like I couldn't breathe. I am not abandoning them now.

Burn the rules.

I steel myself, and look at Elirra, making sure I'm showing her the exact face she expects: angry but resigned, desperate but obedient.

"I understand."

But I am not going to obey.

CHAPTER TWENTY-SIX

I want to leave as soon as Elirra dismisses me, but I force myself to wait until night falls and I'll at least have a chance of doing this all alone. All I know is that if anybody manages to wipe that ridiculous grin off Lochlan's face, Layde Kerrin is going to find out just how adept I am with a blade.

I'm changing into my spying outfit when there's a knock at the door. I stiffen, but before I can say anything, Milla steps into my room.

I tug my jacket on and straighten, daring her to say anything, only to notice her outfit looks like mine. It is dark and simple and perfect for sneaking around at night. Two long daggers are strapped to her back.

She shuts the door behind her. "I get it, all right? This life was chosen for us. That doesn't mean we have to die for it."

Relief slips sharp into my chest. I didn't want to do this

alone. I'm opening my mouth to thank her when she says, "But get sappy on me, and I'm slapping you upside the head."

She turns away from me and slips out the window as if it's the most natural way to exit a room.

I follow her out.

Once we're on the ground, Milla leads the way. I hide the supplies I packed for Lochlan in the city, then we climb over the palace wall and slink across the lawn.

Together we crouch in the bushes closest to the door we need and look over the two guards standing there. I carefully make sure the fabric hiding my features is in place.

"Have you ever broken into the prison before?" I ask Milla in a low voice.

"No. Until now, I've chosen life."

I shoot her a glance. "Do not make me more nervous than I am." I don't want to think about what might happen. The only room I have in my brain right now is for the minutiae of this mission.

"How long do we have?" I hope Milla knows, because I had no time to scope out this place myself. "When is the next shift rotation?"

"The guards change every hour, but they're not the problem. The wall, that's our problem."

I look over my shoulder at the wall across the dark patch of grass.

"Patrols range past here every quarter hour," Milla says. "They'll notice if no one is at the door, and if we're not out by the time they notice, we aren't getting out."

A quarter of an hour to get in and get Lochlan free. I take a deep breath.

I've had worse odds.

Actually, that's a complete lie.

"Inside?" I ask.

Milla shrugs. "No idea."

Wonderful.

We are absolutely going to die.

Milla pulls a blow dart from her belt pouch.

I raise a brow. "At this range?"

Her teeth flash in her grin. "Prepare to be amazed."

We wait until the moment the patrol on the wall passes, then she blows. One of the guards teeters. The other barely has time to look surprised before he's down too.

Milla gives me an amazingly smug grin that just makes me love her more, before taking off across the lawn. I follow, confiscating the keys and unlocking the door. We drag the guards through.

A quarter of an hour starts now.

The prison steps descend into the ground, as if they're hiding what's below. We slip down like ghosts. There are torches, but they're far enough apart that we can stay in the shadows. Both Milla and I know how to move in the dark.

Another light bobs at the bottom. It's a guard. But we can see her while she can't see us, plus it's two on one.

And we are trained well.

I hit her hard across the windpipe. Then Milla's arm wraps around her throat until she slides into unconsciousness.

We unlock the door and slip through.

The prison looks like I'd expect it to, nearly identical to ours. There's not much to the design of places like these. Each door is made of thick wood, with a grille at the top to see through and another at the bottom for food. I glance in and see prisoners, emaciated and asleep. There are slits in the roof that must filter air, judging from the pittance of moonlight that slips in. Besides that, the only light comes past a corner at the end of the hall.

As we approach, I hear a voice. Layde Kerrin.

"What are you doing here, Arisian?"

"Sitting in a cell and being interrogated by a spoiled little laydeling."

Lochlan. My heart lifts in relief at the amount of attitude I still hear in their voice.

I peer around the corner and look down the hall into the cell. Lochlan sits on the ground, their hands still shackled, and Kerrin stands in front of them. Gianna lingers just outside the open cell door. A flickering torch in a wall sconce throws distorted shadows over the scene.

Kerrin pulls his sword and brings its tip beneath Lochlan's chin, jerking their face up with the flat edge of his blade. "I could kill you right now, rat," Kerrin murmurs. "And no one would hear your screams as you died."

In the light of the torch, Lochlan's eyes glitter with anger. "Well, that wouldn't be very conducive to getting answers out of me. You're not good at this, are you?"

One day, Lochlan's mouth is really going to be the death of them.

I gesture to Milla and we jump towards Gianna. She's fast as she draws her dagger, but I catch it on my own blade. Milla ducks beneath our entwined knives, grabbing Gianna's arm and wrenching it. She goes down but manages to sweep out a foot, tripping Milla. But it's too late. I'm already there, delivering a swift punch to her gut and knocking her off balance. She lurches back. Her head makes a painful thud as it bangs against the wall and she slides unconscious to the floor.

Kerrin's gaze flickers between us. I step forward, but Milla pushes past me. "He's mine," she growls beneath her breath.

She's a work of beauty, her daggers flashing in the torchlight. Kerrin tries to attack, but she traps his blade between hers and twists, his sword flying from his hand and clattering against the wall. In a moment, she has him pinned against the wall, her blade against his throat.

Kerrin's eyes go wide. Milla flips one dagger to her other hand and punches him square in the face. He goes down.

"I have wanted to do that for years!" she crows. She turns to Lochlan. "Thank you for getting captured, so I could have that moment."

Lochlan quirks a brow. "You're welcome?"

I grab the keys from the guard at the door, and rush over to Lochlan. "Are you all right?" I look them over as I unlock the shackles. A couple of bruises. The puffed cut on their jaw. But overall, nothing too bad. The terrible tension in my chest slackens. I wasn't too late.

The shackles fall away and Lochlan rubs their wrists. Their eyes meet mine and there's a potent relief there, even as they grin. "I've been better. But you shouldn't be here. What if someone saw you?"

I grin back. "You were the one who told me to break the rules."

I take their hand and help them to their feet. They wince, but they're upright.

Behind us, a sharp whistle splits the air.

I jerk my head around. Kerrin is conscious, blowing a whistle around his neck.

Milla curses and bashes him in the side of the head with her dagger.

"Let's go!" I shout, grabbing a spare dagger from Gianna.

From deeper in the prison, there's the echoing shout of guards. We run as fast as Lochlan can move. The pounding footsteps get louder as we reach the door at the bottom of the stairs. As we rush through, I see the guards charging us.

I slam the door shut behind us, jamming my dagger through the catch. The door shudders from the other side. That won't hold for long.

Somehow, we make it back out into the yard—but the soldiers up here must have heard either the whistle or the commotion because there are already yelled commands sounding across the lawn.

"We need to get through the palace wall now," I say, my voice high and tense.

Milla hesitates. We both know we're too far from a safe spot to climb over. "This way."

I only realize where she's leading us when we're halfway to one of the doors set in the wall. There are always guards at those doors.

"Seriously?" I hiss at Milla.

"It's fighting our way through or getting caught."

Lochlan stops and reaches out a hand. "I'm in the worst shape, so I'll take the blow dart. Milla, I know you have one."

She slaps it into their palm. "If you accidentally shoot me, I'm killing you."

Then she nods at me and we both take off.

There are four guards. One goes down with a dart in her neck before we've reached them, but that still leaves three, and we're not on them when one shouts. Three guards are about to turn into a lot of guards.

I launch myself into the air, my feet slamming into the chest of the nearest guard, using the momentum of his fall to roll to the side. I lash out with my dagger and it goes into his leg. He screams. Down but not out. Good enough for now. Milla's still engaged with her own guard and I spin on the last one, breathing too heavy.

This one is fast and his sword nearly skewers me before it slides past. I manage to grab the hilt and yank, hoping to pull it from his grasp. Instead, he holds tight and the momentum pulls him down on top of me.

His knee slams into my chest and I choke. The man leers down at me, raising his sword above my head.

A dart punctures his neck and his eyes roll back into his head. He topples.

I gasp down air, fuzzy panic shaking through me.

That almost ended badly.

Milla's man falls to the ground. The one I knifed is still yelling until Milla steps over to him and hits him hard in the skull. He goes silent.

It lets us hear how close the other guards are.

Milla clasps my hand and pulls me to my feet as Lochlan staggers over. "Come on!" she yells.

We go through the door. I just remember to grab the pack I'd hidden as we flee through the darkened city streets. We can still hear guards behind us, but the noise grows more and more unfocused.

Our race to the Monuments seems to last forever, but we make it. The towers shine brilliantly in the dark, bathing us all in their light. Yet, it only reminds me of what's past them. It makes me afraid. Lochlan has so far to go, and they aren't at their best. I don't want them to leave.

Lochlan must have read the worry in my posture because their hand covers my own. "I'll be all right out there, Dev," they say. "I've been in worse shape than this."

"When?"

"There was that time Layde Drey made us spar all night, and then run to the barrier and back."

"That was a training exercise, not the Peaks."

"That was plenty terrifying, thanks. And we both know why I need to go."

I swallow. I do know. We're days away from Aris falling. We need to find that second spire, and we need to find it now.

"All right," I whisper.

I look at Milla. She's already dug out the silver tool I packed in the bags. "You're sure about this?" she asks. "There's a chance they'll notice before the gala."

I know that. But I will not risk sending Lochlan through the main gate again.

"Yes," I say.

For a moment I wonder if Milla will actually do it, this act of defiance against her mother. But she nods. "All right."

She jabs the tool against a segment of filigree and there's a flash as the magic activates. Moving quickly, she draws a searing line. It flashes again when it reaches the end and an entire piece of filigree detaches and falls forward. Milla catches it and sets it on the ground.

She did it. She made a hole.

"I guess that's my cue then," Lochlan says.

I look out into the dark at how far they have to go—all by themself.

Before the worries can consume me, they pull me into a hug. "I'll steal a horse and go as far as it'll take me, and I'll be all right in the Peaks. I can still sense those monsters better than most." They pause, and a rueful smile tweaks at the corners of their mouth. "You know, I didn't understand why you were always looking so torn here. But after what happened in the throne room, I think I get it. It's Layde Alyse, isn't it?"

I stare at them in surprise. "I…" My mouth is dry. Lochlan is like everyone back home. They hate Cerena.

"Dev." Lochlan's voice is as serious as I've ever heard. "What's going on? You know you can tell me anything, right?"

I glance at Milla, but she's stepped back to give us privacy.

What am I supposed to say? Lochlan is about to carry the news that the spire can steal magic back to the Whisperer. As soon as she finds it, she'll use it. Aris will be safe.

And Cerena will be left in ashes.

No matter what I do, there's a part of me that just keeps hearing Alyse's words in my head: that together the spires could get rid of the Mists.

"Dev?"

I wet my lips. I can't believe what I'm about to say. "Lochlan, if I were to ask you not to tell the Whisperer about how the spires can steal magic, what would you say?"

Lochlan frowns.

I rush on. "I mean, of course she needs to know about the

spire, and you need to find it, to light it and protect Aris. But maybe we should wait to tell her about everything else." I'm rambling, but I don't stop. Maybe if I keep talking, I'll figure out what exactly I'm trying to say. "I should do more research about it first, and I should be the one to tell her, just in case. Think of how she reacted when I thought I saw a phantom, and that even ended up being the truth, and—"

"Dev." Lochlan clasps my shoulders. I shut my mouth. "Are you sure about this?"

I look into their eyes, fixed on mine.

Am I really trusting that Alyse is strong enough to see this through?

I swallow. "I'm sure."

They nod, letting go of my shoulders. "All right then."

It's what I wanted, but I'm still surprised. "All right?"

"Well, you did save my life, so I do kind of owe you."

Milla steps towards us. "Sorry, you two, but Lochlan needs to go and we have to get back."

I want to grab Lochlan's arm, to force them to stay because I'm scared. I don't know if they'll make it, or if I'll make it without them. But Lochlan just gives me a jaunty grin.

"You know," they say. "You're different now. Freer. It suits you."

Before I can respond, they slip through the hole and they're gone.

Dawn is breaking by the time we get back in, and if Elirra knows we were out, at least she isn't demanding we account for it. I don't even care that I've spent yet another night sleepless, because Lochlan is safe.

By the time I've changed out of my incriminating outfit and have come down the stairs again, a messenger is waiting for me. I recognize Alyse's neat print on the envelope as he hands it over. I step to the side so I can open it:

I'm in.
Alyse.

So much has happened in the last day that it takes me a moment to realize what she's referring to. She'll break into the Royal Vault.

The paper crinkles as my fingers curl around it. No, this is good. I'll just gather some more information about the spires. Regardless of what happens, I'll still have the chance to tell the truth to Elirra and my mother and everyone.

Everything will be fine.

CHAPTER TWENTY-SEVEN

I head to the gallery, breathing deep to calm my thudding heart. Alyse and Everett are hunched over a sketch that seems to be of the palace. I don't ask how they got it. Knowing the two of them, they probably walked up to a librarian and requested it. Good thing I've already done my own research in Elirra's library.

Alyse sees me and a new determination lights her eyes. "You're right," she says, before I have the chance to speak. "We can do this. We have to do this. If there's a hint of where the necklace remains after all of this time, it must be in that vault."

Everett meets my eye too, so I can see just how much he disapproves of all of this. But when Alyse glances at him, he smiles at her. No matter what he might think of me, he's still risking everything for the dream his sister believes in. Love certainly makes people do strange things.

Of course, I'm one to talk. I just risked life and limb to rescue my best friend from a prison.

Alyse turns back to the plans, rubbing at her temple. There are bags beneath her eyes, a grayness to her skin.

"Alyse," I ask quietly. "Are you all right?"

"Sorry, it's this whole thing and..." She shakes her head. "I've been having to do a lot of maintenance on the Monuments lately. The filigree is in rougher shape than it usually is. And the monarch knows, and she won't do anything about it."

I'm so used to thinking of Alyse as having so much magic, but she has to have her limits like any caster. "Are you sure you can do this?"

Alyse nods. "This is what matters. And I think I've come up with a plan on how to get into the vault." There's a bit of excitement in her voice now.

And I get the odd feeling that I'm corrupting her.

Her fingers trace the map. "I walked past the entrance to the hall, subtly of course—" I manage not to wince. Define *subtly*. "It seems there are always guards posted there. So, I thought that you and I, Devonia, could pretend to have an emergency. Like there was a thief in the castle. They'd run off to protect us and I could destroy the lock with filigree and sneak in."

All right, so for a complete beginner, it's not an absolutely terrible plan. It is pretty bad, though. And that isn't how I choose to die.

"Alyse," I say as gently as I can, "I don't think that's going to work. If we do that, the guards will see us. As soon as they come back to the door, they'll see the broken lock. They'll know we had something to do with it. If we're going to leave any evidence, we cannot be seen."

Alyse deflates. Everett actually gives me a grateful look.

I have most of a plan worked out in my head, but the crux of the problem is the guards. I could potentially take them out myself, since there are only two and I'll have the element of surprise. But those guards are the best trained in the monarch's service, not to mention there is absolutely no way to explain how Layde Devonia would be able to win that fight. I don't see Everett's skill set being much help either.

Which leaves Alyse.

It's time to find out how good of a liar I am.

"I think we should actually approach from the elevated hall. I took a walk below it and there are some hidden spots. Alyse, if you could make some sort of stair or even tower out of filigree, you could get us up high enough and then… I think you might be able to use filigree to knock out the guards."

Both Alyse and Everett stare at me. I know it's possible. She did something similar to defend Lochlan. But I also know that for her, there will be a difference between knocking guards off their feet to defend someone and knocking guards out who are just doing their job. I worry that I've reached too far.

But I don't see that I had a choice. We have four days to find this spire. Four days for me to decide what to do next. Because if I don't have some kind of answer by the gala, Elirra will learn of my betrayal and everything will fall apart. I need Alyse to be brave right now.

Maybe then I can be brave too.

Alyse nods. She looks a bit sick, but she says, "I can do that."

Everett gapes at her. "What?"

She glances at him. "Do you have any other ideas?"

"What about if the other guards hear?" Everett demands.

"We'll just have to be quiet," I say. "Besides, all doors lock from both sides. So once we're in we should be able to lock the North Wing door and shut them out. As soon as Alyse moves to knock out the guards, I'll go to that door and make sure it's secure."

Everett sighs. "No, I'll do it."

I look at him in surprise. "I can…"

"I'll do it," Everett says. "Just stay with Alyse."

If he's sure… "All right. Then all that's left is the lock on the vault door. The current combination is always written in code, which the guards should have on them. We'll need to get the combination and figure out the code."

Everett stares at me. "Figure it out as in decode it?"

This was the one part I couldn't see us getting around. According to Elirra's notes, there is always a two-part code hidden on the guards. I'm just going to have to decode it as subtly and as non-spy-like as possible.

"It'll be fun," I say. "Like a puzzle."

He looks skeptical.

"Final thing," I say. "The guards outside in the North Wing knock on their door and check in with the other guards every half watch. That's our time limit."

Both Alyse and Everett have gone a little green. But then Alyse takes a deep breath. "All right. So, when do we strike?"

I head to Alyse's room early. I want to help her prepare. And I'm glad I did, because when I get there, she's obviously nervous. As we wait for Everett, Alyse suggests a walk through the gardens. I'm not sure how good of a plan that is since she isn't acting very subtly right now, but she's already clasping her capelet around her neck, so I follow.

The gardens closest to her room have a sort of wildness that's different from the rest of the well-groomed lawns. The grass isn't so clean-cut and the flowers aren't contained to their beds. I wonder if that was her choice.

She looks at me and smiles, and there are nerves there, but also a sort of thrill.

I am definitely corrupting her.

"I want to show you something." Alyse leads the way down the path before taking a turn hidden by hedges on both sides. We emerge into a small, walled-off section of the garden.

It's a wonder. Even after being in Cerena for this long, I can see that. The garden is full of aspens and bluebells, with marble benches placed among them. There's filigree through-out the garden: hanging from the trees in delicate strands and twining around the benches. Filigree flowers bloom along their counterparts. In the growing dusk, with Alyse beside me, it glows with a brilliance. It's moonlight grown into filigree.

And it is so beautiful.

In that moment all I want is for everyone to have this won-der and possibility.

I turn in a slow circle. "Did you make all of this?"

Alyse kneels down, running her fingers along one of the filigree flowers. "Yes. I'd come out here and work on this, on nights when I couldn't sleep. Maybe I can soon do this in the city, if we get rid of the Hush."

Her dream for the future makes her look so soft. I wish I

could believe that easily. In a way it terrifies me that she lets herself hope like that. That she's so open with me. I'm not that open with anyone. Not even Lochlan. Certainly not my mother. For one moment, I wish there didn't have to be these secrets between me and Alyse.

But that can never happen. The only way for there to be no secrets would be for me to tell her that I was sent here to steal her away. That I was sent to use her.

She wouldn't forgive me. It's a terrifying thought all of a sudden.

I kneel down beside her. "It'll happen, Alyse."

She looks down. "I'm scared," she whispers. "Of tonight. If we get caught. Or even if we succeed. What happens if we find this spire, and it's old or broken? What if we can't save us?"

I'm scared.

I can't think of the last time I said those words, even though there certainly were times that I was scared of missions I was assigned or of Aris falling. But I could never bring myself to give voice to that fear, because I had to be strong, with no cracks. Looking at Alyse, though, I realize there's this strength in being fragile and vulnerable. I always thought that I had to be strong to be accepted, but maybe that isn't true. Maybe I'm glad that isn't true.

"We're going to do this," I say.

She shakes her head. "You don't know that."

"No, but I believe it." If she can believe, then why can't I, with that stubborn streak that has gotten me out of more than one scrape? "You know…" I play with the end of my belt. "I was there, in the court, when you defended that spy. And I was proud of you." I look at her. "I was so proud when you stood up to the monarch."

She blushes, but is already shaking her head. "I shouldn't have done that. I shouldn't have gotten angry like that."

I wonder how much she actually believes that, and how much is just the conditioning she must have received every moment since she arrived here. "Why not? The monarch was in the wrong."

"I'm not allowed to get angry," she says softly. "When I first came here, when I couldn't control my magic… I can't do that again."

I grin. "You're not that same child, Alyse. Anger is human. It changes things. If the monarch doesn't want you to be angry, she might as well tell you not to breathe. Anger tells us when something is unjust. It convinces us to do better."

Looking back now, it's almost strange, thinking of the anger I had against Cerena and even Alyse when I first came here. The only way we're going to succeed tonight is if she and I work together: she using what she knows as a Cerenian, and me using what I know as an Arisian.

Footsteps tread into the garden behind us, and I turn to see Everett. He looks nervous, but he nods. "Well, are we ready?"

Alyse takes a deep breath, then gets to her feet, brushing the dirt off her pants. "Yes."

She heads out of the garden. I go to follow her but Everett reaches out, stopping me. "Tell me that this is going to be all right," he says in a low voice. "That Alyse is going to be safe."

I could lie and say that, but what would be the point? "I can't promise that."

His breath leaves him in a rush, and he looks away from me.

It isn't much, but I give him the only thing I can. "I don't know what it's worth, but I'll do everything I can to protect her."

He tilts his head, studying me, and for once the dislike is missing from his expression. Which is progress I suppose. "You know, we haven't always seen eye to eye and yet somehow I believe you."

"Everett? Devonia?"

Alyse pokes her head around the side of the hedge. "Are you two coming?"

Everett smiles. "On our way."

I take a moment before I follow. Alyse will be fine. We'll all be fine.

I'm going to make sure of it.

CHAPTER TWENTY-EIGHT

The sun is just going down as we head out. Sneaking is always easier in the dead of night, but whatever Alyse is going to build will glow, and it'll be the most subtle at sunset.

I have to give it to Alyse and Everett: for two people who have never done this before, they are passably sneaky. At least they instinctively use the quieter, out-of-the-way corridors. We step from the palace wing out into the yard, and slink along the wall until we've reached a spot where we can see the windows in the hall above our heads, already growing shadowy.

I give a last glance over at Alyse and Everett, making sure they have their gloves on and their faces are fully covered. They aren't exactly wearing spy clothes, but their tight, dark clothing is passable. I turn to Alyse. "Now, you're sure you can do this?" The hallway is three stories above us, and whatever Alyse makes has to be climbable.

She nods, stepping forward. She flexes her fingers and fili-gree grows at her feet. It loops up in spirals, twisting its way into the air. Alyse's face is creased in concentration, sweat dotting her brow, as I stare transfixed.

I don't think I'll ever get tired of watching her work her magic. There's a beautifully delicate spin to the filigree and yet there's a strength to the structure, both of those things coexisting perfectly. And in this moment, I don't resent her for it. I can't.

The structure reaches the bottom of the walkway, and Alyse staggers back, gasping. I reach out to her, but she flaps her hand at me. "I'm all right." She heaves in breaths but there's a triumphant smile on her face.

"I'll go up first," I say. "I always used to climb the apple trees in our orchard so I'm good at it. And we cannot have you breaking your neck."

"But we can have you?" Alyse asks, and her expression is so surprisingly impish I can't help but return the expression.

"I'm like a cat," I say airily. "I always land on my feet."

I pull myself up onto the structure. When scaling walls, I'm used to ever so carefully picking my way up via cracks and bricks. This is so simple compared to that. Alyse really did build this well.

At the top, I peer over the windowsill just enough to see. Sure enough, there are two guards standing by the vault door.

The window is locked, and I slide my knife under the sill to flip open the catch.

I help Alyse up until she's balanced beside me on the top spiral, making sure she's crouched down enough that her head stays below the level of the sill.

"All right," I whisper. "There are two guards. If you send the filigree from the vault door, you can just hit them hard enough to knock them out."

Now Alyse looks truly nervous. I'm sure that intentionally hurting people is the most difficult thing I could ask of her. But all she has to do is knock them out. I squeeze her hand, trying to grant her the comfort she's offered me so freely before. "I know you can do this. Wait for the watch to call and then do it." I look at Everett, who has climbed up beside me. "You ready?"

He sighs but nods.

We've timed our arrival well. It only takes a moment to hear the far-off call of the watch. There's a loud knock on the outer door, and the soldier on the left of the vault door calls back.

Alyse takes a deep breath and focuses on the guards. She sweeps out her hand and silver explodes out from the wall. Both guards go down.

I pull up the window. Everett is already moving and I have to admit that he's quick. In a moment he's at the door, silently sliding in the bolt that will secure it from this side.

I slip in, surveying the damage. Both of the guards are out. There's filigree sticking from the wall. That will be evidence, but it was unavoidable. We just have to make sure we're not seen so they can't pin it on us.

I step over to make sure the guards are both well and truly out.

"Are they all right?" Alyse squeaks from behind me.

One of the guards' eyes flutter open. Making sure Alyse can't see past my body, I deliver a quick jab to his temple that knocks him right back out. "Don't worry, they'll be fine. Guards have hard heads."

I search through their pockets until I find the two pieces of the code.

The others look over my shoulders as I spread out the papers next to each other. It's a complicated code. Time ticks through my head. I can do this. The code is number based. I scan the digits. Pattern based. A Rielli code, named after the spy who created it.

"Got it: 17-5-22."

Everett stares at me. "How did you get that from those papers?"

I ignore him, stepping up to the lock on the door.

"Shh," Alyse hushes him.

"You aren't at all curious?"

"Now really isn't the time, is it?" Alyse asks.

I should probably be paying attention to why Alyse isn't curious. But it's too late. I can't change it now and the door is already open.

There's no lamp in the vault but that doesn't matter, because the amount of filigree in here is still bright enough to see by, and it only glows all the fiercer as Alyse follows me in. Filigree crawls over the marble walls, looking like intricate veins of silver. All through the vault there are pedestals with rich red cushions and treasures sitting atop them. There are gems and necklaces, swords and staves, vases and busts. Every piece is a testament to the art form that produced it.

Everett pauses to look at a tapestry. As soon as I see it, I flinch. It's of Monarch Amelia and Naomi. The sisters are facing away from each other. Amelia is stitched elegantly, cupping flowers in her hands, in a colorful dress that looks so delicate and soft. But for Naomi, there are no flowers. Instead, she wears white and silver lightning crackles around her form. Her eyes are downcast and hard.

I turn away.

We head deeper into the vault, passing treasure after treasure. I want to soak it all in, the history that must be in every single piece in this vault. But I don't have time.

We're here for more important things.

It's when we're near the back that we see the artifacts belonging to Monarch Amelia. Most are obviously not what we're looking for: her crown, the shawl from her coronation dress, her portrait.

At the back there's a chest with beautiful filigree ornaments clasping its corners. I readjust my gloves—as much to protect this ancient thing from my fingers as to not leave any more evidence—and crack it open.

"Alyse, Everett. Over here."

They come up, one on each of my sides, as we look at the letters in the chest, the bundle neatly tied by a faded ribbon.

"Monarch Amelia's letters," Alyse whispers. "Here they are."

My preference would be to steal them and leave right now, but suggesting that might actually send Alyse into a dead faint. So instead we all settle on the ground and take a pile.

I brush my fingers over the first letter, and in that moment I hesitate. There's this sheer age of history that I'm holding in my hands, the papers crackling beneath my light touch. So much of our story came down to these two sisters and the decisions they made. They broke things that not even the intervening centuries could fix.

I open the first letter. As I flip through the correspondence, I catch glimpses of reports and words from Amelia's advisers and her court. I wish I had time to really read this all.

"Wait," Alyse says. "Look at this."

She shows us the letter she holds. I look at the date and see it's only a few weeks before Amelia's death.

I read over the page. It's from the commander of Amelia's forces, outlining a report about a layde who was attempting a coup, his forces already besieging the capital city.

I think back to what Alyse had once told me: that not everyone thought that Amelia was strong enough to lead Cerena.

"Why haven't I ever heard about this?" The words are out of my mouth before I realize that maybe as a supposed Cerenian I should have known.

Alyse shakes her head. "The crown must have buried it. After Amelia died, her chosen successor, a cousin from her family, definitely inherited. Not this layde whoever he was. I didn't hear of this either."

"Well, good thing he wasn't successful in the end," Everett says.

I scan farther down the letter and catch one line:

I understand you've asked Monarch Naomi for help, but we're running out of time.

I press my finger against the ink, worn and pale. She asked Monarch Naomi for help.

And what was her answer? To do whatever she did to create the Mists? Was it truly an attack to take out her sister and rival monarch while she was vulnerable?

Could it be that she did what I've accused Cerena of doing all this time?

I sit back. It's like every clue I find just confuses everything more, all these pieces of history that I never knew.

Maybe in the end, we're all villains.

I numbly reach for another letter, but then my gaze snares on the chest. There's something about it that's bothering me. It takes me a long moment to pinpoint what. The dimensions of the chest are wrong. The wood of the sides is fairly thick, but still, the inside of the chest is too small for the outside.

I pull the box onto my lap.

"Devonia?" Alyse asks.

Is there a hidden compartment? As I turn the box over, I don't see anything obvious. There's no catch or hinge. I run my fingers over the silver edgings of the box, because if something was hidden, that's where it would be. My fingers find a small impression beneath a decorative curl of filigree. I dig my nail in and the bottom of the box pops open, sending a piece of paper fluttering into my lap.

Monarch Naomi's crest stares up at me.

I flip open the letter and see it's dated two months before the last one. It's a short note that looks as if it were scribbled in a hurry.

I'm called to an adviser's meeting but I wanted to get this back to you as quickly as I could. My casters did manage to fix the pendant in the end. I'm sending one of them back, to teach your own how to fix filigree this fine. I don't like the thought of the pendant being away from you for too long.

Amelia, you said you might need to hide the spire, but it could be your greatest defense against these imposters after your crown. Promise to keep the pendant with you. Your bit of magic close to your heart, just like we said when we were children.

Promise me.

I don't understand. Monarch Amelia and Monarch Naomi have always been painted at odds. Naomi was accused of murdering her sister. But then what is this? This letter sounds… fond.

I shift my hands and see the hint of ink on the opposite side of the letter. I flip it over. The words *"Can you fix it?"* are written across the top. And illustrated on the paper is the outline of a flower made of filigree, with a small imperfection in the top corner.

Alyse lets out a squeal that makes me really glad we knocked out those guards, and takes the paper. "You found it!" She looks over the drawing. "I think I can make this. I mean, I'll need to study it. It's so fine and complicated. But I think…"

She lets out a cry and crumples forward.

"Alyse?" Everett shoves the chest aside to reach his sister.

She looks up, her eyes wide with panic. "No."

She jumps to her feet and bolts towards the front of the room.

"Alyse!" I shout after her.

I chase after her as she bursts from the vault and down the walkway. I expect her to turn at the window, but instead she flips the lock on the other set of doors and grabs the handles.

The guards. There will be two more right on the other side of that door.

I don't even have time to yell before she yanks them open.

The guards move to attack but Alyse tugs down the cloth covering her face. Both of the men freeze, and then she's already past. Then I'm past them too, lowering my head so they won't see my eyes beneath my hood.

That's when I hear a piercing shriek and feel a sudden pressure. A pressure I know too well because I've felt it so many times in the Mists.

Alyse takes the steps of the main staircase three at a time and runs out a side door into a yard, me on her heels.

And I see it.

A phantom.

It stands here, a Mistless place at the center of Cerena where this all should be impossible. Only nothing seems impossible anymore. This one resembles a bull elk, with antlers that send frenzied light shooting into the sky.

It's enormous. The largest I've ever seen. Just like Lochlan described.

There are already a dozen soldiers in the yard, but they're in chaos, the ones closest to the beast barely keeping their feet without being killed. One of the guards slashes out with his sword and then narrowly escapes back as the phantom lunges.

I freeze.

How can a phantom be here? Aris I can at least understand because our magic has been failing for years. But here we're a half day away from the Mists, and we're protected by the strength of the Monuments, in the one place on this entire continent where these monsters shouldn't be able to reach us.

I freeze, but Alyse jumps into action. She faces the creature, just like I once did.

Alyse flings out her hand and filigree bursts into life, spearing towards the beast, only for dark to flash through it. She gasps, doubling over. The phantom swings its head at her, and it charges.

"Alyse!" I grab her arm and throw us both to the ground. A sear of energy sizzles over us as the phantom flies past. Alyse lurches up to her knees and with a sweep of her arm she brings up another burst of filigree. This one forms and connects, spearing straight through the phantom's heart. With a scream that rakes pain through my skull, it's gone.

The yard is so piercingly quiet.

Alyse is breathing hard, her face ghostly. Even the soldiers don't dare to move. It's like a moment in a painting, deathly still.

Then the stillness breaks. The guards spring back into action. Some try to contain the handful of bystanders who were caught in the yard. Two of them come to Alyse. They gently help the caster to her feet and guide her back into the palace.

I take the moment to ease into the shadows of the wall where I can't be seen. It's only then that I realize how hard I'm shaking. I wrap my arms around myself, as if that can make the shudders stop.

How did a phantom get here, with the Monuments so strong and complete?

That's when I realize my mistake. The Monuments aren't complete. When I told Milla to cut that hole, we disrupted the filigree pattern.

We let that phantom in.

CHAPTER TWENTY-NINE

That phantom getting into the palace yard and nearly taking out Alyse is my fault. She could have been killed because of what I did. I can feel things slipping through my fingers. I always thought Cerena was so safe, but it isn't. When Lochlan had been captured, Alyse had tried to convince the monarch the magic of Aris protects Cerena too. It's only now that I realize the opposite is true as well. Cerena protects Aris, just like we protect them. The more magic there is on the continent, the stronger we'll all be to fight the corrupted magic.

By the time I get back to the manor, the house is abuzz. I tense as two servants pass me in the front foyer, and then relax, slightly, when I realize they're talking about the phantom attack.

Elirra is going to hear about this soon, if she hasn't already. Will she figure out I was involved? If she learns just how uncertain my loyalties have become, it truly will be all over.

Even without the precedent of my father, how can I expect her to trust me after...?

The precedent of my father.

I stop, my foot already on the first step of the staircase, and I turn to look towards the library. I think of that cabinet that Milla pointed out. If it does contain Elirra's papers, it might hold my father's secrets too.

I shouldn't. But there's this pressure in my chest, unyielding and unbearable. Thanks to today, everything could fall apart. I could be seen as a traitor in this very house. Just like my father was, by so many back home. Maybe if I understand why he did it, I'll understand why I'm risking all of this.

Giving a glance around the now-empty foyer, I cross over to the library. I pick the lock on the hidden door and step over to the cabinet.

And then I hesitate. A part of me is scared even now of what I'll find. Maybe some secrets are meant to stay buried.

But I can't turn away from the truth, not this time.

I need to be brave.

Elirra knows how to choose her locks, and as I add pick after pick, my frustration grows. But I'm my mother's daughter and I refuse to quit, and finally the lock pops open in my hand.

I pull open the doors. I'm sure there's a wealth of secrets here, but as I shift through the papers, I don't care about any of them. All I care about is if there was correspondence between my mother and Elirra. If there was something, anything, that could tell me what happened that night.

And then I find them. Letters. From my mother to Elirra.

They're in the most complicated cipher my mother uses, one that needs a code word to unlock it.

When I was a child, I'd watched my father decode some letters. Laughing, he'd teased me about the code word he'd chosen. But surely my mother wouldn't have used the same key. Surely it wouldn't be that easy.

Only when I try the word against the scrambled letters, it works.

Silvershade.

I flip through letter after letter, catching glimpses of the woman my mother must once have been, with the one person besides my father she could open herself up to. Then I find a letter that isn't like the others. For one thing, it's riddled with mistakes, when I've never known my mother to make mistakes. For another the writing is erratic and messy, still my mother's hand, but clearly distressed. The date marks it a week after my father's death.

I sink to the floor, struggling to read the messy print, her grief scrawled out in every line.

I still don't understand why you gave him those papers. I don't care if he asked for anything you could find. I don't care if you were friends as well. You should have discussed it with me, just like he should have discussed it with me.

Do you know what he said before he left? He said that this was all wrong. This fighting. That the Mists weren't what we thought. He said your papers showed him there was a way to save us in there. That he was going to find it and fix it. He left. He left us. He left me.

And he didn't come back.

249

The letter ends there. I read the paragraphs over again, not understanding. He didn't agree with the fighting and he thought there was a way to save us, in the Mists.

Could it be…?

A shadow falls over me.

I leap to my feet and spin around. Elirra stands behind me, her expression burning. Before I can move again, she grabs my arm and throws me across the room. I stumble, my hip jarring into the table.

"What are you doing?" Elirra hisses.

"They're my parents," I say, and I hate how my voice shakes. I hold up the paper in my hand. "I deserve to know the truth about them. What did you give my father?"

Elirra snatches the paper and rips it in half. It takes everything in me not to cry out as the torn pieces flutter to the floor.

"You should know better than anyone, Devlin," Elirra says, and my name sounds like poison in her mouth, "that the truth belongs to no one. Do you not care that Aris is falling? That the barrier could be days away from dying and taking Aris with it?"

The words are knives in my heart. Everything that I'm doing is for Aris. "Of course, I care."

"Yet I find out you broke into the Royal Vault, and now Layde Alyse has been confined to her rooms. Tell me, how exactly are you planning on stealing her away from the palace when she's now under lock and key?"

Alyse is trapped in her rooms. I won't be able to get to her. I won't be able to get the necklace even if she can make it.

Elirra gives a sharp shake of her head. "I should have known that you were too much like your father. You will be locked in your room for the remainder of your time here."

Too much like your father. Those words drive into my chest. I thought they would hurt but instead I take them and hold them tight. My father didn't just run. Like I knew he wouldn't have just run. He was trying to save us, even as the Mists broke through the barrier. He risked everything for a better chance for all of us. That's all I'm doing right now too.

But I won't succeed unless I can convince Elirra.

"No," I say.

Elirra has already stepped away, but she turns back to me. "Excuse me?"

"You need me," I say. "I'm the only one who has a good-enough relationship with Layde Alyse to stand a chance."

"If you think I would ever trust you now that—"

"Then Aris will fall." I meet her gaze squarely. "You said I was like my father. But trust me when I say I'm my mother's daughter. I miscalculated breaking into the vault. Layde Alyse asked it of me and I knew it would make her trust me even more. I thought I might even be able to learn more about the spire, as we had discussed. However, I will not misjudge again. Layde Alyse will be let out for the gala. Monarch Cora wouldn't dare hide her strongest caster away for that. So, nothing with the plan has changed. I will go to the gala and I will take Layde Alyse."

Elirra stares me down for so long I'm sure I haven't convinced her.

"If you make a single other misstep," Elirra finally says,

"then I will go to Layde Alyse myself, and use your name to convince her to come with me, no matter the risk."

And then she sweeps out the door.

Elirra is going to attempt to take Alyse at the gala if I don't, and with my name she might succeed. I can't let that happen. Whatever I decide, it needs to be my choice.

No one hauls me away as I walk through the palace, but when I reach Alyse's rooms, her guards bar the entrance.

"I'm sorry, my layde," one of them says in a flat voice, "but Layde Alyse is forbidden from having visitors."

"Forbidden by whom?" I demand.

"By the monarch herself."

I stiffen as I turn at Gianna's voice.

She stands behind me in the hall, once more playing the layde.

"Strange tidings, Layde Devonia," she says. "I hope you weren't too near the excitement last night."

It's obvious she suspects me. But she can't have proof or else she would have used it.

"I wasn't," I say smoothly. "Luckily, I was at home all evening with my cousin and aunt."

Gianna smiles as she cocks her head. "That is lucky indeed, if it's true."

If it's true. A warning goes off in the back of my head.

Gianna steps closer, her footsteps so quiet she's like a phantom as she ghosts forward. "You see, Layde Devonia, I've heard whispers this morning that the wildelight attack wasn't the only thing that happened last night. You wouldn't know anything about that, would you?"

"Why would I have?"

"Well, you are good friends with Layde Alyse. And yet, the morning after a wildelight attack, when surely Cerena needs the strength of its casters, she is confined to her rooms."

Gianna's eyes probe me, searching for any weakness. But I'm a spy too. "I'm afraid I haven't heard anything," I say with a smile. "I would be happy to ask Layde Alyse, but I can't seem to get in."

Gianna leans in, so close her breath whispers against my ear, raising goose bumps on my skin. "I know you're not who you say you are, Devonia." Her voice is unsettlingly calm. "And I will unmask you, one way or another."

She pulls back, and I see the change in her eyes: they're deep and dangerous. Then she's past me, her dress shushing over the floor as she leaves. I'm left standing in the middle of the hall. The guards are still staring passively into the distance, and I can only hope they didn't hear that.

I turn, my harried footsteps taking me away. There's a pulsing heat in my head. Gianna suspects the truth, which means Kerrin does too. I have days left until the gala and all of my plans hinged on Alyse's help. Now I can't reach her. But if I can't reach her then what am I—

My gaze catches a mirror, and I stop.

The girl looking back at me from the polished surface is dressed in brightly colored silk. Her hair is piled atop her head and bracelets are strung about her wrists. She looks like she belongs in these clothes. She looks like a courtier. Except for the way her eyes are sharp, watching everything. The way she stands, ready to react in a moment.

She's not Devonia, and not Devlin anymore either: not fully Arisian, but definitely not Cerenian. I don't know who she is.

Gianna's words echo in my head, and so do Elirra's. I risked everything on Alyse's plan. But the spires will only get rid of the Mists if they're both lit. I haven't even found one, never mind the second. We just need more magic, all of us. We're running out and…

Amelia, you said you might need to hide the spire, but it could be your greatest defense against these imposters after your crown. Promise to keep the pendant with you. Your bit of magic close to your heart, just like we said when we were children.

Her bit of magic… What was it that Alyse had said?

I've always felt close to Monarch Amelia when I stand here. She feels like magic to me.

I know exactly where the pendant is.

I go to the Hall of Royals and stop before Monarch Amelia's statue. After reading that letter from Naomi, I no longer know what to think about the two sisters. I don't have the answer to what went wrong between them but at least I have enough answers to do this.

I pull out the spare blade I keep strapped to my leg. My heart thuds in my throat as I dig the tip of the knife into the seam. I work it around, sweat prickling down my back. I should be doing this at night, but I'm running out of time.

The silver crest pops out and as I grab at it, something else falls into my hand.

I look down at the beautiful outline of filigree roses, even more delicate than I could have imagined. It's so delicate I'm afraid my fingers will crush it.

The pendant.

CHAPTER THIRTY

I wait until nightfall, the pendant nestled into my pocket. I slip out of my window, only to run into Milla, who's waiting for me at the bottom.

She raises an eyebrow. "What are you doing?"

I scrabble to come up with a plausible story as I open my mouth but she cuts me off. "Lie to me and I'm calling my mother right now. I know there's something you're not telling me and there's definitely something you're not telling her."

I hesitate as I look at Milla, standing across from me in the gardens. She's dressed in casual Cerenian clothes, a delicate emerald pendant at her neck. I know now that Milla's feelings for this place go far deeper than a spy in a hostile country.

Alyse had told me the truth, hoping she knew me well enough. I just needed that little push of someone to show me what the future could be. Maybe I need to be that person for Milla. It's what Alyse would do. She'd choose to trust, to hope.

And if Alyse can't be here right now, I at least need to do what she'd want.

"The two spires—the Arisian and Cerenian ones—they were meant to be connected. But the sister monarchs... Monarch Naomi did something that caused them to separate. Whatever it was, it caused the Mists. Layde Alyse believes that if we can light both spires we might be able to reverse everything that's happened. And now I'm about to find the Cerenian one because of this." I pull out the necklace and hold it up. "This is the key to finding the spire. We can find it and we can light it."

I don't know how Milla will react to what I'm about to say next. But I've gone too far to turn back now. "I know that you don't look at Cerena the same way as your mother. This is your home, and there is nothing wrong with that. So help me save it, before it's too late."

It's the barest moment but I see a hint of vulnerability crack over Milla's face, and she must realize it too, because she glances away to hide it.

"So this is what you've been doing?" she finally says. "You were supposed to come here and sabotage Cerenian filigree, to ensure it didn't grow stronger."

There isn't enough inflection in her voice for me to know what she's thinking. She's right. I was supposed to make Cerena weaker. And what's even worse is I haven't told her the whole story about how the spires could be weaponized.

I raise my chin. "Yes."

Milla looks back at the house and I think this is it: she'll call her mother and everything will crumble in my hands.

"All right," she says.

I blink. "All right?"

"I'm coming with you. If we find this spire, if we turn it on, then I'll take that as proof that you aren't a traitor and this plan of yours has merit. Besides." She pauses. "You're right. My whole life has been in Cerena. If there's a future where I don't have to choose between my home and my heart, maybe it's worth looking into."

Those words are sentimental for her but I don't comment. Knowing Milla, she'd just smack me for it.

And then I'm leading the way into the dark.

The Rose Garden is quiet in the night, so quiet that the tread of our footsteps on the grass rustles too loudly. I brought a lantern, just in case, but I don't light it. There's enough silver filigree to lend a soft glow to the place, paleness seeping out over petals and flowers.

"You know," Milla says quietly. "There's nothing wrong with creating things to be beautiful."

I glance over at her. "I never said there was."

She shoots me a look. "Don't give me that. I saw the way you looked when you first came to Cerena. I know what Aris thinks of filigree and art."

There's no point in pretending that isn't the truth. "Well, maybe I was wrong." I think of Milla painting in her room and the way she made such beauty. "Is that why you haven't told anyone about your painting? Because of Aris?" I don't ask what I really want to know: Is it because of Elirra?

Milla's quiet for a moment. "I didn't want my painting to be part of the lie that was my life," she finally says. "When I painted, it was just for me. It was the one part of me that felt truly real."

"Well maybe after this, you can be a little more honest. Besides—" I flash her a grin "—it would be a shame to waste such skill."

Milla sniffs, but she looks pleased.

We stop before the wall with the quote and the crest.

"The Rose Suitors," Milla murmurs, running her fingers over the grooves of the letters. There's something wistful in her voice.

"Had you heard it before?" I ask. "Before I told you?"

"Of course." She tosses her hair over her shoulder. "In fact, when I find the girl I'm going to marry someday, that's how I'm going to propose." She glances at the flower necklace in my hand. "I don't suppose I could keep that afterward, could I?"

I go to elbow her, but she's already moved out of the way. She grins. "I'll just steal it when you're not looking."

I roll my eyes. "All right, so I guess I just..." I try to see how the filigree might line up with the flecks of silver in the crest. I press the necklace against the stone. Nothing happens. I twist it a bit.

Milla sighs. Heavily. She takes the necklace. "Up is clearly this way."

She presses the flowers to the crest and this time the silver lights up. She smirks. "This means I get to keep this, right?"

I don't answer, because a pale line of light shoots through the wall, lighting up more silver flecks as it goes. Milla and

I look at each other and then dash after it, the beginning of the line already fading into darkness. We reach the end of the Rose Garden, only for the light to scale a wall. Milla and I follow, even though the stone is covered with roses and it hurts. We come to a faded door in the outer wall of the palace, the light disappearing around its edge.

This garden did not look this big when I first came into it.

The door has a lock, but it's rusted and old and we don't have time to pick it with the light already fading. I use the hilt of my dagger to smash it. Pain reverberates up my arm but the lock falls away.

On the other side of the door there's a stairway. The land falls sharply away, and the stone steps are cut steeply, that line of light coursing down their center. Taking them at a run isn't exactly ideal.

Good thing we both have excellent balance.

We race down the steps and we've just reached the bottom when the light we've been following snaps out.

I stumble to a halt. We stand on a small platform that was perhaps once cut out to be a balcony, if the twisted metal pieces on its edge are any indication. I don't see any hint of a spire, though.

"This was where the old wing of the castle used to be," Milla says softly.

I follow her gaze up the side of the cliff and as I do, I can make out hints of the remains now that I know what I'm looking for. There's that groove in the rock that is too cleanly cut to be natural; that bit of cracked marble still clinging to the cliff side; that stone that doesn't match the rest of the cliff.

This was where Monarch Amelia died all those years ago,

her death ushering in a new era, one where she never saw what happened.

"So where do we go now?" Milla asks. "Has the entrance been destroyed?"

I refuse to believe we've come all this way only to be blocked at the very end.

I pace around the stone wall, and then I see the carving in the shape of roses.

"Look."

Milla steps closer. "Huh, smart." She presses the filigree pendant against it. There's a flash of light through a crack in the rock and then a horrible grating noise. A section of the cliff face moves the smallest bit.

We grab the stone and pull it out, just enough that we'll be able to get past it.

Milla squats by the door, and I see a mechanism of silver filigree, broken now into pieces. She frowns. "Since when has Cerena known how to use filigree mechanisms?"

"No idea."

The tunnel behind the door looks like it must have once been beautiful. Marble tiles with silver running through them lie cracked and shattered on the ground and not too far in, one whole wall has slumped.

"Well, I vote you go into the creepy death tunnel first," Milla says.

"Thanks."

I light the lantern and slink inside, as if by just being quiet enough I can stave off the roof from collapsing. It's a ridiculous thought, except that Milla is doing the exact same thing. Our soft footsteps echo around us. It's eerie being in here, the light from the lantern casting flickering shadows against the wreckage.

In front of us the tunnel opens into a larger space. The tiles beneath our feet wind in an intricate pattern towards the center of the room.

And there the spire stands.

It's bigger than I thought it would be; at least twice as tall as the barrier back home. Its three feet are all larger than me and Milla put together, and they twine up towards the cavernous roof. As massive as the structure is, though, the filigree is still so fine I wouldn't be able to fit more than a finger through the gaps in the silverwork. There is just layer upon layer of it, so delicate it looks like lace. Even though the magic in it is broken and inert, it still shines.

The sight of it steals my breath away. Even after coming to Cerena, I could never have imagined that filigree could look like this. This is our history right here, what we once would have been capable of doing before everything went wrong.

If we fix the spires and get rid of the Mists, we could be capable of that again.

"It's beautiful," Milla whispers. I've never heard the quiet awe in her voice that is there now. "And you say there's something like this in Aris?"

"There's supposed to be two of them. That's the whole point."

I walk around the spire, running my fingers over the metal. As I reach the back, it becomes very obvious what shut this thing down. A foot of the tower is broken, the filigree warped and sticking out at wrong angles. This whole part of the cavern is actually in ruins, the wall at my back nothing but a mass of debris and fallen stones. Something very violent happened here. Could it be the explosion Naomi caused?

"What do we do now?" Milla asks.

I look at her. All this time, I'd been thinking my only hope was Alyse, but now Milla knows the truth, and she's a caster too.

"We fix it."

We go back to the house to retrieve some of the filigree tools that Elirra has, and then we come right back. I'll cut off the broken pieces and Milla will regrow the filigree behind me.

For a moment, though, I just stand there.

Lighting this spire is the only chance of lighting both. But I know that by lighting it, I could also be handing the Cerenian crown all it needs to take the magic. If the monarch gets a hold of it before I light the Arisian spire, that's it. But if I wait until I find the Arisian spire, it could be too late. We're all running out of time.

I think of my father. He'd found something in the Mists. Maybe I am right and he did somehow know about the spires. If he was standing here right now, what would he do?

I already know that answer. He had known this fighting was wrong too.

Milla is the caster, not to mention the artist, so she takes the lead. She shows me where to cut, and I draw the searing lines as she follows behind me, regrowing the filigree. Sweat prickles out on my palms. It's nerve-racking to work on something this ancient. It's not like we really know what we're doing.

"All right," Milla says, rubbing her arm across her forehead. She looks tired. "This last piece should be it."

Silver blooms from her fingers and a final piece of filigree curls up, filling in the pattern.

Light bursts up the spire. It is pure silver pouring out of every swirl of filigree and highlighting every swoop of the pattern. It's more beautiful than I could have imagined, this sight of something broken for so long coming blazingly back to life.

I let out a shaky laugh as my knees give. I plant my hands on the ground. "We did it. I can't believe we did it."

Milla grins, the spire lighting up her face. She looks so young and free.

We've lit one of the spires. Half of the magic that we need is back.

Now there's just one more to go.

CHAPTER THIRTY-ONE

The night of the gala, I feel giddy. We fixed the spire. I wonder if Alyse can feel something like that. Now all we have to do is find and light the Aris one.

I get dressed in my room, wearing purple to honor my friend. I've finally gotten used to these bright colors, just in time to leave them behind. Maybe I should have headed out during the day to get back to Aris, but I need to warn Alyse. Elirra meant her threat. I'm scared that if she uses my name, it'll get her close enough to Alyse to steal her away.

And as I pin my hair in place, I know there's something else I need to say. I need to tell Alyse the truth. Even if she can't forgive me for it, at least it won't be a lie.

Doesn't she deserve that from me?

By the time I'm ready, Milla and Elirra are waiting downstairs. We hustle into the carriage and it's only once we're seated on the plush seats and the door is closed that Elirra speaks. "The plan, Devonia?"

I made sure to come up with one, to throw Elirra off the scent. "I'll find Layde Alyse as soon as we get to the gala. I'll tell her that I made a new discovery about the spires and that she needs to come to the Monuments with me. I'll help her sneak out of the party and through the city. Before we've reached the Monuments and they react to her magic, I'll put this on." I pull out the bracelet from where it's hidden in my skirts. Once I thought it a marvel of crafting. Now it feels wrong to hold it. But better in my hands than in Elirra's. "The Arisian delegation will be waiting on the other side and I'll hand her over."

Elirra nods, and I think she's satisfied, but then she says, "Milla will accompany you."

It takes every bit of training I possess not to stiffen. I wonder if Milla told her mother everything, if this was all a betrayal, but when I look at Milla I can tell by her slight pause that she's surprised too. "Mama?" she asks.

"I'm simply ensuring Devonia's success after the recent slipup." There's a threat in Elirra's expression.

This just got a bit more complicated.

At the palace, Elirra sweeps up the steps with a warning glance. Milla loops her arm in mine as we follow. "If you get me executed for treason, I'm coming back and murdering you," she mutters.

"You know if we're executed for treason, you won't have to."

She shoots me an unamused look. At least she didn't give me up. "I can pretend to knock you out," I offer. Milla still has to live here afterward. I'm the one who gets to sneak away into the night.

But Milla flashes me her usual wry smile. "Please, I've been lying to my mother since I could talk. I am more than capable of concocting my own story she'll believe."

That's actually quite impressive, considering who her mother is.

We enter the ballroom and if Milla hadn't immediately tugged me forward, I would have stopped just to gape. I thought I'd gotten used to Cerenian extravagance, but not like this.

A tree, which can only be Alyse's work, blooms in the center of the ballroom, reaching filigree branches to the roof. Silver filigree blossoms cup flowers carved from gemstones. On the ground, the tree roots become patterns in the floor, only to rise up into tables and chairs. Decadent desserts of spun sugar and layered cakes, of whipped creams and chocolate decorations, are beautifully arranged on tiers of plates.

There's a filigree stage upon which a band plays, beautiful stringed music accompanying a clarinet, its dulcet tones drifting over the crowd. An upper balcony circles the back of the room, and bunches of lilies and candles decorate its arches. The windows are propped open to the gardens on both sides, and the crowd spills out onto the grounds. Outside, the palace lawn is lit with silver lanterns that are reminiscent of Arisian ones, though these simply hold flickering candlelight.

And the crowd...it's an ever-shifting mass of bright fabrics, of filigree and golden jewelry, and coiffed hair. Fine embroidery is everywhere: flowers and birds and filigree patterns.

"Please tell me we have time for a food break," Milla says, eyeing a couple of swans spun from sugar.

"Oh good," I say. "So, this isn't a normal level of Cerenian celebration." If even Milla's impressed with the spread, it can't be.

She snags a swan and unceremoniously bites off its head. "No, this is pretty lavish even for them." She waves the bird. "Did you know they call the twentieth celebration the swan celebration? If the monarch makes it up to thirty, she gets to be a peacock. Imagine the decorations then."

We don't have many traditions in Aris and I wonder if even the older generations remember anything from back before. Maybe after all this is over, we'll have room to relearn things like this.

I keep my voice low. "And you're still all right with the plan?"

"Am I all right covering your treason, you mean?" Milla's tone is joking, but the words are enough to tip my stomach.

She nudges me. "I felt it, you know, the magic of the spire. This could work."

I nod. This will work. "Let's find Layde Alyse."

We search the crowd. As we do I hear people talking. Two laydes chat about how they could see the Monuments from their homes and how much stronger they glowed. A trio of casters mention the surge of magic they felt the previous night.

It's this burn of pride in my chest. We did that.

There are so many people here, and the swirling dancers and the giant tree in the center of the room make it seem as if we've entered a different world. Despite the fact that I need to be leaving, I want to drink all of this in. This beauty. This grandness. This world that might soon be ours. I feel dizzy with it all.

Once we've ruled out the ballroom, we head outside, and I take a breath of fresh night air. There are filigree sculptures on the lawn, dancers that glow like moonlight. I stop to look at them.

"They're beautiful, aren't they?" Milla asks.

I glance over at her, and see the shine of the light reflected in her eyes.

"Once this is all over," I say, "maybe you can bring a little bit of Cerenian beauty and wonder to Aris. Teach us all you know."

There's a gleam in her smile. "Well, I'll teach others," she says. "You're beyond hope."

I snort. "Thank you for that."

"The soldiers who were out patrolling said that the Hush had retreated significantly this morning."

Milla and I glance at the group of young laydes who have joined us on the balcony.

"I heard that it's now well into the Peaks," another says.

Milla catches my eye and gives me a wink. I smile back.

"It's given us the perfect opportunity."

And just like that, some of my triumph is stripped away. Kerrin. I almost leave right then. I don't mind helping Cerena. I really didn't want to help Kerrin, though.

"The monarch's decided to finally rid ourselves of the Arisian menace," Kerrin says. "A battalion is being prepped to cross after the gala."

An ice-cold wave crashes over me. At my side, Milla goes stiff.

"To send into Aris?" one of the laydes asks. "Why?"

Kerrin shrugs, his voice so casual. "Their barrier is all but fallen. They had the audacity to send a spy in our city, and they've been pilfering filigree from us as well. The monarch wants to make sure they never bother us again. Whatever that surge of magic was, it's given us more than enough power to make the crossing safely. The monarch has decided to use it to our advantage. That place has been a thorn in our side long enough."

The world spins around me.

Aris attacked. Ruined. Destroyed.

Because of me.

This cannot be happening.

Milla takes my arm and pulls me away from the group of laydes, which is good, because another moment more and I might have flown at them. She's so tense, her fingernails dig crescents into my skin. She doesn't stop until we're off the balcony and hidden by the palace wall.

She turns to me. For a moment she doesn't say anything. Neither of us do.

I should have predicted this. I should have known that Cerena would do something like this. Cora once said that she thought our monarch was weak and desperate to prove herself strong, but that's been Cora all along. She doesn't know how to deal with the Mists or with a Cerena that isn't impervious. She's the one who wants to prove herself powerful with this attack.

I'd been so naive. If Cerena is sending a battalion at their first taste of what the spires could give them, I know what they'd do if they realized just how much more magic it could offer. Did I truly think anyone would go along with Alyse's plan?

Alyse. I think of her—talking excitedly about breaking into the vault, kneeling before her rose in the garden, her face so worn as she looked at the statue of Monarch Amelia.

If we find Aris's spire, we could still show everyone. Get rid of the Mists. But it took us weeks to find the Cerenian spire. There isn't that much time left. Not with the barrier failing. Not with Cerena marching on Aris.

It's too late.

Milla's the one who finally breaks the silence. "What are you going to do?"

We look at each other, and I know, just like she knows, that there's only one thing to do now. Only one way to save us.

The Whisperer was right. It's always going to be Aris against Cerena and I need to make sure it's my country standing in the end. We've faced our monsters for years, and if there's a chance to get rid of them for good, then I will take it.

No matter what, or who, is left behind.

I straighten. "The plan is what it's always been." My throat is dry, but I make myself say the words. "I steal Layde Alyse. And I fix this."

CHAPTER THIRTY-TWO

It takes me too long to find Alyse. She stands out in the garden on a bit of lawn ringed with lanterns. Their light is enough to show me how tired she looks, and how hard she's trying to mask it. The group of courtiers huddled around her must be asking for a casting because she waves her hands and a flower blooms at her feet, glowing vivid in the night.

A filigree flower. As Aris falls.

"I need to do this alone," I say quietly.

Milla glances at me.

"I don't think she'll follow me if you're there. I'd have to explain that I told you, and that will make her suspicious." I look at Milla. "I will get her out of here. I will save Aris. I promise."

Milla nods. "I know you will."

She leaves and I drift closer to the group.

Alyse looks up and sees me. Despite the exhaustion hidden in her expression, a smile bursts to life on her face. As the crowd disperses, she runs over to me and clasps my hand. "Devonia, I felt it. Did you do something?"

I can only nod, trying to appear normal, not entirely remembering what normal around her is anymore.

Alyse's face glows brighter. "I was thinking we could send a letter to Aris, explaining what we've found and helping them find their own spire."

A letter. Either she hasn't heard the news or she doesn't care. She isn't brave enough to do what needs to be done. I let Alyse sweep me up into her dream, but in the end that's all it was: a hopeless fantasy. She needs to be what she should have been from the beginning.

A mark, and nothing else.

"Alyse, there's something I actually need your help with. About—" I put a pause in my words as I lower my voice "—what we've been studying. We need to go to the Monuments so I can show you. I can't believe I never saw the connection before."

She believes me. I can see it in her face. She believes me so easily I want to shake her.

"Should we get Everett?" she asks. "I think he's here somewhere, looking after the filigree."

Everett is going to kill me when he finds out what I've done. Good thing we'll both be long gone by then.

I guess he was right about me this entire time.

I shake my head. "We can tell him after. The sooner we do this the better."

Alyse nods eagerly. "I know a way we can get out of here."

She takes my hand and guilt blooms inside of me. I push it down. It's too late. I have to choose between Alyse and Aris.

And that isn't a choice, not for me.

Alyse pulls me away, heading in the rough direction of the garden wall. She ducks onto a narrow path in a grove of trees and I see a door hidden in the shadows in front of us.

"Layde Alyse. Layde Devonia."

Alyse goes still beside me. Layde Kerrin.

I turn.

He's there with Gianna and I can see the triumph on his face.

"Don't you think you two have strayed a bit far from the festivities? You don't want people to talk now do you?"

His self-satisfied tone grates against me. Beside me, Alyse laughs nervously, but I stare him down.

"Such a forceful look, Layde Devonia. I saw you on the balcony, you know. Don't tell me you're upset about the attack on Aris."

In that moment, I hate him more than I've ever hated anyone. "How could you attack now? When Aris is about to fall? What's the point?"

"Because they did all of this, Layde Devonia. They caused the Hush. Monarch Amelia was murdered by her own sister all those centuries ago. When Aris falls it will be payment for their crimes. And it's strange that you're upset about this."

"No, Layde Kerrin," I say. "It's strange that you don't seem to care half of the continent is about to fall."

Just like what will happen because of what I'm about to do.

I shove that traitorous voice beneath a layer of ice. Kerrin smirks down at me and I can see he still thinks he's the one in control. But unfortunately for him, I don't care anymore. And that makes me dangerous.

It's two on one. Gianna is the real danger here. I don't know who exactly she suspects me of being, but I know I can take her. Because I am desperate, and she is not.

I lunge forward, grabbing her arm as she goes for her knife. I slam my elbow into her gut, knocking the breath out of her and then I sweep her feet out from beneath her. She lands on her back hard and as she looks up at me, her eyes narrowing, I can tell she recognizes me from the dungeons.

"You," she growls.

I drop to a knee and punch her hard, right between her eyes. She goes limp.

Kerrin stares at me. He goes to run and I'm about to give chase when filigree explodes at his feet, whacking him into a tree. He falls to the ground.

I turn to Alyse, who's clapped her hand over her mouth. "I just attacked the possible next monarch of Cerena," she squeaks. "Why did I do that?"

I could take Alyse right now, but I'd prefer to be closer to the Monuments. "Do you trust me?" I ask.

She stares at me as she studies my face, and then she nods.

Well, her mistake, I guess.

There's a door at the end of the grove, and we slip through. Out in the city there are celebrations too. They're not nearly at the level of the palace, but there are ribbons hung on balconies and metallic ornaments in people's hair. The smells of pastries, sweet candies, and caramel drinks waft through the air. We stick to the side streets, but when we pass a group of children, Alyse waves her hands. A filigree horse springs to life and the children shriek in delight, trying to clamber onto its back. My heart gives a sharp pang. I bury it.

It takes too long, but finally we're out in the quiet of the orchards and the farms.

As soon as the noise is gone, I miss it. Because then I have room to think, and I don't want to think. I shouldn't have ever let Alyse in. I should have known a friendship like hers and mine could never work.

This was wrecked from the beginning.

We're quiet as we walk through the orchards, but eventually I see the Monuments shining against the night sky. They really are stronger than they were before. I spent so much time going along with Alyse, and all I succeeded in doing was making Cerena stronger than it already was and possibly dooming Aris.

It's time. I can't risk Alyse getting closer. At any moment her magic will cause the Monuments to light up even brighter.

So, I stop. She turns. "What is it?" She looks over her shoulder then back at me. "The magic is so much stronger now."

Alyse's face is so open and hopeful. For one moment, I mourn the dream she had. The dream we had.

But eventually we all have to wake up.

I step forward and snap the bracelet onto her wrist.

CHAPTER THIRTY-THREE

I wasn't sure what was going to happen when I put that bracelet on her. So I don't really expect Alyse to crumple like she does, gasping in a breath as she falls to her knees. She stares at her hand, as if expecting magic to bloom from her fingers, but nothing happens.

It worked.

She looks up at me, and the confusion on her face is painful. "Devonia?"

My heart quivers in my chest, but I shove my every thought and emotion away. Just like I was trained to do.

"Even if you scream, we're not close enough for any soldiers to hear you," I say. "And you don't want to make this more difficult for yourself."

Alyse flinches. She tries to get up, but then falls back down.

I hadn't been counting on the bracelet weakening her.

Hopefully it's just the shock. I can't exactly drag her the whole way.

I grab the pack I'd hidden earlier from beneath a nearby tree. My dress is a sewing marvel and with one rip the skirt is off, revealing the pants I have on underneath. The bodice is a bit constrictive, but I'll get changed into something else once I rendezvous with the Arisian soldiers. I grab Alyse's arm and pull her to her feet. Her fingers find the bracelet, but without filigree she won't be able to get it off.

"Come on." I refuse to look at her because I can't right now. All I want is to hand her over so I don't have to do this anymore. Let someone else drag her kicking and screaming back to Aris.

Alyse stumbles and it's only my grip on her arm that keeps her up.

"Devonia," she says weakly.

"Begging won't do you any good," I say, pulling her closer to the Monuments. "You have no idea who I actually am and why I'm here."

"I know you're from Aris. And I know you're a spy."

I come to a dead stop.

She knows?

I turn, staring at her as her arm falls from my grasp. She stares back at me, even though she's hunched over in pain.

Was it my mistake, when I said my father was dead? Something else? I had everything planned out. I'd hardened my heart. I knew that if I was going to do this, I had to be in control, to be perfect. Now Alyse has stolen the breath right out of me.

"No…" I whisper. "You couldn't… I mean…"

She slowly straightens as she looks at me, her face pinched and pale. "I suspected the first time we were in the gallery. I was pretty sure by the time you showed us the clue about the Crown constellation. Why do you think I asked you to help? Why do you think I trusted you with all of this? I knew, of everyone, an Arisian might listen."

She had known practically since the beginning. All this time I thought I was the clever one, manipulating her to win her trust. I thought she was naive, and that I'd been taking advantage of that. And she had known.

"Devonia, I know the recent news was bad," she says softly. "I know you're scared…"

With that, every bit of sympathy is erased by the cold that encases me. I need that ice, because it's the only thing that makes sense anymore.

"You know?" I hiss. I advance on her and she stumbles back. "No, you don't know, Alyse. You've lived here, safe in this city. You've never had to worry that you'll lose everything you love. You've never had to live in a world of monsters. Cerena is going to send a battalion. Not to help. To end us."

"I know," she whispers.

"And you thought you'd send a letter. As if that would save us. As if that would ever be enough. All you will ever be is what they want you to be: small and tired and used by them."

"And you think you're different?" she asks. "Is this really what you want? Having to constantly hide who you are and what you want? Terrified of making the smallest mistakes?"

Her words hit a part of me that I didn't think could still be wounded. How could I have let her know me so well?

Alyse steps closer again, her hands held out as if I'm a

spooked animal. "The plan can still work. We can do this together."

She touches my arm and I jerk back as if burned. "Together? You mean like the monarchs were supposed to rule together? That has never worked." Doesn't she understand? I don't want to do this. But I need to do this, for Aris. "It's too late, Alyse. It's too late for any of this."

"We don't have to make the same mistakes that they did, Devonia. You just said that Cerena is sending a battalion. Even if we go to Aris, even if I have time to fix the barrier, what do you think will happen when I disappear? When the battalion realizes where I am? Can Aris really stop them from simply taking me back? Then what? The barrier has fallen once. It will fall again. Just like the Monuments will fall eventually. We are all drowning, Devonia. I know you know that. You can't stop it."

But I have to stop it. I can't watch my home fall, not now after how long we've struggled. My mother always taught me there were things you had to do, no matter the cost.

And I am my mother's daughter.

"I can stop it," I say. "I can light the Arisian spire and take all the magic."

Those words pull the air out from between us. We face each other, a Cerenian and an Arisian finally seeing each other for who we truly are.

And that's when I realize… If Alyse had known I was Arisian, with every clue she helped me connect, she had known exactly what weapon she was handing her enemy.

And she still did it.

Why?

"Is that how you want Aris to be saved?" Alyse finally says. "By dooming an entire nation? All of this—" she gestures behind her "—gone, when we could have saved it? You blame Cerena for what they've done to Aris. Are you so ready to become the thing that you hate?"

Alyse's look snares me once again. It's so sympathetic, even now, when I just betrayed her.

Everything she said swirls in my head. I think of the beauty I've seen here. Of Milla's paintings. Of that child staring in delight at a silver fox. Of a garden full of magic. If I did this, it would all be gone.

But what about Aris then? What about the city and the workshops, Lochlan and Janna and the other spies, the festivals I went to when I was younger? All of it is crumbling away and I don't know how much longer it will survive.

"Dev," Alyse says softly. I freeze. Dev. Just like what Lochlan always calls me.

"You once said you were scared of making mistakes," Alyse says. "But that's not what strength is. I'm sorry I haven't been there for Aris. But we can save everything, together. We can be more than what they've decided for us. Please. Trust me."

Trust me. All this time I was trying to earn her trust—so I could steal her away. But now she's asking for that trust from me, when both sides of our relationship have been built on lies.

I'm talking about flying.

I pull the key from my pocket and unlock the bracelet. It falls onto the grass.

Behind Alyse, the Monument blazes even brighter. Someone will notice that and come soon. I'm not sure if it will be the Arisian or Cerenian forces first. Either would ruin me. Just like Alyse could ruin me right now. Because if she made a run for it, I don't think I could summon the energy to follow her.

Only then she looks at the hole that Milla made in the Monument. I wonder if she could feel it the moment we got close, or even before that. How much did she know of what I was planning? She rubs her wrist where the bracelet was.

"We should go," she says quietly. "They'll be coming for us soon."

She doesn't wait for an answer, simply ducks through the gap, pulling her skirts through.

I follow her into the dark.

As soon as we're far enough away from the city for the bushes and trees to provide cover, I give Alyse my spare set of clothes. I'm a bit taller than her, but at least they're not her dress. Once we're both changed, I take the lead, winding through the forest as quickly as I dare in the dark. A few times I hear shouts behind us, but with all the tree cover, I can't pinpoint the exact direction they're coming from.

The sun is lightening the sky by the time we reach the foot of the Peaks and begin to climb, the tree line dropping away. I'd be exhausted if not for the nerves coursing beneath every inch of my skin. This is going to be the worst of it. Once we're in the Mists we can hide.

I keep up a grueling pace, and even though Alyse starts breathing heavily, she doesn't complain.

They said in Cerena that the Mists had retreated, and as the hours slip by, I realize just how true that is. We need cover.

We need it now. Then Alyse pulls in a sharp breath behind me and I know, even before the path rounds a bend, what I'll see.

I stop, the wall of white only a few feet out. It seems even more solid than usual and deep in its mass there's writhing silver light.

Alyse draws level with me, wrapping her arms around herself.

"Have you ever been this close before?" I ask.

"Once," she whispers. "Just once." She tentatively steps forward, stopping only when the Mists touch her toes.

She presses a hand to her temple. "It's been so long, but it feels wrong."

"That's normal," I say. "My friend Lochlan, who…" I hesitate. Start again. "They're the…"

"The spy you saved," she says quietly.

The spy she helped save too. "Kerrin was right about one thing. They used to be a caster. And they always said that when they still had magic, stepping into the Mists was like being plunged underwater."

Alyse looks over her shoulder.

"You know, if you do this…you might not be able to go back," I say. "If they learn that you betrayed them, you'll be an outcast. A true outcast. And this won't be easy. Nothing in there is going to be easy." Does she truly understand what that means?

Alyse turns to me, and I see my own stubbornness reflected in her expression. "No, but it'll give us a chance. Besides—" she flashes me a smile that's a shade mischievous "—I did just attack the man who might be my next monarch, so I'd say I'm pretty far gone already."

That had been pretty epic, honestly.

Alyse takes a deep breath. "So, shall we head in, Devonia?"

"It's Devlin," I say. Because there could be anything waiting for us in there. And I want her to know. "Alyse, will you promise me something?" I don't have the right to ask her for anything, but I have to try.

And she doesn't immediately say no. She just waits for me to say what I'm going to.

"If something happens to me, do you promise to keep going? On to Aris. To try to help."

Pain crosses her face. "Nothing's going to..."

"Please," I whisper.

She hesitates, but then she nods. "All right."

She reaches for my hand and I'm so surprised, I take it without thinking. Suddenly I'm so glad that she's here and that she convinced me to do this. I'm glad for this closeness that asks nothing of me except myself.

And together we head into the Mists.

THE MISTS

CHAPTER THIRTY-FOUR

The Mists slide like smoke over my arms and face, raising goose bumps everywhere they touch bare skin. All the colors in the world go so pale and undefined it's hard to even see Alyse beside me, or the mountain at our side.

Something has changed in here. I'm no caster, but even I can tell that. Except when there's a storm, I'm used to deathly stillness in the Mists. But now there's an uneasiness in the very air, with the Mists pulsing around our legs, and flashes of light at the edge of my vision. When the Mists get stirred up, that's when the phantoms appear. And especially now, when it seems like the phantoms have grown so strong they don't have to obey any rule I thought we knew, I can't stand any more risk from this place.

I push us as hard as I dare. I didn't bring a good pair of shoes for Alyse and I curse myself for my shortsightedness.

That I was so bitter and angry that it might be what slows us down when we can't afford it.

We walk for hours, and with every step it becomes more obvious how much we're both lagging. We've basically been going since early last night and, as hard as it is to tell time in here, it must be close to noon now. We'll have to stop. And that'll mean leaving the path.

There aren't that many routes through the Mists anymore. Cerena abandoned theirs when they stopped traveling through the Mists decades ago. Even Aris has abandoned some of ours, so we could focus on maintaining the main paths. I took the quickest route, knowing that despite the risks, it was our best chance of making it through this. But we can't risk setting up camp and sleeping on the path, not with the soldiers behind us. So, I pull us off.

I find a cluster of rocks leaning against each other, just positioned so that we can crawl beneath them. There's barely enough room inside for the two of us, but we fit. I slide off my pack and sit down as Alyse all but collapses beside me.

I dig out some of the food I packed: rolls and cheese from Elirra's pantry. "Here."

"Thank you." Alyse takes the food, nibbling tiredly on one of the rolls.

"We should rest for a few hours." I know we should post a watch, but we also need speed. We'll just have to risk it.

She gives me a weak smile. "I'm not sure how I'll be able to sleep in this. I didn't…" She shakes her head. "I didn't think it'd be this bad. I've never been in this far." She glances at me. "You probably think that's pathetic."

Maybe once I did. But not anymore. "I don't think it's pathetic. It is lucky, though."

She rubs her wrist. "Can I ask...what was that thing that you put on me?"

Guilt delivers a sharp stab right beneath my ribs. "It's a magic nullifier. They made it in Aris."

Alyse pulls her knees to her chest. She looks so tired, but there's still this brightness to her eyes. "You know, I've always admired Aris. The things they've made. I always wanted to learn about them all."

Can I admit to her that I admire things about Cerena too? That it was beautiful in a way I wasn't expecting?

Instead, what comes out is, "I'm sorry."

She looks at me, startled.

I swallow. "I'm so sorry. I should have just told you the truth about everything. I shouldn't have lied to you or tried to trick you."

Alyse looks back down at her hands. I'm scared she'll confirm that I broke something that can't be fixed between us. In that moment, I'm terrified of losing her friendship. I don't know how I'll deal with it if I become nothing to her.

"I'm sorry too," Alyse says. "I should have told you what I knew about you, far earlier. I shouldn't have been so scared about how you'd react. I thought you were just there to gather information, and that if you knew your cover was blown that you would leave. I never imagined that you might have actually been there to..."

"To steal you away." I'm ashamed at the words even as I say them.

Alyse nods. "Right." She plays with the hem of her sleeve.

"And you know, I should have done something for Aris. I should have been brave like you." She smiles at me. "You made me brave, you know."

Bravery? Is that what this is? Sitting here beneath these stones that don't hold out the Mists, with this permanent pit of fear in my stomach? Is Lochlan safe? Is my mother?

Will we leave the Mists and see a stretch of destruction where my home used to be?

I don't want to think about that. I can't. So, I try to be like Alyse and to believe like her. I need that hope, that things will get better, or my heart will crumble.

"Well, Everett is going to be absolutely furious at me," I say, aiming for a joking tone and not quite succeeding. "I guess he was right for never actually liking me."

Alyse's expression shifts as she bites her lip. "He can be overprotective, but it's only because he blames himself."

"For what?"

She hesitates. "Do you know how I got my magic?"

I shake my head.

"I was six, and Everett was eight. We were visiting our aunt and uncle in Krisilla, a village right at the foot of the Central Range. Everett had always wanted to see the Hush, and so one night he snuck out. And I followed him.

"Everett was only a few steps into it when a wildelight found him. I saw it knock him to the ground, and I was so scared for my brother. There was just this pressure in my chest. I flung out my hands, and magic burst from them."

She rests her chin on her knees. "People have always assumed that I found my magic young because I had such a

strong connection. But it isn't true. I found my powers because I was desperate to save him."

That hadn't been what I was expecting. "But why would
he blame himself for that? Casters are born with their powers
and sooner or later you would have found yours."

"I've told him that. But when the soldiers came for me and
brought me to the capital, Everett and my parents weren't
able to follow until a year later. So much happened during
that year, when I couldn't control my magic, when I was so
lost. No matter what I've said to Everett, he's always thought
that if I was older when I discovered my powers things might
have been different."

I have the sudden image of Alyse, young and all alone.
Everyone looking to her to strengthen the Monuments with
her magic, when she couldn't even control it. Surrounded
by court rules that were probably more foreign to her than
they'd been to me. And yet, today she is who she is. And I
can't help but think that a caster born in Wysperil, who had
never had to save her brother from the Mists, might never
have thought of saving Aris too.

"I'm sorry," I say quietly. "But, Alyse..." I search for the
right words. It's true there are times when court life and the
monarch have seemed to smudge Alyse away. But that isn't
all there is to her, not by far. I know that now. "You're stronger than you look."

She smiles at me. "Thank you for that," she whispers.

It feels so nice to just be sitting here with her. But I'm me
and I have to ask. "What gave me away in the end? That I
was a spy?"

"It was little things," Alyse says. "The way you talked about art, and Cerena and Aris. When I saw you skulking around my room. When you kept conveniently finding clues. I don't think you're as sneaky as you think you are."

I can't help it. I snort. Then I'm laughing for real, so hard my shoulders shake. It seems unreal that I'm sitting here in the Mists with the strongest caster on the continent, who is somehow my friend, and she just insulted my spying skills. And here I thought she was the unsubtle one. "Well, no one has ever told me that before. I wonder what my mother would think if she heard that."

As soon as the words are out, my laughter dies, as if it's been strangled away. Alyse's face scrunches up. "Your mother?"

I could lie. If there's one thing that I could do right now, it's lie. But I've tried lying to Alyse and it didn't work.

"The Whisperer of Aris. The head spy. She's my mother."

Alyse's mouth drops open. I stare down at the ground, twirling my finger in the dirt. "I wasn't always a spy. But eight years ago, when the Mists broke through the walls, my father disappeared. He disagreed with the fighting, with all of this. He was like you really. He thought he'd found a way to save us and he went into the Mists." My voice sounds so thin, even to my ears. "He didn't come back. And after, it was just her and me. Only she didn't have time for me anymore, so I just became one of her spies. I lived in the dormitories. I was trained by her instructors. Not by her."

Out of the corner of my eye I can see the sympathy in Alyse's face and it nearly breaks me. It's not something anyone has really given me before. Lochlan knew I needed jokes from them. But maybe I needed this too. "I'm sorry, Devlin," she says. "I didn't know."

"It doesn't excuse what I did to you. It's just…" I grasp for words. "I felt I had to do it, that I have to be perfect all the time, for her."

"Why?" Alyse asks quietly.

"Because." And I say the words I've never said to anyone before. Definitely not to my mother. Not even to Lochlan. "Because I thought that would make her love me."

A long pause follows those words. Then Alyse shakes her head. "But that's not love."

I don't realize I'm crying until Alyse reaches up and brushes the tears from my cheek. "You don't have to be perfect to be loved," she says. "It's all right to make mistakes. There's a strength to being able to admit you were wrong. There's a strength to picking yourself up even when you fall."

I sniff. "Shouldn't I be the one comforting you, after what I did?"

"Probably. But I have the feeling you'd be as bad at that as you were at drawing."

I laugh. And it's ridiculous. Suddenly I can't remember why I was so insistent on taking Alyse in the first place. Because this…this is so freeing. It's like I've been underwater for years and now I can finally take a deep breath of air. She gave that to me. Now that I have it, I don't ever want to let it go.

"We should get some sleep," I say quietly. "We have a couple of long days ahead of us."

We curl up, two spots of body warmth in the silent Mists. And slowly, we fall asleep.

CHAPTER THIRTY-FIVE

I'm woken by Alyse's scream.

I bolt upright, nearly bashing my head on the overhang of rock just above me. Alyse is curled over herself, her face a rictus of pain. The Mists whip around us, scuttling in and out of the cracks.

A phantom is coming.

There's another roiling flash of energy and a shriek that touches some primal instinct in me to run. I thought that having the rocks as protection would be safer but it's a hundred times worse because I know it's out there. And I can't see it.

There's a second shriek and it appears at one of the cracks. It lunges out with claws as sharp as knives, and I barely avoid being skewered. I scoot back, my hand whipping out my filigree knife.

It disappears again and I wait, trying to hear it over the thundering of my heart.

A slam shudders through the rocks. My eyes widen. It's trying to bring down our shelter.

Another slam, and the stones over our heads shift precariously.

Alyse is still bent over in pain, and I grab her arm and haul her up. I drag her out right before the structure comes crashing down, the force of it throwing us both to the ground. Out here, the storm rages even stronger. The Mists fling my hair and grab at my clothes, and all around us there are bright cracks of silvered lightning.

The phantom stalks out of the white. It's twice as tall as I am, standing on two legs and looking like some sort of great ape, with claws at the end of its fingers. Its eyes fix on Alyse.

"Alyse!" It lunges at her at the same time that I move. I swipe out with my filigree knife, but it's a glancing blow, barely nicking the thing's skin. Still, it must feel it because it shrieks and turns on me. I take a few steps back, trying not to panic at its sheer size as it looms over me.

It lunges and I roll out of the way, but I'm not fast enough. Its claws catch my arm and blinding pain shoots through my shoulder. I crumple to the ground, the knife falling from my hand.

The thing stands over me, raising its claws.

"Devlin!" Silver filigree bursts from the ground in front of me, knocking the beast back. I see Alyse, on her knees. Her face is pinched and pale but she flings her arm out with another blast of filigree.

I need to get up but pain is tearing apart my shoulder. I have the hazy thought that I'm losing a lot of blood. I can see it on the ground, pale in the Mists. Too pale. But Alyse and the spire… I need…

There's a shout and white-clad figures flood our patch of mountain. Everything is going so fuzzy I can't tell if it's Arisian soldiers or Cerenian soldiers that found us. And I don't care, because either of them finding us might mean life for a few more seconds and right now that's all that matters.

Then I see another figure. I know her, from the way she holds herself to the way she radiates command, because I've studied both for so long.

"Mother?" I whisper.

She shouts at her people and they swarm like a well-directed hive, half of them herding the thing with lanterns, and the others moving in with knives.

"Devlin? Dev!" Lochlan drops to their knees beside me. They probe my shoulder and curse, before yanking off their gloves.

"That isn't regulation," I whisper.

"Dev, focus on me. You're going to be all right." They tear off a strip from their cloak and bind it around my shoulder.

There's another shriek and a flash of light as the phantom disappears. The storm and the tension in the air abate.

I look over, and see Alyse being pulled to her feet as another bracelet is snapped around her wrist.

"Lochlan," I manage. "Alyse."

They look over their shoulder and their face creases.

And then it all goes dark.

I wake up to a throbbing pain in my shoulder. I'm supposed to snap to alertness, but right now everything is so fuzzy that all I can do is groan.

"Dev."

Lochlan's voice sounds close and I don't understand what they're doing back in Cerena.

Only then I remember: I'm not in Cerena. I tried to steal Alyse away and she convinced me to trust her and a phantom attacked us. And then Lochlan—then my mother—came.

I jolt up, only to hiss as pain from my shoulder shoots through me from head to toe. "Dev, easy." Lochlan takes my shoulders and presses me back down.

I crack open my eyes. I'm sitting in a tent, that all-too-familiar spread of beige canvas above me. Lochlan picks up a cup from the side table and helps me to drink. Whatever it is tastes so bitterly of herbs I have to blink back tears, but it takes the edge of pain away. "Where are we?" I gasp out.

"About a day farther into the Mists than where we found you. The storms are raging up ahead and the Whisperer wants them to weaken before we head out again towards Aris."

"And Layde Alyse?" I whisper.

Lochlan sits down on the bed and gently wraps an arm around me. "You took it worse than she did. You're the one who almost got her arm clawed off."

"I had no choice. I heard about the barrier, that it was falling."

"That's why we came," Lochlan says. But there's something in their voice. Something they're trying to hide from me.

And that can only mean one thing.

"Is that actually why you came?" I ask.

Lochlan is silent.

"Lochlan, why is the Whisperer here?" Even something as important as stealing Alyse shouldn't have been enough to pull the Whisperer away from coordinating her people to protect the monarch, not with the barrier on the brink of failing. Not if she truly believed I could do this.

"Dev," Lochlan says softly.

"She didn't think I could do it." I press my hand to my eyes. Well, I guess she was right. Because I failed. I have no idea how much she might know or guess, or how I'm going to convince her this isn't what it looks like.

Then again, maybe I shouldn't try. Now that I'm back in this camp, I can feel the claws closing around me and cutting off my air.

"Dev."

There's something about Lochlan's voice that makes me raise my head.

"Layde Alyse didn't have her bracelet on."

We sit there, so close together, and for the first time, there are lies hanging heavy between us. My lies.

"What aren't you telling me?" they ask quietly.

My throat is so dry. How am I supposed to tell them about this, when I know how much they resent Cerena like everyone else?

"Lochlan…" I whisper.

The tent flap opens and Reinolds steps in.

"Good, you're up. The Whisperer wants to see you."

My mother wants to see me. Despite the fact that I almost got my arm torn off, despite the fact that the camp is evidently at a standstill, she wasn't here waiting for her daughter to wake up. She just wants to talk to her agent.

And why wouldn't she? She sent her agent on a mission, one that could have saved Aris. And as far as she knows, her agent failed to rendezvous when she was supposed to and nearly got her mark killed. Her agent failed.

But that's not love.

I gingerly slide off the bed and follow Reinolds.

Outside, I get my first look at the scope of the camp. There are five beige tents set up, two in the inner ring, three in the outer ring. One of these tents holds Alyse, but I can't tell which. Lanterns are set up on the periphery of camp, each as large as my torso. There are wisps of the Mists within their boundary, but it's not too thick in here. Traveling the Mists is never safe, and especially not now, but with the magic the lanterns are emitting, at least we won't have to worry about a phantom attacking the camp.

I hope.

My mother's tent is one of the two inner ones. It isn't marked, of course. If a Cerenian assassin ever makes it into one of our camps, there's no point in painting a bull's-eye. But Reinolds gestures so I guess this is it. It's time to see how good of a liar I really am, to someone who I never thought I'd have to lie to.

I take a deep breath and step inside.

There's not much here. You don't take anything you don't need into the Mists. There's a small cot. A camp table with some papers. The mahogany chest the Whisperer always travels with. And the Whisperer.

Seeing her twists my heart in my chest. Because I've been so confused these past few weeks and I thought I wanted what she wanted, but maybe I don't.

And I can't say any of that to her.

She looks me over, and I try to believe she's making sure

I'm all right. But when she speaks, it isn't about that. "Devlin, what happened?" The edge in her voice makes me realize just how much trouble I'm in. "Why didn't you meet with the delegation and why didn't the caster have the bracelet on?"

I have to decide, right now, whether or not to lie to her—when my head is still foggy with pain medicine and my shoulder still burns. No matter which way I choose, there's no going back. Even now, there's a part of me that wants to tell her the truth, because she's the Whisperer. She's my mother.

My mother, who doesn't seem to care that I could have died. Who doesn't seem to care that her family of two was just about a family of one.

"There were complications at the gala," I say. "Layde Kerrin caught me sneaking Layde Alyse out and I had to break my cover in order to steal her away. I knew there would be soldiers right behind us and I had to take a different route away from Cerena. So I did the only thing I could: I tried to take Layde Alyse through the Peaks on my own. But then that phantom attacked. I couldn't fight it alone, so I took Layde Alyse's bracelet off."

I'm surprised at how smoothly the lies slip from my lips. Lies rooted in as much truth as possible. A face that stays neutral.

Everything I only know from the Whisperer's service.

"What if she'd used her magic to incapacitate you and escape?" the Whisperer asks.

"I weighed the risks. If I hadn't released Layde Alyse, she could very well have died and she's the only one who can fix the barrier. I was confident that her attention would be drawn by the phantom and that I would be able to retake her afterward."

"Until you were injured."

The words land between us like weights. Because she says them like I'm a commodity, not her daughter.

I try to hide it, but the pain that cracks through my body must show on my face, because she sighs. "How is your shoulder?"

"It's fine, Whisperer," I say stiffly. "I'm sorry to disappoint you, or if I misjudged."

Her expression relents with the tiniest bit of softness. "You did your job, Devlin. You stole Layde Alyse out of the city and far enough into the Peaks that we could claim her. You did well. I'm… I'm proud of you."

I'm proud of you.

Something thick and heavy sticks in my throat, and I'm not sure whether to laugh or weep. She's proud of me. I've waited years for those exact words; done everything in my power to get her to say them to me. Now finally, after all this work, she has.

And all it took was me lying to her face.

"Sit," the Whisperer says. She gets up from her chair, the only one in the room, and brings it to me. "You must be tired and you shouldn't be standing."

She pours me a cup of tea. I take a sip and it brings me back, to when I was a child and I would join her in her office, drinking tea and swinging my legs on a too-big chair. She would read her reports and quiz me on the subjects I was being tutored in. Even after all this time the memory is warm, like she hasn't been in years.

"Since we have some time due to the Mist storm," the Whisperer says, "I need to ask you about your mission."

Of course. The report.

I sit up straighter. "As soon as I arrived in Cerena, I headed directly to my check-in point with Layde Elirra and I…"

The Whisperer waves her hand. "Not the report. I want to know about these spires."

The spires.

"Yes," I say. "I discovered the existence of the Cerenian spire through Layde Alyse. Originally, I assisted her because I thought it would help me gain her trust. Then, when I learned how important the Cerenian spire was to them and that there was an Arisian spire too, I realized that I needed to find out more information for Aris. Unfortunately, though, right before the gala…" I swallow and it goes down hard. Even with the choice I already made, admitting a mistake to the Whisperer goes against everything I've worked at for so long. "I made an error during the search and it resulted in Layde Alyse being confined to her room. That put a stand-still to our investigation until the night of the gala, at which point, it was too late."

"And that's it? You didn't hear any word about power surges or changes in the magic?"

Power surges.

I'm so used to hearing nothing but a perfect level of control in the Whisperer's voice. Now something has broken through: a hint of desire I would have missed if I hadn't spent years look-ing for scraps of anything in her tone. I remember the last time Lochlan and I had run a mission together, what she had asked when we'd come back: *You saw no indication that they were try-ing to find an existing structure, did you?*

Does my mother know more than she's letting on?

"At the gala, I did hear some courtiers mentioning the Mists had retreated farther from their border," I say. "Could that be from a surge?"

I can't believe I'm trying to probe the Whisperer for in-formation. But I don't stop. There's something she's hiding even now.

And I'm tired of living in the lies she created.

"Perhaps." The Whisperer drums her finger on the desk. "Tell me, do you think it would be possible for Layde Alyse to have found and lit the spire on her own?"

"As far as I know, she was confined to her room until the gala, which is when I took her. She wouldn't have had the chance."

"And yet evidence points to the contrary." The Whisperer stares at the tent wall, as if she can see through it. "Do you understand the gravity of the situation, Devlin? If the Cere-nians have indeed lit the spire, it could spell ruin for Aris. The amount of magic a structure such as that could grant to them, when they already have so much, would destroy us."

Of course, I understand. I was there when they decided to send a battalion after us at their first taste of that magic. They didn't even know where the spire was or what had caused the power surge. I wonder what the Whisperer would say if she knew that I was the one who lit it. I'm terrified of her find-ing out. "I understand, Whisperer."

"Do you?" My mother turns back to me, her body strung tight as a whip. There's something off about it. I want to say that maybe she is afraid of what these spires can do. Only I'm perhaps the only person who has seen her afraid, the night my father left, and this is not how she wears her fear.

"Of course, I do," I say. "An influx of Cerenian power would be disastrous for Aris. That's why it's so critical that we light our spire before they light theirs."

"No, it's critical they don't light theirs at all. There's no telling what these spires can do."

There's no telling what these spires can do. I would have thought that was true, that no one really knew enough about these spires to understand what they are capable of. But my mother is the Whisperer. If anyone in Aris knew about these spires, wouldn't it be her? And then there's those letters she sent to Elirra, about my father going into the heart of the Mists, to find something that could save us.

What if she knows about the spires, because he did too?

"Devlin, you need to think back," the Whisperer says. "To ensure you missed nothing."

If I told her everything, I have no doubt I would gain her respect forever. And with what I know and she knows, we could find the spire. Only, then what? Why am I so uneasy?

Why do I not believe that, given the choice, she would save Cerena too?

I shake my head. "I'm sorry, Whisperer. That's all I know."

CHAPTER THIRTY-SIX

The Mist storm could settle at any time. I need to break Alyse out, and I need to do it now, but there was something about my mother's words. I have to find out the truth, and depending on how things go, this might be my only chance.

So, I take it.

I hide in the shadows of a tent, looking at the one I stood in just a few hours ago. My shoulder throbs dully, in tune with my pounding heart. I didn't tell Lochlan about this. They'll be furious, but I couldn't ask them to risk this for me. And maybe this is something I need to do alone.

The Whisperer exits the tent, Reinolds on her heels, and the two of them head deeper into the camp.

There are no guards. Everyone here has been handpicked by my mother, and no one is expecting a betrayal. Especially not from me. I slip over and into the tent. It's just as bare as before, but without her presence filling it, it seems even emptier.

Unlike so many of my missions, this time I know exactly what I'm after. I pad over to the chest sitting on the table and pick it up.

My father had this made for her. There's only one key, which she always wears around her neck.

But I wasn't raised to need keys.

The lock is so delicate I go with my finest pick, gently feeling around the inside of the mechanism. Time ticks through my head. The Whisperer could be back at any moment.

It pops open.

Right at the top there's an image drawn in pencil. It's not as good as the one that Alyse drew, but it's still unmistakably a spire. It has to be Aris's because why else would my mother have it? Beneath it there's a packet of letters, every one written in my father's hand.

My throat closes up. I flip through the papers, wanting to savor every word and knowing I can't because I don't have time. As much as it hurts, I skip to the last one, because that's when it all went wrong. That's when he went into the Mists and didn't come out. And I have to figure out why because somehow that has to be the key to all of this.

Celia.

It's in there. I know it is. The papers I received from Elirra contained the last clue I needed. The spire is at the old castle. We could light it. We could fix this. We would just have to

convince Cerena to do the same, to share the magic once again,
and then everything would change.

My throat is so tight. I touch my father's words. He'd been looking for the spire. He went into the Mists for the spire. He wanted to connect them, not use them.

He was doing just what I am now.

A hand clamps around my arm. I pull my dagger, but my injured arm is already being twisted, and I gasp from pain, the knife slipping from my grasp.

My mother stares down at me. She's caught me in the greatest act of rebellion I've ever committed. I don't even care.

"How could you not tell me this?" My voice trembles with anger as I hold up the letter. "How could you not tell me that this was the reason why he died? That he knew about the connection between the spires?"

My mother's eyes narrow. "So, you lied to me," she says coolly. "You did know about the spires."

The Whisperer's look pierces me—not just because of its coldness, but because I broke something between us. All this time, all I wanted was her approval. I wanted to be perfect for her. And yet in this moment, it's just Alyse's words that come back to me: *But that's not love.*

I'm done with this. I'm ready to take up space in her world.

"You lied first," I whisper.

My mother's eyes flash and I see how deeply I've wounded her. For a moment I quaver.

But she started all of this.

My mother snatches the letter and I don't even have time to flinch before it's out of my hand.

"What are you going to do?" I demand. "To Layde Alyse? To the spire? Tell me the truth."

She stares down at me, and a tremor goes through her face before she stills it. "It's too late to save the barrier. But with Layde Alyse's magic, we will find the spire. We'll turn it on. And then we will use it to take all of the magic for Aris."

CHAPTER THIRTY-SEVEN

This whole time, I'd been so terrified of Monarch Cora taking the magic away from us, and instead we're going to steal it from them. Once we do, the Mists will crash over Cerena like a wave. It will wipe out all of the beauty and the life until there is nothing left.

"This was your plan all along?" I whisper.

Something almost hesitant passes across my mother's face. "Devlin, you're young. What happened with the attack, with your father, was only one of the many tragedies of our past. I don't expect you to understand this."

She's seriously pulling that on me? After sending me on a deadly mission to the heart of a hostile nation, now she's trying to pretend that I'm too young?

"No, I don't understand. You would condemn Cerena and—"

"They condemned us first," my mother snaps.

"I know we've been at odds for a long time, that they didn't send help when they could have but—"

"I'm not talking about that. I'm talking about who tried to steal the magic first."

"What?"

My mother looks at me. I know she's debating whether or not to tell me anything. Which is what makes it so surprising when she goes on. "I spent years, combing through every record I could find, especially after your father... Especially after your father died. And finally, just a few days ago, I found proof. It was a report of a group of Cerenian loyalists who were afraid that Monarch Amelia was the lesser monarch, and that she wouldn't be able to protect them if Monarch Naomi chose to reclaim her entire country. One of them, a Layde Eliezer, decided to seize power himself. His plan was to attack the palace, force his way to the spire, and steal Arisian magic. Once they had control of the spire, the crown would be theirs. They made it all the way to the spire before they were stopped."

She shakes her head. "Despite all their lies, it has always been them. They were the ones who would have stolen the magic from us centuries ago."

I sit down heavily in the chair. I knew from Monarch Rina's letters that, at one point, Cerena had debated stealing Arisian magic. I just didn't realize how close they were to achieving that. How close Aris had been to falling all those centuries ago, even before Naomi had done whatever she did.

"I didn't even have a chance to tell the monarch that before I had to leave." My mother looks at me. "You see now, though, don't you? For centuries they've blamed us, denying us help because they said the Mists were our fault, when in reality, they nearly stole everything from us."

Her words sound so distant. That's what happened? When all the lies are stripped away, that's what's left behind? Yet one more betrayal that has been cracking apart this continent for centuries.

"Now…" My mother circles the desk, picking up her quill. "Tell me what else you know about the Cerenian spire, so that we can end this."

End this. I look at my mother, standing across the desk from me, focused down on her work. The truth is finally out. Laid bare between us.

But all I can think is what she said. *Them. Us.*

Those casters did what they did because they were afraid their monarch couldn't protect them. Against who, though? Us? Did they really think Aris would attack?

Our entire history has been shaped by the fears of people who looked across their borders and saw enemies rather than allies.

And I'm tired of it.

"No," I say.

My mother's gaze slowly lifts. "Excuse me?"

I stand and gesture to the letters on the table between us. "We don't have to do this. Reconnecting the spires would get rid of the Mists. It could save us all."

My mother scowls, slamming down her quill. I flinch. "Don't tell me you're that naive. There can be no working with Cerenians. Even now they're marching on Aris, to destroy us. Our only choice is to destroy them first."

Maybe Cerena did break things. But we broke things too.

I circle the desk so that we stand face-to-face. "Father didn't think so. He wanted to light the spires."

"And he died for that plan."

"It could work. If we just talk to the Cerenians—"

"There is no point."

"Whisperer—"

"He died because of them! Because they turned their backs on us."

She didn't mean to say that to me. I can tell by the way she stiffens.

Before I can react, she grabs my arm in her steely grip. "Reinolds!"

Reinolds ducks into the tent.

"Reinolds, it seems that Devlin's trip affected her more than I thought. She is to be placed under guard and watched from this moment until we arrive in Aris. I trust your discretion on this."

I knew something like this could happen, but I didn't quite let myself believe it. Then again, maybe I should be grateful. If I were any other spy, I would not have gotten away with a punishment this light.

And, given the choice, I would do it all again.

"Do you really think you can hide this?" I'm angry, and I clearly don't have anything left to lose. "About the spires? About the truth?"

The Whisperer looks at me. "You are treading a very thin line," she says. "Take another step and you will fall."

Then her grip is exchanged with Reinolds's and I'm being pulled from my mother's presence.

* * *

There's a heavy shackle around my ankle, attached to the tent pole I'm leaning against. Reinolds stands just inside the tent flap, studying some papers but looking up every few moments as if I'm going anywhere. As if I could. I think of all the tight situations I've gotten out of: the locks I've picked, the dungeons I've escaped. But these are the people who trained me. They know every tool I've ever been taught. And without those tools, I'm helpless. I wonder if this is how Alyse felt when I snapped that bracelet around her wrist and I took away her magic. When I betrayed her.

I'm so tired. Alyse could be in the next tent over and there's nothing I can do. I should have saved her when I had the chance. Now they'll take her to Aris, and use her to steal the magic away. The spires are our one shot at getting rid of the Mists. If my mother does this, Cerena will fall. And I know that one day Aris will follow. Even with the magic, we won't be able to stand against the Mists alone. It will leave our entire world in ash.

He died because of them!

Those words twist inside of me. I knew that my mother's heart broke when my father disappeared, but I don't think even I realized just how deep that went. How much she was willing to destroy to pay that back. That almost hurts more than anything else that she said, because she still had me and I still had her. If only she'd let that be enough.

Only it wasn't. Nothing I did was enough. I was the one who held every key: to the spires, to the magic. And I messed it up. I fatally messed everything up.

313

I pull my knees into my chest, pressing my forehead to them as if I can just smear every thought out.

Why did I think I could convince her? It took Alyse weeks to get me on her side. Did I really think I would say a few words and my mother would put away a lifetime of hating them for what she thinks they took from her?

Reinolds lets out a cry and I hear a thump. I rocket up to my knees, looking for the attacker that must have come.

Lochlan stands by the door, grinning at me. "Need some help?"

I gape at them as they confiscate Reinolds's key. They come to me, reaching for the lock, but I tuck my shackled leg beneath me.

"Lochlan." I shoot a glance at the tent flap. "You have to get out of here."

"Not without you."

"You don't even know what I've done."

They squat in front of me, quirking a brow. "I mean, I'd rather unlock you first and then you tell me, but all right, if you want to do this now."

A headache pulses against my temples. "This isn't funny."

"Who's laughing?" they retort.

I stare at them, sitting in front of me, in this dreary tent, with a shackle around my ankle.

"You ready to tell me what's really going on?" they ask quietly.

I don't want to. I don't want to see their face when they learn what I've done, that I've gone along with a plan by a Cerenian caster. But maybe if I tell them, they'll leave. Because the only thing worse than ruining my life would be knowing I ruined theirs too. Someone should be free of my mistakes.

"The spires, the ones I told you about: if they're both lit, it will get rid of the Mists. That's what I've been doing. That's why I didn't want you to tell the Whisperer about how the spires could steal magic. Because I was scared she'd use them that way. Alyse isn't my prisoner. I lit the spire in Cerena, and the two of us were heading to light the second one too, when we were caught."

Lochlan's face doesn't change as I speak. They simply watch me. When I'm done, their fingers wrap around the shard at their neck. Not tugging it for once. Just holding it.

"Do you hate me?" I whisper.

Their brow furrows.

"For working with a Cerenian?"

A smile quirks the edges of their mouth. "I could never hate you, Dev. And that Cerenian, you know, she saved my life." Their voice drops quieter. "You could have told me all this."

Could I have? Would it really have been that easy?

"Did you say any of this to the Whisperer?" they ask.

My laugh comes out strangled. "Like she's ever cared about what I think." I can feel it again, the despair wrapping around my chest. I'm back to standing in front of my mother, seeing the way she looked at me. "Just go, Lochlan. It's too late for any of this. And maybe this is better. I can't ruin anything else if I'm stuck in here."

There's a pause and then, "Since when have you given up?"

"Lochlan, I'm done, all right? I can't do this anymore. Say it however you want, it's too late. Cerena is advancing on us, and the barrier is failing, and my mother wants to steal the magic. Everything is falling apart. I don't see how I ever thought I could defy her."

"So, you're just going to let her win?"

"She's already won!" My voice rises. I know I need to stop before I alert anyone outside of the canvas walls, but I can't. Because there's just this anger inside of me, thudding against my chest and roiling under my skin. At everything. At everyone. At myself, for how badly I failed. At Monarch Cora and our own monarch, and their parents, and their grandparents, all the way back to Monarch Naomi and Monarch Amelia. At the brokenness that has spanned centuries. At everyone in Cerena who turned their backs on us and everyone in Aris who's going along with a plan that will doom half a continent. At all of the fear that has slowly been strangling us away.

At my mother.

"She's won and I am so angry at her for it. I have been angry at her for years!"

The words, when they finally spill out of me, bring relief. All this time, I hadn't even admitted the truth to myself. That I was angry at her, for not being my mother when I needed her because I was drowning in grief. When I just wanted to talk to her and for her to let me know that it was going to be all right.

In the silence, Lochlan reaches over and unlocks my shackle. They stand and hold their hand out to me.

"Come on, let's go."

I look up at them. I was so sure they'd hate me when they learned what my plan was. But instead, they just stand there waiting, that half smile on their face that I've missed so much. I was wrong about how they'd react to all this.

Maybe that means I'm wrong about our chances too.

I am so tired, and my injured shoulder burns, but I've never quit on anything in my life. Why would I start now?

I take Lochlan's hand and I get to my feet.

CHAPTER THIRTY-EIGHT

This is a horrible plan. No, that's not even true, because there's no time to make any sort of plan. Just time to move and hope that we somehow stay far enough ahead of my mother and her people.

Because that went so well last time.

Lochlan leads the way. We creep from shadow to shadow until they stop. "She's in there."

The tent they point to looks exactly like the other ones, except now there's a guard posted in front of it. I must have rattled my mother enough that she wanted to take extra precautions.

It's Benji. He's a good spy. But he favors his right side, ever since a phantom attack three years ago nearly separated that leg from his body.

"We can take him," I say.

"That's not a fair fight."

I give Lochlan a look. "Really? Since when has that mattered to us?"

They shoot me an amused look. "I'll distract him since I'm not the supposedly jailed one. You sneak around the side. I'll give you a couple of seconds to move."

"On it."

I drift closer, staying in the darkest patches of night, until I'm crouched a few feet from Benji.

Lochlan strolls over. "Benji, did you hear what happened to Devlin?"

I nearly snort. Nearly break my cover right then.

I'm going to kill them.

Lochlan's foot whips out, catching Benji on his bad knee. I dart forward, hooking my arm around his windpipe and pressing tighter until he slumps unconscious.

I glare at Lochlan.

"All right," they say, "but in fairness, it is the only thing anyone's talking about."

Oh, just wonderful. What happened to Reinolds's discretion?

We drag Benji into the tent. I drop his limp body and turn. The space is empty except for the figure sitting in its center, looking so small. There's a shackle around her ankle and that bracelet is still around her wrist.

She looks up and our eyes meet. I see the emotions flicker over her face: the fear, and the surprise, and, more than anything, the relief. Maybe there was a part of her that wasn't sure I would come for her. Maybe there was a part of me that wasn't sure I'd be able to. But we're both here. We can still do this.

She opens her mouth, but I press my finger to my lips. My tent was on the outer edge of camp. Alyse's is in the center. We cannot afford to draw my mother's attention.

I grab the keys from Benji and unlock the shackle and the bracelet. At least she has on a solid pair of boots now. We have a long way to go and we'll have to do it in a hurry.

I take her hand and pull her to her feet, and there's something solid about that connection. There's hope in the way she smiles at me.

Going out the front of the tent will be too obvious, so I slide my knife into the back, tearing a strip small enough to see through. It's clear. I cut the tent from top to bottom.

I lead us out, Alyse following, and then Lochlan. I see the edge of camp, just beyond the last tent, thrown into bright relief by the lanterns.

That's when I hear the shout.

The cry is taken up. I'm about to make a dash for the edge of camp when two spies come running around the side of the tent. They see us.

Alyse sweeps her arm up, knocking them both clean off their feet with filigree.

Lochlan grins. "Oh, I like you."

"Come on!" I grab Alyse's hand.

There's no point in being quiet anymore. I race past the lanterns and plunge into the thick of the Mists.

"Dev!" Lochlan calls from behind me, their voice slightly deadened. "You're going the wrong way. We need to stay on the path."

I don't slow. "We're not taking the path." My mother's people already caught us once that way.

"Dev." Lochlan grabs my uninjured arm, forcing me to stop as they throw a harried glance over their shoulder. "We will get lost in here without the path—you know that."

"Not if we travel inside the Storm Corridor."

Lochlan's eyes go wide.

The Storm Corridor was once a narrow pass of a canyon that served as an important trade route between Old Isteria and Wysperil. That was before the Mists filled it. That much corrupted magic trapped in one space only made it stronger. There are more storms there than anywhere else. It's a risky plan. But this could work.

"What?" they hiss.

"I found something in my mother's tent. My father knew about the Arisian spire—so did my mother. He thought it was at the old castle. The Storm Corridor leads right to it."

Hesitation crosses Lochlan's face. They know what that truth means to me. How long I've been looking for it.

"Dev," they say quietly. "Your father died in the Mists. No one has ever survived the Storm Corridor."

"No one's ever gone in with a caster as strong as Alyse either," I say, looking at her.

I'm asking a lot; I know that. It's only recently that she's thought of using her magic to fight. It's terrifying: the knowledge that all our fates will be so completely out of my hands.

I can see that Alyse is afraid too. But then she straightens and nods. "Let's do it."

I keep up a harsh pace, knowing we need distance between us and my mother's forces. The Mists reveal nothing. They could be ten feet behind us or a hundred feet and we would

never know. The only sound I can hear is Lochlan muttering under their breath. Probably about me. I suppose I deserve that.

We shouldn't slow, but as we get closer to the corridor, I
find myself beginning to lag. Lochlan grimaces. Alyse's face
clenches in pain. Around us, the air turns harsh and painful.
I remember once coming upon a skirmish, when I had first
become a spy. There was nothing there except dead bodies
and the scent of blood. That is what this reminds me of.

The Mists are so thick that my foot lands right on the edge
of the corridor before I realize we've arrived. I freeze.

Staring down into the canyon is like looking into the belly
of a storm. The crackles of lightning are so constant they light
up our faces and raise the hair on my arms.

"We're really doing this?" Lochlan asks.

"Yes, we are," I say.

I wander along the edge, until I see a spot where we should
be able to descend, a bit of a slanted rock shelf that hopefully
continues past the little I can see. "Okay, here's the plan. Alyse
will cast three lanterns, as large as we can carry. Then, Alyse,
as long as we're down there, you'll need to keep putting as
much of your magic as you can manage into the filigree."

She's pale but she nods.

"We move as quickly as we can," I continue. "In and out.
Everyone understand?"

Alyse and Lochlan nod. There's a beat and then Alyse says,
"Um, I don't actually know how to make a lantern."

Right.

Lochlan steps forward. They walk Alyse through the steps
of forming the cage, then pulsing more magic into it. It's fas-

cinating watching Alyse make one, curls of magic blooming at her feet.

It takes Alyse a few tries, which makes me nervous—we don't exactly have a lot of magic to waste—but she's a quick study. She flushes at the three completed lanterns, letting her fingers drift through their light. "They're beautiful."

Lochlan smiles but there's loss in that look. "Filigree naturally glows. It's just about enhancing that aspect of it."

I lash one of the lanterns onto my belt. "I'll head down first." Taking a breath, I make that first careful step to the top of the slanted rock shelf. Not too bad so far. I reach up, and help Alyse down. "Stay close," I murmur, once we're all standing together again. I keep my voice low. Whatever might be in this place, I don't want to attract its attention.

It's slow going. As the Mists swirl around us, at times I can't see my feet, even with the lantern. Around us, the flashes of lightning are almost blinding. My muscles ache from being clenched so tightly for so long.

I take a step and the ledge crumbles beneath my foot. I nearly go down, but Alyse grabs my arm and jerks me back.

I look over my shoulder at her, clutching my arm, and laugh weakly. "Thanks."

The Mists are so thick, I don't see the bottom until we reach it. Even though I know that means we are well and truly trapped down here, I'm relieved to not be climbing down into the unknown anymore. At least now I know what's beneath my feet, even if what's beneath my feet is terrifying.

We all look at each other, and then we head deeper into the storm.

CHAPTER THIRTY-NINE

I keep my hand against the wall of rock beside us, scared that if I let go, I will lose it. The flashes of lightning down here are constant, each a too-bright burn of light that makes me flinch. They play on my nerves, tricking me into thinking I'm seeing things deep in the misty white: figures and phantoms and fears. The charge in the air around us fills everything with terrible energy.

I expected this place to be swarming with phantoms. Instead, their absence seems ominous. What does it mean if there's a place that even those creatures won't go?

It's impossible to know how far we've traveled, but Alyse is lagging. Sweat drips down her forehead and she's as pale as the Mists around us. She cradles her hands to her chest, magic curling around her fingertips.

The lantern in my hand flickers.

"Alyse?"

Shudders quake through her body. "The magic… It's so suffocating… I feel like it's smearing me out."

Lochlan and I exchange a glance over her head, their own face tight with pain. "We need to hurry," I say.

We each take one of Alyse's elbows, pulling her forward. The lanterns' flickers grow more distinct. This horrible keening cry grows in the air all around us. Just a bit farther. We must almost be out. Almost…almost…

Alyse lets out a pained cry and the lanterns go dark.

No.

A roar explodes, right as a gale-force wind slams into us. It rips me away from the others. My lantern skitters away into the storm. Then there's only the white screaming around me, so strong I can barely keep my feet beneath me.

"Lochlan!" I cry, not even able to hear myself over the din. "Alyse!"

I don't see them. I can't even see my own hands as I reach forward. They were just here.

Silvered lightning crashes down beside me, so close I lose my feet, falling hard to the ground. The air burns where the silver light hit and I scramble back, coughing. The lightning in the Mists has always heralded phantoms. I've never heard of it hitting someone.

Another bolt strikes too close, searing my eyes with its leftover light. I somehow manage to get myself upright despite the storm and the wind, choking on the feeling of burning surrounding me.

"Alyse!" I croak.

Silver filigree erupts from the white, bursting from the ground towards me, then past me.

For one solitary moment the storm abates and the white slackens. I see Alyse, arms thrown out in the epicenter of what looks like a filigree explosion. Lochlan is nearby too, off to the right.

Already, I can see the storm beginning to crash back down.

"Lochlan!" I scream. "Get to Alyse!"

I dart forward, the wind already picking up again, trying to buffet me back. Bringing with it lightning and wind and torrent. Alyse reaches towards me, and our fingers touch right before the Mists wipe everything back out.

"Lochlan?" I have to bring my face right up to Alyse's to get my words across.

"I've got them," she shouts back.

The only sensation is Alyse's hand in mine. I pull her forward, running as fast as I dare.

Silver lightning bursts all around us, making my eyes water and my ears ring, but Alyse throws silver filigree ahead, keeping the worst of it at bay. And then I feel it, the ground sloping beneath our feet. The end of the corridor.

It slants up steeper and steeper, making my chest burn, but I don't stop, because I can feel the storm slackening around us.

I reach level ground without realizing it and it's like coming out of a cloudburst. The Mists no longer thrash about. The lightning is gone.

I collapse down onto my hands and knees, the other two beside me. Each of my breaths feels too shallow and frantic. Behind us there's just a roiling mass of silver and white.

"I hate you," Lochlan mutters to my left. "I hate you, I hate you, I hate you."

They pull me into their arms, their heart thudding against

my ear, and I just take that sound in. We're both alive. We made it.

Where we made it, though, remains to be seen.

Slowly we separate. Beside us, Alyse looks around. She's still shaking, but she's upright. I don't want to know how much casting it cost her to get us through that. I reach out to her and she clasps my hand, offering me a weak smile.

"Do either of you know where we are?" she asks.

The Mists are still thick here, but I can make out the edges of splintered stones and fractured walls. Far up above me in the white I can see what must be some sort of guard tower. The effect is incredibly eerie.

"The old castle," I murmur. "Which means…"

"We're at the heart of the Mists," Lochlan finishes.

I glance over my shoulder, as if I can see Aris back there somewhere. It's the closest I've been to my home in months. This was the plan, to use the corridor to escape my mother. Yet I feel so exposed. Maybe a part of me never actually expected to get this far.

But we did. I push myself up to standing, here before the old castle.

"So," I say. "Let's go find a spire."

CHAPTER FORTY

We creep closer to the castle. Being here isn't anything like the storm we just left, but there are still flashes of lightning, and I hear the unmistakable scream of a phantom.

"Well, we're all going to die," Lochlan says in a low voice.

On my other side, Alyse sucks in a sharp breath. I elbow Lochlan, shooting them a look. They hold up their hands.

"Are you ready?" I ask Alyse quietly.

She flexes her fingers, magic sparking at their tips. "I think so." I pretend not to hear just how weak her voice sounds.

"Hood up, and stay right behind me. With any luck, the phantoms—wildelights—won't notice us."

The wall in front of us, which I'm guessing was once an outer guard wall, is broken enough that I'm able to hoist myself over it, helping Alyse climb behind me.

On the other side, I see what must have once been the palace lawn. I can just make out scattered remains of rock that I'm guessing fell from the castle when the explosion happened. And the filigree structures. Even in the Mists and even though they've long gone dormant and many are twisted, I can still see their grandeur. One, an arch off to the left, stands taller than the castle. Another squat one by the wall looks mechanical, with intricate pieces woven in among one another.

These would have been the structures built before all of this happened. Before the magic corrupted. I wonder what they were used for. Seeing their scale almost reminds me of Cerena.

I wave us forward, tracking to the first pile of stones I can see. The next stack looms out of the Mists. I'm about to move again when I freeze. A phantom. There's so much pressure and tension in the air that I don't notice the monster until I actually see it. I flatten myself against the rock, the others beside me.

It comes closer, so big I can see the arch of its back over the stones sheltering us. Beside me, Alyse's eyes are closed, her face white. But magic curls around her hands. Plumes of silver light, just waiting to make filigree.

There's a bloodcurdling scream and the thing disappears as quickly as it came, in a flash of white.

I slump in relief. My muscles feel like jelly, but I force them to get me up. The only thing worse than moving farther into this place would be sitting still and waiting for something else to find us.

Two more darts across the lawn take us to the palace. Here at floor level, it's clearly more intact than it is up above, where broken spindles of stone poke through the Mists. But more intact is still barely intact, and we don't have to walk far before we find a gaping hole in the wall. We slip through.

The hallway on our side is caved in, so we go the other way, the tattered remains of a carpet beneath our feet. It's unnerving being in here. Walls on both sides mean no escape either way. Broken pieces of old furniture litter the floor: tables and drawers and even the snapped-off arm of a candlestick.

Three times we have to backtrack because Alyse and Lochlan sense phantoms. I'd say we're making painstakingly slow progress, except that since we don't actually know where we're going, I can't say we're making any progress at all.

My father could have walked this way. He'd wanted to find this spire too, even if it meant running into a storm. Did he make it this far? Could I be following the same path that he did?

I wonder if he would be proud of me.

Beside me, Alyse stops.

"Alyse?" I whisper.

She bites her lip. "I feel something. Faint but there, like when the spire was lit in Cerena."

My heart nearly collapses in relief. That's good enough for me. "Which way?"

Now she takes the lead. As she does, the Mists only grow thicker. It's like we're swimming through a sea of white, the air dragging at our limbs. The charge around us builds, sending prickles all over my skin and making every step and thought anxious.

Finally, Alyse stops. "Here."

We stand in front of a door. It's locked, but the door is rotting and old. Backing up, I slam my good shoulder into it. It gives and I stumble through, only to freeze.

"Dev?" Lochlan asks. "What…?" They step up beside me and then they also stop, their mouth dropping open.

I look behind me. The Mists are clearly still there: a solid wall in the doorway. But it's as if they can press no farther into the space. In front of me, I can clearly see a plain stone hallway.

Alyse, who's stepped up on my right, looks around. "Is it the spire?" she asks.

A burn of hope lights in my heart. If the spire can do this even when off, I can only imagine what it'll be able to do when it's lit and we share the magic once again.

"Come on," I say, energized. "We must almost be there."

We walk down a hallway and emerge into an office. Broken bookcases litter the ground, spilling curling pieces of parchment and filigree ornaments across the ground. A desk, mostly intact, sits in the center of the room. One entire wall is taken up by a single painting, askew but still whole.

"The sister monarchs," Alyse says, looking at it.

The two monarchs look younger here, I'm guessing around coronation age. Amelia sits on a chair and Naomi stands behind her. Amelia is in Cerenian white and blue, Naomi in Arisian green and gold. Both wear the crowns meant to mirror one another. They look…happy. It reminds me of that letter. Was that a trick of a painter's brush, or were they truly happy at some point?

"Where are you feeling the spire?" I ask.

Alyse turns in a slow circle. "Um, everywhere?" Her face scrunches up. "I can't pinpoint it."

"All right," Lochlan says. "Well, Monarch Naomi must have known where the spire was. So, let's see what we can find in here."

Lochlan and I head to the bookcases.

"Is rooting through personal possessions a spy thing?" Alyse asks.

Lochlan and I look at each other. We grin. "Yes."

I methodically sift through the shelves, uncovering reports and draft laws and decrees. Pieces of history that would be fascinating under any other circumstance, but nothing useful now.

Lochlan pulls out a sheet of paper next to me. Their eyes go wide as they read farther down the page.

"Lochlan, what is it?" I step up to them, and they wordlessly hold the paper out to me.

I take the page. The notes must be Naomi's because the writing matches every other sample in this room. At the top it says: *"An Account of Monarch Irea."*

I frown, confused. "Who is Monarch Irea?"

Lochlan shakes their head. "Dev. Read it."

I turn my attention back to the faded ink.

The earliest casters in Moraina used magic in its raw form. There was no filigree. The rulers of various fiefdoms sent casters to pillage and kill and steal, using blasts of magic to attack one another. This raw magic caused great harm to a caster's body. Many died. It was also affecting the magic itself, causing it to react in unpredictable and often violent ways.

A powerful caster named Irea grew tired of the killing and the death. She gathered the most gifted casters she could find and developed a form of magical casting based off of the patterns she observed in nature. She called this casting filigree.

This was a different time. Magic was wilder and freer. However, this also meant that it shifted, ebbed, and flowed. Irea, realizing filigree could anchor the erratic nature of magic, created two powerful spires, stabilizing the magic of Moraina. She had enough foresight to hide them from those who would seek to use them. She even laid a trail of filigree between them, deep in the earth, so that the spires and the magic that they anchored could be shared.

Irea, now in control of the most stabilized access to magic, was eventually given the fealty of the other rulers.

She became the first monarch of Moraina.

I look up at Lochlan, their eyes shining. "This is it, Dev. This was when filigree casting was invented."

Alyse has joined us on my other side. "Irea must have been the caster in the story of the Silver Spire."

"And Naomi knew it," Lochlan says. "All of it. If she hadn't died so early, just think how different everything would be now."

They're right. If Naomi and Amelia had lived, then all of these secrets, which have been buried for centuries, could have seen the light. Our entire world might not have changed that one night.

I look away from the page and as my gaze shifts around the room, it catches on the desk. It's a beautiful piece of furniture. Silver casements cover the corners and edges of the rich wood. There's actually something familiar about it. Perhaps I saw it in a painting of Monarch Naomi somewhere.

I tilt my head. Or perhaps I saw it just a few days ago. The more I look at it, the more the desk looks like a large version of the chest we found in the Royal Vault. The filigree pattern along its edges is the same; I'm sure of it. Which means, if that's true…

My fingers probe beneath the filigree on one of its corners, and a catch is right there. I pull it and a hidden door in the side of the desk drops open.

There's only one thing inside the newly revealed compartment: a leather-bound journal, so old its cover is a spiderweb of cracks. I gently pick it up and flip it open. Its pages are full of notes and schematics, and for a moment I can't believe what I'm holding. These are Naomi's original notes about grafting and lanterns and filigree patterns. About the spires.

The dates written on the journal's pages spill forward, until I reach the ones right before the attack. I turn the page and there's a letter tucked inside, which can only be the one Amelia sent to her sister asking for her help.

Even though I'm so close to learning what happened, I almost don't want to keep reading the journal. I don't want to see what led to those consequences that cut our world so deeply.

But I look. There's only one entry left, and I don't understand its date: a good six months after the attack. That would have been right before Naomi's death.

I flip the page back, as if I missed something. But there's nothing, so I do the only thing I can and read the last entry.

I thought it would work. The rebels attacking Cerena had nearly reached Amelia's spire. Cerenian magic was in chaos as too many people drew too much at once in the fighting.

The magic had reacted violently in the past, during Irea's time, and I knew it would soon react the same way in my sister's country. I thought that if I could deliver a pulse of power to Amelia's spire that it would give balance back to the depleted magic of Cerena. That would allow my own forces enough time to reach my sister.

However, I miscalculated. Cerenian magic was already in chaos and the pulse I sent made everything worse.

An explosion ripped between the two spires and Amelia... my sister...

They all think I killed my sister on purpose. What is the point of correcting them, when this is all my fault? All of this was my mistake.

I'm so sorry, Amelia.

A finger reaches out and brushes those last words. "I can't believe it," Lochlan murmurs.

I hadn't realized that Alyse and Lochlan had come to stand on either side of me. I numbly lower the journal.

We'd been wrong. This whole time, we'd been horribly wrong. Naomi hadn't killed her sister out of revenge or jealousy. She'd tried to save her sister.

She'd tried and she'd failed.

"That's how this all started?" Alyse asks. "After all this time, that's how it started?"

"With a single mistake," I say.

Who had spun all of this so out of control for so long?

When did something that started out as a mistake stop being a mistake and start being an intentional way for us to hate one another?

And Naomi. She couldn't have known what would happen. All she was trying to do was save someone she cared about. And in the last months of her life, the fear and the regret of that mistake were clearly destroying her.

Just like the fear of mistakes has always destroyed me.

And why? If she had just told everyone the truth, would the world we live in be different now? That fear didn't help Naomi. And it's never helped me.

My gaze strays from the paper, and I see something peeking out from the edge of the portrait. "Look."

We heave the painting off the wall. Behind it is Naomi's seal, glittering with flecks of magic. All of the filigree in the Mists that I've seen so far has been dead, but this glows with the faintest shimmer of light.

Alyse steps towards it, running her fingers over the stone. "There's magic in this wall. Ancient magic."

"Do you remember the filigree pattern of the pendant?" I ask her.

She nods, determined, and flexes her fingers.

That's when I catch a shadow hovering near the door.

I'm opening my mouth to shout, but before I can, figures explode into the room.

I use the wall as a launching point, slamming into the nearest man and knocking him down. The momentum takes me back to my feet, even as from the corner of my eye I see Lochlan go down beneath three different people, another already grabbing

Alyse. They're Arisian. Soldiers and spies. I even recognize some of them. My hand finds my knife and I pull it.

"Devlin!"

A voice I know as well as my own rings out across the room. And even before I turn, I know who I'll see.

My mother.

CHAPTER FORTY-ONE

The Whisperer strides through her people until she stands right in front of me. I'm not sure what I thought I'd see in her expression. Anger. Disappointment. Instead, there's just a flatness that hurts me more than any of those other emotions could have.

My knife is between us, my blade pointed at her heart. She doesn't so much as glance at it.

"Stand down," she says.

I shake my head. "No. The magic needs to be shared between the spires—why can't you understand that? Even Father thought so."

Something flashes in her eyes: hurt, regret. Then it's gone.

"Your father died for a hopeless dream. Once we have all the magic, we'll find our own way to rid ourselves of the Mists."

That won't work. I know it in a way I can't explain. The

spires were meant to be two sides of one whole, just like Cerena and Aris. Unbalancing them like this cannot possibly fix anything.

"Mother."

My calling her that gets to her. I can see it as she pauses.

"What we know was a lie," I say. "The explosion was an accident. Naomi was trying to help her sister. Everything is right here." I hold the journal out as a peace offering to her. My mother looks at it, and for a moment I think she'll take it. Instead, her gaze lifts to my face.

"I didn't raise you to be so naive."

The words are a slap. My blade wavers and in that moment, my mother moves. She fights so rarely nowadays, I forget how good of a warrior she is. She grabs my arm, twisting it behind me as she snatches the knife from my grip. In a moment, she has me pinned.

"You and I will talk about this later." She pushes me towards Reinolds and as he catches my arms, I hate him a little deeper.

My mother walks past us, examining the silver in the wall. She turns to Alyse. "Well, my layde, it seems that we meet again."

Alyse's jaw is set and I have to give it to her: she doesn't quail beneath my mother's look. She just stares right back. I have never been prouder of her or of how brave she's become— how brave we've become together.

My mother nods at the seal. "Open it. I assume you know how."

Alyse throws a quick glance at me.

"I'm not a cruel woman, my layde," my mother says. "But

don't think for a moment that I'm incapable of it. And it won't be you who feels the blows."

I shake my head at Alyse, even though I'm not sure if my mother would make good on her threats when it comes to me. But it doesn't matter. Alyse steps up to the wall.

"You're making a mistake, Whisperer." Alyse looks over her shoulder. "You could stop this. All of this."

"I don't put hope in fairy tales," my mother says crisply. "And neither should you. It makes you weak."

Alyse shakes her head. "No. My hope is the strongest thing about me."

She turns back to the door and her fingers brush over it. Beneath her touch grows a perfect imitation of Monarch Amelia's filigree necklace. The silver in the stone sparks with light, and just like in Cerena, a section of the wall shifts. Two of my mother's people haul it away, revealing the beginning of a tunnel.

My mother nods. "Layde Alyse is coming with us. Guard the other two here."

"No."

I don't actually believe it's Alyse who's spoken until my mother looks at her.

"No? You're not exactly in a position to make demands, my layde."

Alyse juts out her chin and though it quivers, her voice is steady when she speaks. "Aren't I? There could be other doors in there. You need me, and I'm not doing anything for you if you leave your daughter and Lochlan here, risking attack."

A tense silence settles over the two of them, before my

mother inclines her head. "Fine. Bind their hands. They're coming with us."

Reinolds ties my hands. I stare at him as he's doing it, even though I know I shouldn't be confrontational. Alyse is right. I don't want to be left defenseless here.

We head into the tunnel. The only light comes from the lanterns two of my mother's spies hold. The farther we walk, the more deterioration we see from the explosion. The rock is riddled with cracks and rifts. In places, Alyse has to create a floor of filigree just to get us across. Finally, the cavern opens up and I see the second spire.

It's beautiful, a sister to the one in Cerena. And just like the other spire, there's a large break on its one side.

I can't believe it. We've come all this way, and the second spire is right in front of us, and this is how it ends. All the mistakes of our past are finally going to culminate in the one that destroys us.

Because of her.

I try to jerk away from Reinolds but he holds me tight, his fingers digging into my arms. "You're really going to do this?" I demand, my voice gone ragged. "You're just going to take all of the magic for Aris?"

I don't actually expect my outburst to sway my mother, but she turns to me.

"You'll be condemning Cerena," I say.

"Like they were so willing to condemn us?"

"We have to stop repeating the same mistake over and over again. The only way forward is together."

"You can't trust Cerena, Devlin," she snaps, her calm mask slipping. "And believe it or not, I am actually doing this as much for you as for anyone. You shouldn't have to live in a world constantly threatened by them."

As much for me as for anyone. I wonder if that's true and there is a part of her that is simply trying to make a better world for her child.

But I don't see how I'm supposed to accept the way she's going about it.

So, as she turns away from me, I try the very last thing I can.

"If you do this, then Father died for nothing."

It's the worst way I could hurt her, and I know how deeply I buried the knife when in front of all her people she falters.

She doesn't turn back this time. "What happened to your father led us to this. It made us smart."

"No," I say. "It made you afraid." I let that fear, that anger, rule my life for years, because of her. Now I'm done. I want to move on.

And more than anything, I want her to come with me.

"That's all we've ever done," I say. "Let ourselves fear the Mists and the phantoms and each other. And it was wrong. It was always wrong. Because we could have fixed this together years ago and we didn't."

Reinolds shifts behind me. I'm making him nervous. Judging from the looks I'm getting, I'm making a lot of people nervous. Good.

But my mother steps forward, her back rigid. "Alric."

I recognize the name. He's one of the few Arisian casters left. He joins her.

"Fix the spire. Then pull all of the magic into it."

Alric goes to the spire and places his hands against the filigree.

Only to double in half with a sharp gasp.

Off to the left, Alyse staggers against the wall of the cavern. I tug at Reinolds's grip. "Alyse?"

She looks at me, eyes wide in panic. "The Hush... A storm..."

A distant roar reaches my ears, shaking the walls of the cavern and dislodging pieces of the roof. I don't even have time to open my mouth before the Mists flood in from the tunnel, turning the cavern into white and wind.

Reinolds's grip loosens on me and I jab my elbow into his gut. With a grunt, he stumbles back. Spinning, I grab his filigree knife and use it to cut through my bonds.

I run towards Alyse. We're so close. We just need to fix the second spire and then...

A bone-chilling shriek rattles the cavern, and the largest phantom I've ever seen plunges through the roof.

CHAPTER FORTY-TWO

I stop and stare at the thing, the wind whipping at my hair and clothes. Flashes of lightning crackle at the edge of my vision.

The phantom resembles a bird, with a long tail of lashing light and massive wings. Despite the Mists around us, the phantom is so large that its body illuminates the whole cavern.

The ancient filigree that Alyse felt in the door—that must have been keeping the Mists out. Until we opened it.

"Take it down!" my mother shouts. Her people rush forward. But the space is small, and it's so big. Its tail sweeps out, hitting four spies. It lunges at two others, its beak snapping, but then silver filigree explodes from the ground, knocking the thing back. It shrieks in rage and turns on Alyse.

Oh no, it doesn't. All I have is the too-small blade, and I don't know if something that big will even feel it. But I stab the knife into its tail.

Judging by its shriek, it notices. It turns on me.

That's not good.

It dashes towards me, and I don't even have time to move before its foot catches me across the chest. It's like being hit by a bolt of lightning. I scream as I tumble head over heels, crumpling to the ground in a pile.

"Dev!" Lochlan shouts.

Filigree shoots towards it but it dodges, stalking closer to me.

I gasp, the floor shifting in and out of focus, the tang of blood heavy in my mouth. It raises a clawed wing.

A hand latches around my arm and yanks me back. I only have time to glimpse my mother, fierce and angry and proud, before its wing hits her, not me. She goes flying, slamming into the far wall.

Chasms shoot through the ground and an entire section of the floor, the section my mother is on, collapses, half separating from the rest. The phantom staggers back, unbalanced.

"Mother!" I scream, lurching to my feet.

She tries to get up but then falls down, clutching at her ankle. The floor cracks again, shifting precariously.

I'm standing right on the edge of the largest chasm, looking at the slumping floor just on the other side. I don't know if my weight will shift its precarious balance, but I have no rope to throw my mother. No way to get her except to go get her.

Our eyes meet.

"Devlin," she says, "do not come over here. That's an order."

Yes, because after all but declaring me a traitor, giving me orders is obviously going to work.

The floor she's on cracks again, and I leap over the gaping

air of the chasm to land on the other side. The ground shudders but holds. I run to my mother.

"Devlin—"

"I'm here," I snap. "So either you help us make it back or we both die, all right?"

My mother grits her teeth but I manage to haul her to her feet.

The floor shifts, slipping backwards now. We are definitely going to die. Five feet away from safety and we're going to die.

We lurch forward, rocks crumbling beneath our feet—so close. I'm a step away, when the whole thing falls. I lunge forward, but my foot only finds air. I'm opening my mouth to scream when something solid erupts beneath us.

We're sitting on a shelf of filigree. I see Alyse, panic on her face, arms thrown out, before her expression splits in relief.

Then Lochlan is there, dragging both of us back onto the safety of blissfully solid stone.

I pant as I look around. The situation has gotten worse. Five spies are on the ground. The remaining ones are barely managing to avoid being skewered by the thing's claws.

"Nothing we're doing is affecting it," Lochlan gasps. "Not knives. Not filigree. It just brushes them off."

But that's all we have. If we don't stop it, it's going to eventually damage the spire beyond repair and then…

The spires.

"Alyse!" I call. "We have to fix the spire. We have to share the magic. It's the only way to stop that thing."

Lochlan reaches down, grasping my hand. They pull me to my feet. "Then let's do it," they say.

A hand catches me by the elbow. I look down at my mother, and her expression is so painfully raw. She's afraid.

She's afraid for me.

"I have to do this," I say.

She shakes her head. "I can't lose you too."

There's a stone in my throat. "You never lost me."

I pull out of her grasp and run with Lochlan towards the monster. "Alyse!" I shout. "Knock it this way, and then go. Lochlan and I will distract it."

She hesitates for only a moment and then throws out her arms, silver filigree buffeting it towards us.

"This is your plan?" Lochlan shouts.

"Go right!" I yell. The two of us dodge as the thing's claws come down, raking across the stone. Behind it I see Alyse reach the spire and fling her hands against it. Magic grows in the broken gap and light begins to seep up the tower.

The thing shrieks, as if it can feel it. It turns.

I stab it through its leg and it bucks in pain, before its wing sweeps out, knocking me and Lochlan off our feet.

"Alyse!"

It goes to lunge at her as with a cry, she shoots a final blast of silver light into the spire. A wave of pure magic, of light and energy, explodes.

I just manage to flatten myself to the ground as it hits, squeezing my eyes shut against the burn of brightness. The phantom cries, a bloodcurdling sound that pierces me to my core.

And then stillness. Quiet. I blink the light from my eyes as I look around, but the phantom is gone.

Then I see the spire.

It shines blazingly bright, as if it's pure moonlight set on fire. The glow bathes us all in luminescence, turning the decrepit cavern into something beautiful.

It's lit. They're both lit and the magic is shared. Because of what we did.

I meet Alyse's eyes as she slumps to her knees, letting out a laugh. The light from the spire dances across her face.

Beside me Lochlan raises themself up with a groan and then freezes.

"Lochlan?" I scramble over to them. "What is it? Are you hurt?"

They stare down at their hands. "My magic…" they murmur. "I can feel it again." Taking a shuddering breath, they flex their fingers, and filigree blooms from the ground.

Their connection is fixed.

"The Mists…" Reinolds says.

One by one heads are turning to look up through the hole in the roof where the phantom broke through.

Blue sky. I can see the blue sky, because the Mists are gone.

After all these years, all the deaths and the losses and the fighting, the sun shines bright again on a land no longer blanketed by the monsters we created. This world isn't whole, but it's here.

My mother steps up beside me, leaning on Alric on her other side. She looks up at the sky, and something vulnerable enters her eyes. It's something I haven't seen there since I was very small, and we were both mourning and pulling away from each other.

She looks at me and I can't stop myself from stiffening. I

have no idea what she's going to say. She could take this away right now: steal Cerenian magic and go with her original plan.

"Mother, please. You said you were doing this for me. So do this for me."

She studies me, her face giving nothing away. Then she nods.

"All right," she says. "We'll try this."

CHAPTER FORTY-THREE

"Are we prisoners?" Alyse whispers.

We're sitting side by side on a bench in the atrium before the Arisian throne room. I pluck at my sleeves. My mother is nearby, talking to Reinolds. She's leaning heavily on the staff that was found for her, but at least she's up and with me.

"Um, no?" I say.

Lochlan snorts from my other side. "Very convincing."

I give them a look. Not that they seem bothered. Ever since we got back from the spire, they've had this goofy smile on their face. Even now, they're twisting their hand, watching as magic spills around their fingers.

I elbow them, because this is serious, but they just grin at me. At least one of us is having a good time.

The monarch's page steps out. "Her Royal Majesty is ready for you."

We get up, and my mother steps forward, her staff clacking on the ground. The top of it has been sharpened already. "Chin raised and shoulders back, Devlin. You're meeting royalty."

I raise a brow. That was oddly maternal for her.

The doors to the throne room are pulled open and my mother sweeps through. I follow, taking a deep breath.

I've been near the monarch practically my whole life, working in the same palace, treading the same halls, but I've never seen her up close. In her portraits, Monarch Chloe has always seemed so serious to me, too serious for her age. But today, her eyes are lit up.

We all curtsy to her, and I have to admit—I always thought my mother was graceful, but nobody matches Alyse.

"I have heard the reports and seen the evidence myself," the monarch says. Her voice is young but it carries through the room. "The Mists are gone. The phantoms are finally banished from our lands. This is a joyous occasion. However, I also understand that even now a battalion is advancing upon us and that laws were broken in pursuit of this. Tell the court what has happened."

My mother nods at me. I step forward and curtsy again.

It was a lie that got us into this mess. Whatever happens next, I don't want to start that with a lie too.

So, I tell the truth, about everything. The spires. The sister monarchs. About me and Alyse, Lochlan and Milla and Everett. All of these people who got us to this point. And as I speak, I try to make Monarch Chloe and all of them understand. I know this won't be easy. The suspicion and the anger aren't just going to go away. But that doesn't mean we can't try. We need to try if we want to move forward, if we want to stop making the same mistakes over and over again.

Monarch Chloe listens intently. For someone so young, she's good at hiding her emotions. Then again, that's who I was at her age. But maybe now, because of this, she can be someone different. We all can be.

When I'm done, she turns to Alyse. "You are the great caster Layde Alyse."

Alyse nods. "I am, Your Majesty."

"As the only spokesperson for Cerena here, what do you say?"

Alyse steps up to stand beside me. The two of us, side by side before this court.

"Your Majesty. I'm not going to pretend that this will be simple or easy, but it will be worth it. The Hu— The Mists are gone. The phantoms are gone. Thanks to the spires.

"I understand the mistrust and hostility that has been between us for generations, but we need to try to make things better now. Let me go out and meet the battalion from Cerena, to talk to Monarch Cora. As a sign of peace, I make this promise: I won't tell the Cerenian crown where their spire is throughout the negotiations."

There's silence after that. I glance at Alyse.

"Is this a lack of loyalty?" Monarch Chloe asks.

"I am loyal to Cerena, Your Majesty. I just believe that loyalty means more than allowing us to fall back into the way things are. I think it also means recognizing that the original monarchs of our two countries were sisters and friends. I can have loyalty to Cerena and to you too. I want to make a world where we can trust each other, and if hiding our spire helps with the negotiations, then I will do that."

There is quiet in the court as the monarch looks us over. Tension buzzes at my fingertips. Ultimately, this decision is hers. If she orders us to draw all the magic through the connection between the spires, I don't know what I'll do. I can't take the guards in here. And even if I could, then what am I going to do? Get in an argument with a fourteen-year-old?

"We will send a delegation to the battalion, to negotiate and reopen relations," the monarch finally says. "Layde Alyse, you will join our negotiations."

A spark of hope flames in my heart. I don't know how Cerena will react to this. But it's a start. They'll have seen that the Mists are gone, and right now they don't know how it happened, but we do. I hope that will be enough to make them listen. Surely at least some of them are as sick of this fighting as we are.

"Your Majesty?" My mother steps forward. "I would like to nominate my daughter to join the delegation. I should be by your side during this time, but she will help ensure that negotiations go smoothly. She does, after all, have some experience with Cerena."

I stare at my mother, even though I know I should be hiding my emotions. After all this, after I went against her orders, escaped her custody, and called her out in front of all her spies, I never expected my mother to praise me. Not because of a lie or because I was hiding who I was. To praise me with the whole truth out there. I thought after all the ways I've grown, it wouldn't affect me. But it does. A proud warmth blossoms in my chest until it fills me all the way through.

Maybe I did still want it.

"Well, Devlin?" Monarch Chloe asks. "Are you willing to go back to Cerena? After just returning?"

Out of the corner of my gaze, I see Alyse giving me puppy eyes.

I almost crack a grin. Maybe we can't magically fix all the problems of our world, but we fixed this one. Surely that means there's hope for the others too.

After all, we deserve to make our own mistakes.

"Yes, Your Majesty. I am."

CHAPTER FORTY-FOUR

Back to Cerena. As I pack my bags, I think of how different this trip is going to be from before. The last time I was going undercover to capture Alyse. This time I'm traveling with her, as myself. In some ways, that's scarier. As Devlin I won't have any place to hide. But there's something hopeful to all of it too.

A knock sounds at the door. I open it, and see my mother.

There's something different about her and it takes me a moment to figure out what it is: her expression is softer now. Softer than I've seen in a long time.

"May I speak to you?" she asks.

I nod, feeling awkward as I gesture her into my room. I can't think of a single time she's been in here.

She goes and sits on the bed. I timidly perch next to her.

For a moment, she doesn't speak, which is stranger than anything. She's never been at a loss for words.

"I'm sorry," she finally says.

I rub my arms. I'm not entirely sure how to handle this conversation even as I crave it. I don't want things to simply fall back into the way they were before. "You were trying to do what was best for Aris."

"Best for Aris…" She shakes her head. "You told the truth in the throne room. Perhaps it's time for me to tell the truth too. You know by now that your father told me about the spires, about the Arisian one that he believed was at the old castle. What you don't know is that he asked if I would send him in with a contingent of other spies. And I said no."

Maybe there was a part of me that always wondered why he didn't just ask her for backup. And maybe there was a part of me that never voiced the question because I was scared of the answer.

"Back then, I didn't believe in the spires like he did," she says. "Cerena may still have legends of the structures, but whatever we had was long-lost. I knew we couldn't spare the spies on a hopeless mission. And I was scared of losing him. Only then, on the night when the Mists broke through, when it was all over and I heard the report that your father had left, I knew he had gone to try to find the spire. The storms raged for days after that, even after we pushed them back, and I wanted to go after him, but I couldn't because I had you." There is such sorrow in her eyes. "I couldn't allow you to lose me as well, not after what happened to your father. Not after it was my fault that he died."

My throat closes up. "It wasn't—"

"It was, Devlin. If I had granted him the contingent, there is no telling what would have happened, but at least he wouldn't have gone in there alone. I didn't listen to him."

She rubs her finger, which once held a wedding ring, long ago.

"I never wanted you to become a spy. This is a hard and dangerous life. I didn't want to see you go through it. Only then he died, and I was so lost. I didn't know how to handle any of it without him. So, I gave in and let you be raised by the instructors and your classmates. That was wrong of me." She turns and I see the regret in her eyes. I see everything, because she is letting me see it. "I should have been there for you. I should have been a better mother."

There's a pinching sensation in my heart, at this conversation that's taken us eight years to have. I stare down at my hands, conflicting emotions of hope and happiness, regret and even sadness fighting inside of me.

"Imagine my surprise," she continues, "when I saw you in that tent. I realized you knew everything that he did and, more than that, you wanted to go after the same thing that he did. And I thought if you did, that I would lose you too."

Emotion presses hot behind my eyes as I look at her. Finally, there's nothing between us. No secrets. No lies.

"But you didn't," I whisper.

She smiles softly. It's the first time since my father died that I've seen that smile. "But I didn't."

We're both still here. The years before are gone, and there's no way for us to get them back. But we can still change what comes next. I always thought I wanted praise from her, for being a perfect spy. But really, all along, this was what I wanted. For her to truly see me.

"We could try to do better," I whisper. "Once I'm back from Cerena. I'm willing to try if you are. To become a family again."

My mother hesitates then places her arm around me. The gesture is unsure, but it's there. I lean against her shoulder.

Maybe fixing the two of us won't be any easier than fixing Aris and Cerena. But I want to believe that it will be worth it.

I do believe it.

Our horses climb up into the pass, and as we reach the top, I pull back on the reins.

The Mists are gone. For the first time in my life, I can see the mountains spooling out before us. We can actually ride horses in here, knowing they won't be frightened. I would always stop, coming back to Aris, scared that one day it would be destroyed. But here I am now, with everything changed. I know there's a battalion out there somewhere waiting for us, and a Cerenian monarch who hates Aris. This isn't over yet. But it's enough for this moment.

"The Mists," I whisper. "They're finally gone."

Alyse and Lochlan pull up on either side of me.

Lochlan leans forward, arms crossed over the front of their saddle. "It was all thanks to us really."

I raise an eyebrow. "You know, Alyse and I did most of the work."

"Absolutely. I mean, you would both be rotting in an Arisian cell if it weren't for me."

"And you'd be in a Cerenian one," I retort.

"I would have gotten out," they say breezily. "I was waiting for the right moment." They cluck at their horse and it moves off. "Now come on. Let's go make history. Again."

I stay there for a moment, just wanting to drink this all in. "I can't believe we really did it."

Alyse smiles. "I knew we would."

"How?" The word comes out without me thinking. But I mean it. I turn to her. "I'm asking seriously. How did you know this wouldn't all just go horribly wrong?"

Alyse looks out over the mountains. "You have to keep believing that you can create change and a better world. You have to believe before you can act, don't you think?"

"You know, you're a really impressive person, Alyse."

She laughs. "Where is that coming from?"

"No, really. I'm sorry I almost ruined everything. Because I didn't trust you. Because I was so stuck in my ways."

She shakes her head. "It's okay."

"It isn't…"

"Devlin, it's okay." She holds out her hand and I reach across the space between us to grasp it. "We both misstepped along the way. But what we did was only possible because we did it together."

I smile at her. "Thank you. For convincing me not to be so stubborn headed."

"I am good at that."

"So, what do you think is the likelihood of Everett trying to kill me when he sees me again?"

"You're a spy. You'll be fine."

"That didn't answer my question."

"Come on, you two!" Lochlan calls from up ahead, turning around in their saddle. "We're leaving you behind."

Alyse and I smile, and together we head into our future.

★ ★ ★ ★ ★

ACKNOWLEDGMENTS

Writing the acknowledgments for a novel is such a special moment as an author, because the books I write would not be possible without the unwavering support I receive from so many people. A book isn't the product of just one person, but of multiple people, and I have so many I want to thank for *Silver in the Mist*.

First of all, there is my amazing agent, Rebecca Strauss. She has been there every step of the way in my publication journey and I could never thank her enough for all of her support and guidance, and for always answering my many e-mails with good cheer and great advice.

Next, there is the fantastic team at Inkyard Press. I want to offer my wholehearted thanks to Bess Braswell, as well as to Connolly Bottum, Brittany Mitchell, and Laura Gianino. This book and my journey as an author are what they are today thanks to every one them. It is so amazing to be part of a team with such dedicated and passionate people.

It was also wonderful to work with Anna Prendella once again. Every round of notes that she gave me ended up making the story and the characters so much deeper and richer. I couldn't have done this without her.

I want to offer a special thanks to Carlos Quevedo for my stunning cover. It was so special seeing Devlin come to such vivid life and it went beyond my expectations.

As I've grown as an author, I've had the honor of building so many wonderful relationships with fellow writers. I want to give all of my thanks to Kirstie, Brittany, Amber, Bianca, and Kaleen for all of the tea and scribbles. Thank you to Michelle and Rebecca Ann for always being there, ready for a chat. And thank you to Rebecca for being such a brilliant mentee!

Then, of course, there are my friends. To Ella, Nicole, Peyton, Jordan, and Emily: thank you for all of your encouragement, messages, and virtual hugs throughout this process.

Thank you to God, for being with me every step of the way.

Thank you to every reader who took a chance on my book and my world. It is the most amazing thing as an author to know that there are readers out there who are willing to explore the worlds we create. I hope that you enjoyed the time you spent with my book, but no matter what, thank you for taking the chance on *Silver in the Mist*.

And finally, thank you to my family. I am so lucky to have the wonderfully supportive family that I do. Thank you so much to my parents. No matter how far-fetched my dreams have seemed, you've always made me believe that I can achieve them. You have been there for the good times and the difficult times, and I cannot thank you enough. Thank you to my mom for always being there with advice and support. Thank you to my dad for the many puns and jokes. To my sister Sara, thank you for being such a marvelous role model. I look up to you so much, and thank you for showing me what I can be. And to my sister Rebecca. You have always embraced every horizon, and have always shown me what is possible. Thank you for being so brilliant and so much fun. Thank you to my grandparents: you are not all here anymore, but I know you're still watching me. And finally, a thank-you to my dog, Pan, for keeping my lap warm during many a writing session.

Thank you all!